About the Author

During fifteen years of living in different countries across the world, Luise Noring broadened her mind of people, cultures and languages. When asked why she has spent so many years living and traveling abroad, Noring answers "curiosity." In fact, curiosity best captures her pursuit of knowledge that has guided her entire life. In her previous careers, Noring was an academic scholar of economics and ran her own international consultancy company. The book draws on in-depth research knowledge and practical experience with the people, countries and cultures of the world.

Read also, *Going Places, Somewhere and Nowhere*, *Going Places, United and Divided*, and *Going Places, Ebb and Flow* by Olympia Publishers.

Please also visit the author's website: www.luisenoring.net

Hidden

Luise Noring

Hidden

Vanguard Press

VANGUARD PAPERBACK

© Copyright 2025
Luise Noring

The right of Luise Noring to be identified as author of
this work has been asserted by her in accordance with the
Copyright, Designs and Patents Act 1988.

All Rights Reserved

No reproduction, copy or transmission of this publication
may be made without written permission.
No paragraph of this publication may be reproduced,
copied or transmitted save with the written permission of the publisher, or in
accordance with the provisions
of the Copyright Act 1956 (as amended).

Any person who commits any unauthorised act in relation to this publication
may be liable to criminal prosecution and civil claims for damages.

A CIP catalogue record for this title is available from the British Library.

ISBN 978-1-83794-567-2

This is a work of fiction. Names, characters, businesses, places, events and
incidents are either the products of the author's imagination or used in a
fictitious manner. Any resemblance to actual persons, living or dead, or actual
events is purely coincidental.

Vanguard Press is an imprint of
Pegasus Elliot Mackenzie Publishers Ltd.
www.pegasuspublishers.com

First Published in 2025

Vanguard Press
Sheraton House Castle Park
Cambridge England

Printed & Bound in Great Britain

Chapter One

He has done this trip before. He has also promised himself—many times before—that he would never do it again. And yet here he is! He is leaning forward over the steering wheel. Almost clinging to the steering wheel. In a kind of frustrated desperation. He can't do anything else but cling to the wheel. He can't go anywhere other than stay behind the wheel. He must make this dreadful journey, again. And there will be more, just like it, until he quits. *Today! I quit!* he keeps repeating inside himself. The sentence goes in loops. Until it becomes a chant. It removes his focus from the young woman sitting next to him. She is quietly sobbing. She holds her hands to her eyes. She starts wiping the snot that flows from her nose with her right arm sleeve. It is an unbearable sight. "Today! I quit! Today! I quit! Today! I quit!" he chants.

The little girl sitting behind on the backseat gently puts her hand on her mother's left shoulder in an effort to comfort her. It has no effect on the sobbing young mother. The little boy is sitting on the backseat in complete silence, looking out of the window.

"Today! I quit! Today! I quit! Today! I quit!"

"You have to tell me where you want to go?" Juan insists. "Do you have your mother; you can stay with? Or some other relative? Friends? I can take you to a women's shelter if you have called in advance?" She can't reply through her tears, because they will not stop. "Look! The only thing I cannot do is just drive aimlessly around New York. I have other families in your situation that I must pick up today." After a while, he pulls up at a diner. Parks the van and asks the boy if he wants to go in and pick up something to drink for them. The boy gets out of the backseat. Juan lifts him off the van. Hand in hand, they go into the diner. Juan asks the boy, "Where does your grandmother live?"

The boy answers, "In Kentucky."

Juan looks up at the woman behind the counter, while muttering, "Well, that doesn't work!"

When they get back to the van, the woman has stopped crying. "Take me to Grand Central Station," she commands. "Just take us to Grand Central Station," she repeats, and starts crying into her hands again.

He pulls up by the west entrance to the station. He helps carry the fine and heavy mahogany furniture that's been in the back of his van into the station. It's everything the woman owns. A homeless man standing next to the entry helps him carry the furniture. They leave the furniture just inside the entry door. Juan hurries because he knows that soon guards will show up and turn them away. He doesn't want to be there when that happens. On his way out of the station, he slams a five dollar note into the palm of the homeless man, who helped carry the furniture into the station. Juan swears. Again, he spent his own money on coffee and a homeless guy. Juan only gets fifteen dollars per eviction, and just spent seven dollars on extras. *This will be my ruin,* he thinks, shaking his head as he climbs into the van.

Back in the station, the woman is sitting on her bed in the middle of the commotion. Grand Central Station is rapidly entering rush hour. She is holding both children tightly around the shoulders. "I am so sorry!" she says, continuing in a low tone of voice. "So sorry. So sorry." She is shaking her head in despair.

*

Things started going south some years back. It all started when her husband, the children's father, lost his job in the warehouse when it shut down. She had thought that the warehouse must be sitting on prime land that could be developed for greater profit. But that never happened. Instead, the vacant warehouse just sits there and reminds them of better times. Times when her husband and their father didn't drink. Didn't beat. Didn't take prescription drugs. In fact, the doctor and the liquor vendor are the only ones who benefit from the decay and destruction of their neighborhood in Baychester, Bronx.

The empty warehouse just sits there and mocks their pitiful existence. On good days, her husband promises they will move away from under the shadows of the warehouse. She hopes they will move to Hiseville, Kentucky, where her mother lives. "You can get a job in construction there," she says with hope in her voice. Still, every time she hopes, he drinks even more, and the beatings pick up.

While kicking her in the stomach, he screams, "This is not my fault, you lazy cow!"

Whenever that happens, the children hide in the basement by the laundromats. They find themselves in the basement more and more often.

One day, when Saskia returns home from some poorly paid odd job that hardly warrants her travel time and expense, she walks into the apartment to find her husband dead on the living room floor. In recent months, whenever the doctors won't proscribe him sufficient medical drugs, including benzos, Xanax, and fentanyl, he tops up the prescription drugs with street drugs, such as meth, coke, and heroin. A lethal cocktail that finally gets the better of him. It is all so predictable.

Saskia rushes over to his lifeless body. She violently shakes his head, while tears start running down her face. She tries to find the pulse. Either there is no pulse, or she is in such a state of panic that she is incapable of finding it. "Help! Help!" she starts screaming, while bending over his lifeless body.

The next-door neighbor bursts in. "Saskia! Call 911! Call 911!" he yells, pushing her abruptly aside to kneel over the lifeless body. After a short while, he turns to Saskia and shakes his head in a resigned manner. But Saskia has already left the side of her dead husband.

She is desperately searching the apartment to see if her children are at home. "Max! Ava!" she repeatedly calls out, while opening doors, looking under beds, into cupboards and behind curtains. She frantically runs around the apartment, calling out to her children until the neighbor grabs her arm.

"They are not here. Thank God! Just call 911." When he looks at her, he says, "I'll call 911."

"Come fast!" he commands into the phone. He wants the dead body gone before the children get home. "Fast!"

During the time immediately following his death, Saskia walks around in a haze. It is strange how when we lose someone, we tend to only think back on the positive moments with that person. "Oh, he was such a good father," she hears herself saying to his old colleagues whenever she meets them in the local Dollar Tree grocery store. In this catatonic state of sorrow, she doesn't comprehend nor acknowledge the grief of her children. Not because she is a bad mother. In fact, she is a very good mother. She is simply incapable of harboring any more grief and sorrow than she already does. In the evenings, she sits alone and drinks. She can only fall asleep when she is wasted out of her mind. "At least it's better to drink than to take drugs," she reasons as she stumbles into bed.

The school contacts her. Social services start dropping by. They want to talk to her. By the time social services decide her children should move into temporary foster care, they are evicted. Shortly thereafter, she is sitting in the van with Juan, sobbing. Soon they will wander the streets, where no one will be able to find her. They will disappear into thin air. Abracadabra.

As expected, the guards of the Grand Central Station show up within minutes of their moving into the station. "You can't stay here!" one of the guards orders. He is tall and slightly overweight. His uniform is made of cheap polyester and stretches over his inflated belly. His tone of voice is harsh, but his eyes foretell of a kind and compassionate soul. "You can't stay here! This is not a hotel!" he repeats.

"We have nowhere else to go," Saskia musters the courage to reply.

"Well, that is not our problem. Is it?" the other guard next to him intervenes. Saskia notices that he is blushing. She thinks they probably decided between them who should take action first. Then his colleague would back him up. All the three of them struggle with the situation.

"Just give me a couple of hours," she pleads. "Just a couple of hours. I need to think…" The guards look at each other. After a short while, they nod and walk away without saying anything.

Saskia turns to her children. "Don't be scared. I will find a place for us before the guards come back. Just give me some time. I need to make some calls. Can you go and play in the meantime?" It is a stupid question. Ava and Max are very worried. They are scared. They want to ask their mother what is going to happen to them, but unwillingly they decide to leave her side and give her space to make the calls. They walk away, hopeful that she will find a solution.

Saskia frantically calls around different women's shelters. "Please, can you help us? We have been evicted, and now I am sitting in Grand Central Station with my two young children and all our belongings—furniture, clothes, everything! We have nowhere to go." She starts crying.

The voice at the other end is quiet. Then she says, "Hang on. Let me try to see what I can do. Just hang on the line."

This is Saskia's sixth call. "Please, please, please, God! Help me!" she begs.

"Sorry, honey. We are totally full. I don't know what is going on, but there is a surge of homeless people seeking shelter. I am really sorry, but there is nothing I can do. We have reached the breaking point." Saskia hangs up without uttering another word. New depths of desperation are besieging her body. Panic overtakes her soul. She is unable to see the numbers and make the calls as the pressure in her chest becomes unbearable. She grasps for air. She passes out.

"Mama, Mama!" She hears a frail voice in the far distance. Max is calling her. Ava is standing next to him with large, frightened eyes. Her children are in a panic as they shake her.

Ava reaches her right hand out and gently strokes her sweaty forehead. "Mama, it is all going to be fine. Don't worry," Ava says.

While she was desperately trying to make her calls, her children were exploring their new home, the Grand Central Station. They were walking down stairways, pulling door handles, looking behind shields and so on. "We found a door that opens!" Max exclaims with excitement in his voice. He is only eight years old. She loves him so much. The pain in the chest and heart is so real.

"It is true, Mama. The door opens to a long, narrow stairway," Ava confirms. Out of the corner of her eye, she can see the two guards approaching. She looks the guards in the eyes. They stop and wait at a distance. Caught between a rock and a hard place, she gets up and obediently follows her children to the door that opens. The children each hold her hands as they drag her along the station. They walk down to a station platform: platform number three. At the end of the platform, Max ascends a couple of steps and opens a door. "Look, Mama! I told you. The door opens! We can live down there!" He points down the stairway into the unknown darkness below.

Saskia shakes her head. "We cannot live down there. We don't know what is down there. And I am sure that there are loads of rats. Maybe the sewer is down there," she says.

Ava asks, "Mama, do you have any better ideas? We cannot live in the streets. It is raining. And it will be freezing tonight. And we cannot live in the station. The guards will throw us out." As Saskia has no better ideas, she follows her children down into the abyss. The steps of the stairway are narrow and full of dust and dirt. It is difficult to find a footing in the dark. They feel they way forward with their hands fumbling along the walls and into the open air ahead of them. Saskia and her children are holding their breath. They don't speak a word.

Once at the bottom of the stairway, Saskia remembers that she can put on the light of her phone. She searches her pockets for her phone and sighs with relief when she finds it. With the light on, they can see that they are in a small room with a metal floor. She tries to see what is below the metal floor through holes of rusty decay. Cables! Cables are below them, thousands of cables in all sizes. "Thank God! It's just cables," she says, relieved that a river of sewage isn't running below them. Saskia continues, "We cannot live in this tiny, pitch-black hole."

Before Saskia can react, Max opens yet another door. This time, it is a large and heavy metal door that leads into a dimly lit tunnel. They pass the threshold into the tunnel. The tunnel is warm and comfortable. The floor has been swept clean. The walls are covered in old decorative tiles. "What a strange place!" Ava exclaims. "It must be a deserted passenger tunnel. But why is it so tidy, warm and light? Maybe someone lives here?" But Saskia is totally perplexed.

They start walking down the tunnel. "We can live here!" Max exclaims. After about thirty meters, a young boy emerges. He stands with legs apart, and pulls out his left hand, revealing a palm that is filthy.

"Stop!" he yells. In his right hand, he holds a machete that he swings around effortlessly, slicing the air in front of them. They take some steps back till they hit something. They turn around. Three youngsters are blocking the direction that they came from.

Saskia looks at the young man standing in the middle with big, frightened eyes. "What do you want?" she asks in a loud voice.

He looks her up and down, and then the children. "The question is: What do you want? What are you doing down here?" he asks.

Saskia replies, "I don't know. Well, it's a long story… We were evicted."

"That is not a long story," he says, while his buddies laugh. "That is the shortest story in the world," he says and opens his arms. "Welcome to the underground!"

They walk toward the young boy, who lowers his machete and steps aside to let the young man and his two buddies pass. Saskia and her children obediently follow. "Let me take you to our basecamp sub-level 1," the young man says. At the end of the deserted passenger tunnel, there is a large cast iron gate. It is beautifully decorated and polished. It squeaks when he opens it. A girl sitting guard on the other side of the gate is awakened with a jolt by its squeaking. She stands up and straightens her jacket. Saskia looks at her, thinking she cannot be much older than her own daughter. Ava forces a smile to the girl as they pass her. They descend a winding stairway, and, before they know it, they are standing on a disused station platform.

Saskia reckons that at least twenty people are on the platform, surrounded by makeshift beds and chairs tossed randomly around. Most people on the platform are youngsters who are sleeping, looking at their phones, or chatting with each other. There is an open fire in the middle of the platform, where a couple of people are preparing some sort of food. The food stinks, and Saskia and her children screw up their faces as they pass by it.

"We have rules down here!" the young man yells as he swaggers along the platform. He stops to turn around to address Saskia and her children, and the rest of the crowd on the platform. His name is Lucky Luke, but he just goes by Lucky. He is of medium height and stocky build. He obviously trains to stay fit and in shape. He is probably in his late twenties, Saskia thinks. He seems like some kind of leader of this peculiar settlement in the deep underground of Grand Central Station.

Still looking at Saskia, Ava, and Max, Lucky points to a vacant space on the platform floor in the far end of the station. "You can make camp down there," he says. "You will get some blankets and pillows. Whatever we can spare. And help yourself to some dinner."

Saskia whispers into the air between her and Lucky, "Thank you." She is so extremely grateful. Just an hour ago, they were hunted animals seeking refuge. Now, they are welcomed into this group of outcasts.

As the days pass, Saskia and her children start helping with daily chores. In many ways, life in the underground is good. There is shelter, food, water, warmth—including human warmth and compassion. She asks Lucky, "Where do you get electricity and fresh water from?"

"We tap the electricity wires and connect to the freshwater pipes. We tap into all the different lifelines of the city. We have everything we need down here. All for free!"

"Does no one ever come down here, except for you guys?" Saskia asks.

"It happens that workmen from one of the utility companies or the subway company come down here. That is why we have guards at different posts. They warn us. We can vanish into thin air in less than five minutes if intruders come."

Lucky doesn't want to share too much information about their existence down below. Saskia senses that there are many more like themselves down here. On a couple of occasions, someone she doesn't recognize ventures in and walks across the station platform in a habitual manner, heading straight toward Lucky and his two buddies, Trish and Trash. Sometimes, Lucky, Trish, and Trash follow this person out of the station and onward into the unknown maze of corridors, chambers, stairs, and tracks in the underground. Saskia observes, but she knows not to ask any prying questions.

"Where do we get food from?" she asks a woman about her own age, who is camping next to her. The woman is called Becky. She is dirty, even though, no one needs to be dirty down here. There is plenty of water, including for bathing. It is clear that many of the people in the underground struggle to comply with the rules and regulations that dictate life above ground. Here, no matter who you are or why you are here, you are welcomed. No one is required to comply with any of rules and regulations of the society above. Only the codes of conduct of the underground must be followed—the most important one being to keep their whereabouts hidden.

Becky looks at her. "We go on night raids to rob and plunder food. In the daytime, we loot bins for discarded foods outside supermarkets. You'll be surprised at the quality of food we find in those bins!" Becky releases a broad and surprisingly white smile.

Saskia asks Becky, "Are you all alone down here?" They are relaxing on their blankets.

"No. I have a son down here," she replies.

"Where is he?" Saskia asks interested.

"He is somewhere down here. You know, we are not alone. Many other homeless people live down here."

Saskia looks around, acting surprised. "Where are the others?" she asks.

"It's hard to tell," Becky replies. "But they're somewhere down here. I don't know where my son is. I haven't seen him for a long time. I miss him." Even though Saskia is bursting with curiosity, she knows that she will not learn more from Becky or from anyone else at this point in time. Maybe if she stays long enough, she will start connecting the dots.

One of the most difficult things about living in the underground is the lack of daylight. After just a couple of days, day and night flow together like ebb and tide. Saskia loses all orientation. "But you and your children are free to go up!" Trash says. "You just have to make sure that you clear your exit and entry with the guards, so no earthling sees you." The people above ground are scorned. They are called earthlings and do not even warrant being spelled with a capital letter.

On a regular rainy day, Saskia and her children venture up above ground. Trash walks them through the labyrinth of corridors and stairways while giving them detailed instructions. "When you want to get back in, you must knock three times twice. Then we know you are one of us. Make sure nobody sees you entering!" They walk up a winding cast iron stairway till they reach a small plateau at the top of the stairs. A boy who is guarding the door jumps up as he sees Trash. Here, at the top of the stairs, Trash suddenly opens a door onto the bright daylight of Lexington Avenue. He gently pushes them out the door. "Hurry!" he yells and immediately shuts the door behind them.

"Wow, people walking around here..." Saskia looks around at the huff and puff of the Thursday afternoon. "If they only knew what is going on behind this door! Below this ground!" She speaks in a low voice to her children, as they turn around to inspect the door from street level. From the outside, the door looks unsuspecting and insignificant.

They wander around the streets. She knows that she and her children look like homeless people. They even walk around in the apologetic, dejected way people do when they feel they are a waste of space. People in the streets give them a wide berth, as if whatever ails them is contagious. They wander into a random grocery store. The guard at the door immediately gets up from his slumber and starts following them around the store. Some aisles further into the store, Max pulls Saskia's sleeve and discretely points ahead. In front of them, they recognize one of their fellow community members from the platform audaciously slicing open a package of chicken and putting the fresh chicken meat into his pockets. The guard is just a few meters away from him. But with the guard's eyes fixating on Saskia and her children, their accomplice can pretty much do whatever he pleases. Saskia freezes till their accomplice has completed his theft, all the while engaging the full attention of the guard.

Back on the street, Saskia is shocked. In contrast, Ava and Max are bouncing up and down with joy or pride or whatever it is. "He was stealing. No matter what, we must never condone stealing. That is not okay!" she idly explains.

The children ignore her until Ava says, "But mother. How do you want us to survive if we don't steal?"

Saskia answers, "Becky told us that they also loot the bins of supermarkets for discarded food. I think that is acceptable."

"But we are also stealing light and water in the underground," Ava says and continues, "what is the difference between stealing chicken in a supermarket or stealing light and water!" Saskia knows Ava is right. Still, she is sad at the desperation of their situation, and the moral decay in its wake. They have become their circumstance.

Darkness sneaks in over the city. It is within the darkness of the night that the city reveals its true face. The city has reached its boiling point in terms of the number of homeless and distressed people living there. Wandering the streets for hours, Ava and Max complain that they are hungry. She counts the banknotes crumbled up in her pockets. "We can pick up something in there," Saskia says and points to a drugstore. "You have three dollars each."

Ava looks around the store and asks, "Why is everything locked up?"

Saskia replies, "Because there are so many people, like our newfound friends, who have no money. Hunger leads them to make poor and desperate choices, such as stealing. As a result of this widespread theft, the store finds it necessary to secure all its merchandise. Without such precautions, the store would ultimately face closure due to the rampant theft."

Subtle signs, such as the presence of private guards and the secure locking up of merchandise in supermarkets and drugstores, prophesize an imminent future where distress and despair will overwhelm the teetering city.

Back on the street, they see four youngsters lifting the cover of a manhole off in the middle of East 97th Street. The youngsters have put up a makeshift street works rail to prevent cars from running over them. They slide down the manhole. Saskia, Ava, and Max stand on the sidewalk with their jaws hanging open. "They are from the underground!" Max yells and points. Ava lowers his hand and hushes him.

"We don't know that," Saskia says. "But it seems strange that they are going down a manhole. Let's go back and ask Lucky and the others about this." They speed up to get back into the underground.

Back on the platform, Ava and Max sneak around, discreetly trying to get a glimpse of people's faces. Lucky approaches Saskia. "Can you call your kids over here?" he says in a firm voice, while explaining. "People are hiding down here. They don't like to be stared at."

Saskia summons her children while getting up to ask Lucky, "We saw four youngsters crawl down a manhole on East 97th Street. Do they also live down here?"

Lucky explains that there are several routes that all lead to the settlement in the underground. "You are at sub-level 1. And you must stay here. There is a manhole with snowflakes on West 42nd Street adjacent to the terminal, which leads down to our settlement on sub-level 1..." He pauses and continues, "You and the kids can only go down the manhole of West 42nd Street. Generally, the manholes with snowflakes and RTS written on them are safe to go down because they have been installed either by the electricity companies or by the subway company. We will tell you about the different manholes, exits, and entries, when the time comes."

Saskia looks at him in contemplation and asks, "So, the four youngsters going down the manhole on East 97th Street went to another settlement down here? There are other settlements down here. Right?"

Lucky answers on a need-to-know basis, "Yes. But you don't need to know anything about that now. You *earn* your right to advance through the levels."

Saskia hurries to get one more question in before Lucky turns around to leave. "How do I *earn* my right to advance?"

Lucky answers, "You will soon know," before he swiftly returns to his basecamp in the middle of the platform, preventing Saskia from posing more questions.

The next morning, Lucky, Trish, and Trash stand over her, waking her up. "What! What!" she exclaims as she sits up. "We have an assignment for you," Trish says. "You must fetch dinner for all of us. It's your turn. We don't care how you do it. Just do it!" Saskia gets up, feeling hurried and completely disoriented. After collecting her thoughts, she wakes up Ava and Max.

Once back on the street with her children, she says, "Right! Now, we must find some bins outside supermarkets, drugstores, and delis that hopefully hold a treasure horn of food." Becky told Saskia of a couple of places that are a "sure thing."

"There is a supermarket a few blocks over, but the challenge is to get into the storage area in the back of the supermarket, where the bins are located," Becky explains.

The three of them determinedly walk to the supermarket. Saskia tells Ava and Max to stay outside, while she walks into the store to inspect. She wanders around like she is looking for something, but she can feel the piercing eyes of the man behind the counter trained on her neck. There are camaras all over the store. She finds the door at the back of the store and walks through it. "What do you want?" a youngish man confronts her on the other side of the door. She freezes and looks at him, astonished. "You need to leave. Immediately!" She leaves the supermarket.

Standing in front of the store again, Saskia tells Ava where the door is and asks her to try to get into the back of the store, unseen. "You must wait till you see the youngish

28

man in the store. He has dark hair, is thin and rangy, and wears a strange, blue uniform that looks like pjs," Saskia explains. Ava checks the aisles for the man and makes sure the way to the back is clear. Then she rapidly slips through the back door. In the meantime, after the incident with Saskia, the owner has moved from behind the counter to the back room. Immediately, upon Ava's entry into the backroom, he exclaims in a loud voice with a strong Hispanic accent, "Young lady! We get you people creeping around here all the time. This is like a rat infestation! I will call the police now!"

Ava breaks down on the floor. "Please don't, sir. I beg you. My mother, my little brother, and I are hungry. Just hungry. And we have no money."

The man shakes his head in resignation. "I hate this. I cannot help all of you. I, too, have my own family to feed." He looks at her with pity. "I will not call the police, but you need to leave now and *never* come back."

Ava is sobbing. "But you don't understand. We need food! Don't you have discarded food somewhere? Please!"

He sighs loudly and sits down on a crate, shaking his head. "I don't understand what is happening to the world. It is falling apart."

"Please!" Ava repeats.

"You said discarded food?" he asks.

"Yes!" Ava replies, wiping her face while getting up.

He remains on the crate and points to a door. "Go through that door and into the yard. There are two large dumpsters out there with old food. Help yourself." He gets up, while saying, "But do NOT come back! This is a one-off." He walks away, while shaking his head and repeating, "Fucking rat infestation. Fucking rat infestation."

Ava fills her pockets, hands and arms and waddles back through the store and out on the street. Saskia and Max run up to her to help her carry her loot. The man is back behind the counter. He looks out the window. "Fucking rats..." he mumbles.

Back in the camp, they are the heroes of the day. Everybody gets up, clapping and cheering as they walk across the platform. Saskia, Ava, and Max hold their heads high. They dump all the food near the fireplace. "Well done!" Trash is coming over to them. "That is a very impressive first catch!" Saskia reflects on the phrase "*first* catch." It confirms her suspicion that there will be many more dispatches up above ground to hunt for food, loot bins, and get on the wrong side of shopkeepers. As she goes to sleep after dinner, she is still smiling. She thinks with gratitude of how lucky they are to have found this welcoming and generous group of people. Nevertheless, during her sleep, she dreams of running frantically around, searching for food. She dreams of breaking something repeatedly and having to spend endless hours mending it, while the urgency of not having found any food mounts. She wakes up with a shock, soaked with sweat. An eerie feeling has settled in her mind during her sleep. It will never leave her again.

Days and weeks follow. Every day, Saskia and the kids are tossed a challenge: get food for dinner, clear an underground passageway of rubble and stones, clean the showers, wash all the blankets at the laundromat, guard the exits and entries, and so on. No day goes by without a challenge to overcome. Saskia doesn't mind hard labor. She has done that all her life. But she does mind the stress of earthlings, such as subway workers, making a sudden entry into their secret world, or of the constant pressure of having to find food. The unpredictability and uncertainty about their future is also taking its toll. On more than one occasion, she is forced to steal food. She doesn't tell Ava and Max because she knows that she leads by example. Actions speak louder than words.

"Today is the day we need your excellent skills at getting food!" Lucky walks over to her. She feels the panicky fear from her dream pumping through her veins. She has exhausted all the opportunities of scavenging dumpsters outside supermarkets and drugstores. From now on, the only option left is to steal.

A couple of hours later, Saskia is standing in a narrow aisle of the drugstore. She has checked that there are no camaras, which makes her momentarily overly confident. She takes her time looking at the different packages of biscuits wondering which ones both Ava and Max will like. She selects one and stuffs it in under her large coat. Later, she realizes the large coat gave her away. With the weather being warm outside, there is no reason to walk around in a large coat, except if you have something to hide beneath it.

The guard puts a firm hand on her shoulder the moment she bags her loot. She jumps with a fearful shock.

He came out of nowhere. An instant later, she is sitting in the back room of the large drugstore, pleading with the guard not to call the police. "I have no record. I am just trying to feed my children!" She is holding both hands before her, begging him to let her go.

"Do you know how many times I hear this? Every day!" the guard says in an angry tone of voice. "You all come in here. Rob and steal and then beg for your lives. Get yourself a job like everybody else!"

Saskia looks at him for a moment, then says, "But we are homeless. If you don't have an address, you cannot find a job."

"This may sound logical in your world, but we are many people who get up early in the morning to travel far to go to work for pennies. Pennies!" the guard says. "Why should you be allowed off the hook? And what kind of a mother puts her children in such a situation?" The police knock on the door. Saskia feels icy chill creeping up her spine. Her throat is narrowing. *Shit! Shit! Shit!* she thinks, besieged by panic.

The guard walks out of the room to inform the police of the incident. Now, only a young boy is left in the room watching over her. Suddenly, she gets up and charges full force ahead, pushing the young boy to the ground while running out of the door. The guard and two policemen are right behind her down the aisle. She runs out and down the street toward the secret door on Lexington Avenue, all the while thinking how she can get through the door, making three knocks twice, without getting noticed or caught. She passes the door. Her heavy coat opens and some of her loot falls to the ground, leaving clues as to where she has gone. The police are right behind her. Suddenly she makes a sharp right and runs down a narrow alleyway holding large dumpsters with cardboard and empty crates. She crawls behind one of the dumpsters and holds her breath. "Please God!" she prays. "Please!" She doesn't dare to look out. After what seems an eternity, she sneaks out and hurries back to the secret door on Lexington Avenue. Three knocks twice and it opens. Once inside, she almost collapses with relief.

When she's back on the platform, Saskia walks over to Lucky and asks for a private word. He gets up, and she follows him through a door and down a narrow corridor with a myriad of cables hanging above their heads. "I was caught today," she starts with hesitation in her voice. "But I escaped the police, and made it back down here unseen."

"Right! It has happened to all of us," Lucky says, stopping to check if she is okay.

"Yes. But I can't do this anymore…" she says firmly.

Lucky is still looking at her, when he says, "Look! I can offer you combat training, so that you can defend yourself better, in case you get caught again. We can improve your running, both your speed and endurance. That is what I can offer. But you and your kids can't stay here if you do not contribute to the community like everybody else. That is *not* an option."

Saskia anticipated this answer and proposes, "If you tell me all the different assignments there are down here in the underground, I can select the ones at which I could possibly excel."

Lucky looks at her again. "Let me tell you something. We are thousands of people living down here. I probably shouldn't be telling you this. But I like you and the kids, and I want you to stay. There are three levels of settlement. We are at sub-level 1. There are many sub-level 1s. Fewer sub-level 2s and only one sub-level 3, where the leaders are."

Saskia is astonished at the level of apparent organization ruling the underground. "Right. So, what are you saying...?" she wants Lucky to continue.

"The higher your level, the more comfortable your living quarters and general quality of life is. For instance, we at sub-level 1 hand over a portion of our food to both sub-levels 2 and 3. We wash clothes for people at sub-levels 2 and 3. You only just arrived so we were easing this information to you little by little, but now that you tell me you don't want to work with us... Well, I think, it is important for you to get the bigger picture."

Saskia challenges Lucky, "So, if we get their food, wash their clothes, and do other chores for sub-level 2 and 3, what do *they* do at sub-level 2 and 3?"

Lucky stops again and looks at her. "That is for another day. You are getting ahead of yourself." He is smiling, as he continues, "All you need to know, right now, is that I am offering you and the kids combat training. If you accept my offer, you may be able to advance. And you want to advance! Believe me!" Lucky is still smiling.

As they make their way back to the settlement, they pass the young boy that they met on their first day. He is still effortlessly swinging a machete in the air. The air whizzes as he slices it into a million small pieces. Saskia thinks to herself that he must have taken combat training. She agrees with Lucky to stay on and start combat training as soon as possible. Lucky is content.

The subsequent day, they are woken up in what seems the middle of the night by Trash and a young woman, whom Saskia has never seen before. Saskia presumes that she must come from one of the other settlements, possibly even from another sub-level. Later, it is confirmed that combat training is provided by the sub-level 2 settlers. That is their principal obligation. Success at sub-level 2 is measured by the number of sub-level 1 settlers that they can successfully train for combat. Such success is also measured by your ability and readiness to fight. The young woman is, indeed, from sub-level 2, and she is going to train them. Her name is Annona. She is tall, slender, and muscular.

Still, as she walks behind Annona for what seems an eternity, up and down stairways, and along wide and narrow corridors, Saskia doesn't think that she looks strong. Saskia has lost all orientation of where they are, but, overall, she thinks they may have ventured even further down into the underground. Suddenly, turning a sharp corner, they stand in front of a tall and wide double-sided gateway in neatly painted gray metal. They walk through a small door in the massive gateway. Once on the other side, Saskia, Ava, and Max are astonished by the scene awaiting them. They are in what seems to be an old train holding and repairs plant. It is vast! Along the edges of the plant, a gallery with doors runs on the second floor.

Below, on the ground floor, where they are standing, there is an arcade with doors. Saskia wonders where all those doors lead to.

"Welcome to sub-level 2!" Annona exclaims while opening her arms and spinning around on the middle of the floor. Large industrial light tubes dangle from the ceiling, flooding the plant floor in bright white light. There is a shooting range, boxing ring, fencing yard, knife throwing area, and so on. All along the periphery, there is a running track with a bunch of exhausted people dragging their feet to the loud and relentless yelling of a young man.

"You and some of your comrades from your settlement on the End Station—that is what we call your settlement—come here for combat training. Only if you become excellent soldiers will you be able to advance to sub-level 2. Trials and tribulations will determine if and when you are ready to advance."

Max asks, his voice full of excitement, "How long does it take to become a soldier?"

Annona looks at him. "Young man. Rule number one, listen! Listen to what I say! I will only say it once. I will not repeat myself. I said, 'if and when.' Many people never make it to sub-level 2. I don't know *if* you will make nor *how* long a time it might take you. That depends on you." Annona turns around. "First, each one of you must show me your baseline skills in each of the disciplines that we offer down here. Then I will determine which disciplines you will specialize in. You need at least two disciplines, preferably three, that you will perfect. But only one will be your preferred one. That one you must master to perfection! Everybody must be able to run. Run fast. And long. Run for your life! I mean it." Annona points to the people on the running track who, by now, are almost crawling along at a snail's pace.

Saskia is sweating and swearing her way through boxing, fencing, and shooting. After countless hours, Saskia looks at Annona, horrified, when Annona tells her that she must finish today's training with "a steady run," as she calls it, of forty-five minutes along the running track at the periphery of the plant floor. Saskia is slightly overweight. She has short legs; large, heavy breasts, and a voluptuous bottom that seems to pull her backward whenever she picks up pace. At best, she has run for the bus, but only rarely did she catch it. However, she did outrun those policemen, she thinks with a smug grin on her face. Then again, maybe she outsmarted them, rather than outran them. In fact, neither Saskia nor the guard and the two policemen were in any shape or form to run the distance. Saskia is built to move slowly. Since her late teens, she has been slightly overweight and learned how to compensate for her slowness by putting in extra hours. Extra hours cleaning, extra hours of factory work, extra hours of minding the elderlies, extra hours of grocery shopping, extra hours of everything.

Back on the End Station, Saskia feels sick with exhaustion. Too sick to eat. She collapses into deep sleep. In this way, weeks and months pass with simple obligations determined by their sub-level 1 leaders, and combat training mandated by their eminent sub-level 2 leader, Annona. Saskia loses count of the hours in the day, the days in the week, and the weeks in the month. Time hurries by.

To Saskia's relief, her children, who have not yet accumulated and stored excess food on their bodies, turned out to be fast learners and fast movers. In fact, they are thrilled with the training. Soon enough, Max shows talent for knife throwing and machete swinging. Ava seems a refined shooter. However, after weeks of training, Saskia's choice of combat skills remains undetermined. Boxing and fist fighting are off. Shooting is also not her thing. Fencing is totally off.

Saskia is getting moderately desperate, as she asks Annona, "What happens if I find no discipline that I can perfect, and both my children show great talent and advance to sub-level 2 without me?"

Annona looks at her. "You would not be the first mother to see her child or children advance, while she remains on sub-level 1. In which case, you will just stay on the End Station." Saskia remembers Becky, whom she spoke to one of her first days. Becky explained that her son is "somewhere down here," but without knowing exactly where.

The thought of her children venturing on into the underground without her makes her sick. "How can I protect them, if I am not there?" she asks herself, distressed. Then, in that moment, she realizes that her children are doing combat training *in order to go into actual combat*. She may lose her children altogether.

Saskia has noticed that many of the settlers at sub-level 2 are young, some of them even just kids. In contrast, at sub-level 1, there are a few older settlers, who seem to have gotten stuck in limbo on End Station. Some of them appear to have severe mental illnesses. Saskia reflects on what came first: the mental illness or the homelessness? Being homeless is enough to turn anyone, even the most mentally resilient, into a mental wreck plagued by illnesses, especially if you lose your children to the underground in the process.

The mental illness is a veil behind which some of these older settlers hide. They hide from the world and the harsh realities of their existence. Behind this veil are the real people with their sanity perfectly intact. Saskia has sometimes seen and even spoken to the sane people behind the veil of insanity. She has seen some of these elderly settlers in the streets. Like an earthling, she too has given them a wide berth, when confronted with them in the real world.

One of them goes by the name Troll. He stands in the streets and screams from the top of his lungs. "What the fuck of a life! You think this is a life? You just walk away. You just leave me here to rot in hell. Just get on with you fine lives while I rot in hell." Another one of the elderly settlers, who has also permanently stationed on the End Station and goes by the name Preacher. Nobody knows where he came from. He seems alone in this world. Preacher stands on street corners yelling, "You believe in earth! You believe in God! Yeah, yeah," he lowers his voice, and raises it again as he continues, "I feel it! Hail Mary! Save us all! Save us all!" But nobody is coming to his rescue. Little do people passing them know that Troll and Preacher may be among the sanest of all of us. Troll and Preacher know exactly where we are all heading. They have found an effective coping mechanism for surviving the journey ahead.

Saskia is determined to follow her children to sub-level 2. After weeks, even months, of relentless training, Saskia is slimmer than she can ever remember being before. She has a newfound self-confidence. She reflects, "Do I really have a greater self-confidence because I am slimmer? Am I just as compliant to society's norms as everybody else? Am I really that shallow?" At some point, she gives up trying to understand why her self-confidence has grown and instead starts enjoying her increased mobility, energy, and agility. She spends time in front of the mirror looking at her newly defined jawline and cheekbones. Her thighs, bottom, and belly are muscular and tight. Her arms are well-defined. She turns and twists in front of the mirror, surprised at who is looking back at her.

The day has come for them to hear what their specialized combat category is. Saskia is still undecided. She has proven no combat skills whatsoever, despite her newfound strength. But she has become a relatively fast and persistent runner. She is also good at climbing, but that is hardly a combat skill.

"Ava! You have proved yourself an exceptionally good shooter. I have your first assignment…" Annona says in a proud tone of voice. "Together with a special combat unit that, like yourself, largely specializes in shooting, you will break into the Bureau of Alcohol, Tobacco, Firearms and Explosives, raid, rob, and retrieve a large batch of guns and other firearms that New York police confiscated from criminals. The firearms are held in the storage of The Bureau of Alcohol, Tobacco, Firearms and Explosives for analysis. But we can put those arms to better use!"

Saskia is in a total panic, as she loudly interferes, "I do not accept this! Ava is only thirteen years old. It is totally unacceptable."

Ava turns around. She has grown considerably during the past months of relentlessly tough training. "Mum. Don't worry about me. We all have to contribute. And it is for the cause," Ava calmly says.

"What cause?" Saskia asks. "What cause? I haven't heard of any cause!"

Annona looks at Saskia with compassion, as she says, "You will only know about the cause once you advance. Right now, I am sorry to say, it looks like you are not advancing, Saskia. I cannot recommend that you go into combat. It is a question of life and death out there. Not just your life. But also, the lives of your comrades." Saskia feels totally helpless. She is losing her own children to this underground and their cause—whatever the hell that is. "This is not what I signed up for! If you, Lucky, and some of the other leaders had told me that this was the endgame, we would have exited the underground even before we settled. This is *not* what we signed up for!" Saskia insists, without any effect.

"Anyway, if you are done now, honey," Annona says, looking at Saskia overbearingly. "I will continue to congratulate Max, who is exceptional with the knife and machete. There is a large demonstration planned for next week. We need you and some of your comrades from the street combat unit to stir things up during the demonstration. We want the demonstration to end in chaos—and even better, a bloodbath!"

Saskia breathes heavily as she says, "I protest!"

Annona turns to her, again, and says, "It is a bit late for that. We have invested enormous amounts of resources in you three. And to be honest, you are a lost cause and have really just wasted our time, energy, and resources. You can walk away from here, but you can never leave the underground. Not at this stage. Anyway, your children have a bright future ahead of them. I hope you will not stand in their way."

With no further ado, Annona turns around to take Ava and Max in her arms and slowly walks off with them, grabbing each by the shoulders, while gently pushing them forward. Ava and Max are entering the gladiator academy getting prepped for a life of combat. "You will see your mother later. You are always allowed to visit the End Station and your mother. Any time!"

Saskia runs after them. "Wait! Wait!" she yells, as she walks in front of them and stops to confront Annona. "Listen. Give me any challenge, and I will show you I can succeed. I have it in me. I just don't fall into any one of your stupid combat categories. But I know better than most how to fend for myself in this life!"

Annona stops to look at her. "Okay. Fair enough. I will talk to my superiors about your proposal. We will get back to you. Till then, Hammer will follow you back to the

End Station." Annona points at the large man who has emerged seemingly out of nowhere. Saskia sighs.

"But you promise to get back to me with my challenge?" she asks for reassurance from Annona.

"Yes. Yes," Annona replies impatiently.

Saskia insists, "And if I pass the challenge, I will advance to sub-level 2 and live with my children here?"

"Yes!" Annona says while continuing to walk away with Ava and Max in her arms. Hammer walks her back to the End Station.

The subsequent day, Hammer summons her in the late afternoon. He waves for her to follow him toward the door leading the long way back to sub-level 2. Once back in the plant floor, she is greeted by Annona and her children. Ava and Max run toward her, embrace and kiss her. "Mum, Mum!" they exclaim, jumping up and down. However, before she gets a chance to talk with her children, Annona waves at her. Saskia follows Annona into a large meeting room at the other end of the plant floor. Inside, two women and three men are seated around a large mahogany table. One of the women gets up. She has immaculately neat, gray hair that rests effortlessly on her shoulders. She is petite. She is wearing what looks like a gray uniform of sorts. Her name is Kate. Saskia thinks Kate must be in her mid-fifties. Kate rests causally on the edge of the table with her hands in her lap.

"You remember the warehouse that used to employ your husband?" Kate starts. Saskia looks confused. Of course, she remembers the warehouse, but how does this woman know about the warehouse?

"Yes, yes..." Saskia replies with vagueness in her voice. She knows that the time has come for her to hear her challenge. She waits with eager anticipation, ready to face whatever challenge lies ahead in order to be reunited with her children.

Kate continues, "That warehouse, which was shut down and caused the death of your husband," Kate pauses. "Okay... we can debate whether his death was a good or bad thing another day. Anyway, that warehouse was bought, and its assets stripped by one of the richest financiers in New York. That is what he does! That is how he makes his fortune. He profits from other people's misery. Hard-working people, just like yourself, Saskia."

Saskia looks perplexed at Kate and at the others sitting around the table watching her. Saskia thinks to herself that they are obviously trying to make her challenge as personal as possible to her. After Saskia collects her thoughts, she says, "Right. But we know that. That is just the way of the world, right? Some people enrich themselves from other people's misery."

Kate gets up. "No. We are no longer willing to accept being the underdogs of this world. There is no logical explanation why this financier should be rich beyond reason, and at the expense of our livelihood—while we work ourselves to the bone for next to nothing! Here in the underground, we no longer accept this premise. We are fighting for a better world. We are willing to use any means necessary to get ahead in the world. That is 'the cause.'"

Saskia nods. "I get it. So, what are we doing here in the underground, if we don't accept the ways of the world?"

Kate stands up straight with her legs spread wide. "We fight! We fight! That is what we do. Enough is enough!"

A cold chill runs down Saskia's spine. She doesn't like what she hears. She thinks of her children. Then she remembers that she has been summoned to hear her challenge, which will eventually reunite her with her children. Saskia thinks to herself, *This is all about my children. The rest they can keep for themselves.* Kate walks over to her and puts a firm hand on her shoulder. Saskia straightens her back. "We have a challenge for you. You too can fight for the cause. If you pass your challenge, you will advance to sub-level 2 and live a good life here in the plant, together with your children," Kate says.

Saskia is intensely curious. "Okay. What's the challenge?"

Kate embarks on a long tale. "The financier who acquired your dead husband's former place of employment—Dr. Darren Glenmore—recently bought a huge 18-carat diamond at a large celebrity-led auction at Christie's for his young fourth wife, Christel. Your assignment is to steal this diamond. We have a special customer who is willing to pay us five million dollars in cash for the diamond. Money that we can use for the people down here. Money that will give us all a better life, more security and protection. Step-by-step, we are working our way out of this misery."

Saskia thinks she's probably no smarter than anyone else in the underground, but she is certainly more desperate. Now, this desperation is her driving force. "Ohhh…" Saskia hesitates. "Do you know, where this doctor lives? Do you have any information that can help me?"

Kate and the others reply in consensus, "Yes, we have lots of information."

Kate continues, "Annona, whom you already know very well, will help you prep for this assignment. She will walk you through all the information you need. Together with Annona and our specialists, you will find the best way in, around, and out of Dr. Glenmore's residence, *with* the diamond. Do you see? In, move to the exact location of the diamond, steal it, and get out!"

Saskia nods. "Right. I get that. So, when do we start?" Kate and the others sitting around the conference table, reply in unison, "Now!"

Annona places a gentle hand on Saskia's shoulder to indicate that they will be leaving now, together. Annona shows Saskia her new living quarters on the ground floor in the sub-level 2 plant. "You will stay here, while we train for the assignment. You will not be asked to do anything else but prepare and execute the assignment till it is completed."

Saskia sighs with reliefs and asks, "Do my children live close by?"

Annona shows her where Ava and Max live. It is a bit further down the arcade, quite nearby. "But you will not really have time to do anything else but prepare for the assignment in the next coming weeks. I doubt you will be spending much time with your children," Annona says and continues. "Anyway, both Ava and Max are also busy preparing for their first assignment as members of their sub-level 2 combat units." Saskia turns her head away from Annona. She doesn't like to think about her young children being sent out to rob and fight.

Chapter Two

Days and weeks pass with tough physical training and detailed information brain dumps. Saskia is both physically and mentally beat exhausted when she goes to sleep. She is woken up at six every morning. "To give your days structure," Annona explains. After countless weeks of brutal training, Annona asks Saskia to ascend the underground and go live in an apartment in the upper world that is owned by the underground. The apartment is situated on the fourth floor of an old brownstone on West 117th Street, between Frederick Douglass Boulevard and St. Nicholas Avenue in Harlem. The neighborhood has undergone substantial gentrification over the past decade and has recently become quite swanky. Saskia has also undergone substantial transformation. Anyone who knew her in her old life, back in Baychester, would hardly recognize her today. She is slender and muscular. Her hair is kept totally short.

She carries her large duffel bag effortlessly up to the fourth floor and rings the bell. A thin, young man opens the door. "Oh, it's you!" he says, while continuing, "they could have told me you would arrive today." He turns around, leaving the door open. She follows him into the den. "The kitchen, den, and bathroom we share. They must be kept totally tidy!" He walks into a large room. "This is yours! You get the nicest room in the apartment. It is probably the old living room."

The apartment is in a poor state. It has the original wooden floors and panels along the walls. Paint is chipping off the walls, revealing layer upon layer of wallpaper and paint. Instead of curtains, thin tissue bleached into dusty colors by the sun are nailed to the upper window frame. Saskia's large room has greenish walls and pale purple tissue covering two large windows facing West 117th Street. The sun's rays are warming the room. A large mattress is placed on the floor against the wall opposite the windows. Pillows, duvets, and blankets are randomly tossed on the mattress. There is a clothes rag and a small desk. The rest of the room is unfurnished, leaving plenty of open floorspace in the middle of the room. Saskia loves the room. She hasn't had her own room and proper privacy for almost a year by now. The underground doesn't offer such luxuries.

The thin young man has dark hair and eyes, and pale skin. Saskia can't really place his ethnicity. "Where do you come from?" she asks him.

"Everywhere and nowhere. We don't ask that type of question here," he replies and looks at her. "Anyway, my name is Elijah. But everybody calls me Eli. I am here to help you with your equipment, firearms, explosives, listening devices, tracking devises, room sensors, camaras, night vision goggles, and anything else you believe necessary for this assignment... I have also had the floorplan of Dr. Glenmore's place digitalized. In fact, if you are able to put room sensors and camaras in one or more rooms, then we can follow all activity from my screen in the real time. In that way, when you are in the house, I can warn you if someone is entering the room, walking toward you down a corridor, or blocking your exit. You see? But that means that you must get into the place, to install all the sensors, before you actually *do* the theft. I don't know what your plan is?"

Saskia nods. "Humm... I think, before anything else, I should start surveilling the house and shadowing its inhabitants—to get a sense of who's in there and what everybody's daily routines are. For instance, when do they leave the house? I heard that Christel goes running every morning. I need to familiarize myself with the clockwork of the house. Also, maybe I should also start entering the house without stealing anything, to get a real sense of the floorplan, entries, and exits. That way, if I think it's worth the risk, I can place these devices of yours. But under what pretense do I enter the house?"

Eli nods. "This is your assignment. It's *your* life on the line, so you decide how you want to go about it. Do you have a deadline from sub-level 3?"

Saskia sighs. "Yes. I have two months—tops—to steal the diamond. They have a buyer waiting."

The next day, Saskia gets up at six a.m. and grabs a coffee. Afterward, she goes for a run in Central Park. She is ecstatic about being out in the open. Free. Hear the birds, feel the gentle wind caressing her cheeks. Let the early morning sun's warmth permeate her body. By eight, she is back on the street and heading over to Upper East Side and 1067 Fifth Avenue, where Dr. Darren Glenmore and his young wife Christel reside on the four top floors of a late Neoclassical high-rise. The two top floors are the private quarters of Dr. Glenmore and Christel, while the two floors below those house an expansive kitchen, storage, laundry rooms, staff accommodations, surveillance rooms, security staff quarters, and so on. Fifteen people are employed to maintain the private residence of Dr. Glenmore.

Luckily, the fence into Central Park on the opposite side of the street is covered with wood panels that screen the restoration work going on inside the park. Because there are no workers on this particular Saturday, Saskia can set up her surveillance station unhurriedly on the work site. A hole in the fence grants a perfect view to the main entrance of 1067 Fifth Avenue, as well as the adjacent staff entrance on East 88th Street.

For two full, uninterrupted days, Saskia is able to get a sense of the inner workings of Dr. Glenmore's household, at least on weekends. While waiting and watching outside Dr. Glenmore's building, she thinks of how best to go about her assignment. Inside her head, Saskia hears the voices of the leaders of sub-level 3, who handed her the assignment. It's not the first time the underground has planned a theft of this type and magnitude. In their view, a fast "in and out" theft is the most successful. "The more you linger, the greater the risk of getting caught," Annona explained, and continued. "Such an 'in and out' theft must be planned down to the smallest detail." Annona recommends Saskia access the private quarters of Dr. Glenmore through the roof.

While sitting and surveilling, Saskia notices a woman in a maid's uniform exiting the staff door. The woman looks like Saskia's former self. Saskia reflects on the possibility of befriending this servant and maybe, in some way that she has yet to clearly think through, use such a friendship to gain access to Dr. Glenmore's home. Making a split-second decision, Saskia gets up, stretches her legs, and follows the woman down East 88th Street. The woman walks determinedly toward a street cart selling coffee and pretzels. She grabs both, turns around, and briskly walks back toward Central Park. She hits the pavement hard each time her foot touches down. A reflection of both her personality and stature. She is short and overweight. It is a beautiful spring day. The sun is high in the bright, blue sky. Once in the park, the woman sits down on a bench to enjoy what seems to be her afternoon snack.

Saskia sits down next to her on the bench. "What a beautiful day!" she says, inviting a casual conversation. "Maybe now we finally get warmer weather." The advantage of living in shifty climates, such as New York, is that the weather always grants an opportunity to break the ice for any conversation.

The woman turns to her and smiles. "Yes. If we don't suddenly get another blizzard!" They both know that they are out of their element in this wealthy neighborhood.

Saskia audaciously says, "I just had a job interview, but I don't think I will get the job. Damn that! I really needed it!" Saskia stares into the air in front of her in a meditative manner. She knows that if she says anything else, the conversation will seem too purposely forced.

After a short while, the woman asks, "What kind of job are you looking for?"

Saskia replies, while still fixating her eyes on the air in front of her, "Anything, really. Cleaning, washing, cooking, whatever! I worked for three years minding elderly ladies, and did some all-round housework."

After a short while, the woman asks, "Where was that?"

"Oh, that was in Baychester, Bronx. But I moved to Harlem recently, and I am looking for work in Manhattan. But it's not easy."

Saskia and the woman have sat next to each other in silence for a couple more minutes, when the woman gets up. "I must get back to work now. I am a cleaner in the house over there." She points toward the building on 1067 Fifth Avenue. "By the way, my name is Rita." She reaches out her right hand to greet Saskia. Rita continues, while starting to walk away, "We are looking for a cleaner right now. I think."

Saskia gets up. "Really!" She follows Rita along the pathway back to Fifth Avenue. "Do you think I can apply for that job? Whom do I contact?" she asks with excitement in her voice.

"Give me your number, and I will forward it to our housekeeper, Mrs. Charter. She may get in touch with you."

Saskia stops on the pathway. "Thanks a million. I really appreciate it."

Rita writes Saskia's number in her phone. Then she picks up her pace. "I must go now. I hope Mrs. Charter will get in touch with you. Fingers crossed!" She smiles, turns around, and leaves.

Once Rita is out of sight, Saskia is bursting with excitement and anticipation. She is trying to restrain herself, but this almost seems too good to be true. Later that evening, she walks back to the apartment on West 117th Street with a bounce in her step. To her surprise, when she opens the door to the apartment and yells, "I'm back!" Annona appears from the kitchen. Saskia walks into the kitchen, where Eli is also sitting. He looks worried.

"The plans have been forwarded," Annona says firmly. "We need the diamond in three weeks."

Saskia sits down on a chair, utterly deflated. "It's just not doable," Saskia says, shaking her head.

Annona looks at her. "Look! I am just the messenger. These are your new orders. Three weeks!"

They share some plain supper, which Eli has made, while Saskia asks Annona how Ava and Max are. Both completed their first assignments successfully. "Max ended up in ER and got some stitches, but he didn't get caught, which is the main thing," Annona says reassuringly, then continues, "Ava is working with a small group of our youngest, scraping off the serial numbers of the crime guns that they robbed from the storage facility of the Bureau of Alcohol, Tobacco, Firearms and Explosives. It was a great heist! The leaders are very pleased with both your kids' efforts." Saskia feels terrible knowing that her children are becoming professional criminals and risking their lives to survive in the underground. But she knows there is nothing she can do.

She has no alternative means of survival to offer them. You can get into the underground, but you can never leave. Hearing about Ava and Max's ordeals, her resolve to pursue her assignment is strengthened. "Right!" she says, and gets up. "I have an early start tomorrow morning. By the way, I befriended a cleaner of the Glenmore household. Her name is Rita."

Saskia turns to Eli and asks, "Can you find any information about Rita, the housekeeper, Mrs. Charter, and others working at the Glenmore household? I told Rita that I am looking for a job. Hopefully Mrs. Charter will call me for an interview. I told Rita things that are true, where I worked and lived before, so that I'm less likely to be caught in a lie. Who knows! Maybe I will *work* in the Glenmore household. Then we are one giant step closer to getting the diamond!"

Mrs. Charter calls her the subsequent day and asks her to come that same afternoon for a job interview through the staff entrance to the 8th floor. Saskia is nervous, but convinces herself that she is just applying for a job as a cleaner. "It's just a job!" she convinces herself. Deep inside, however, she knows the stakes are higher than that. Yet, at this stage, to calm herself, she can't be thinking about how to steal the diamond.

If she gets the job, great! If she doesn't get it, she will revert to the original plan of rappelling down from the roof into the private quarters of the Glenmores on the top floor. This plan requires that she use explosives to break into the safe, even though that doesn't sit well with her. Saskia asks

Eli, "Is using explosives really the best way of breaking into the safe? There must be a better way that doesn't cause an explosion." They agree that the exact details of the theft are best left till later, when Saskia has a better sense of the situation and of her options.

She practices sentences that she can recite with ease during the interview. She lists all the tasks she did in her former job and learns them by heart. By the time, she walks through the staff entrance, she feels well prepared. Although, she is still struggling to explain why she left her former job and moved to Manhattan.

On the ground floor, right inside the staff entrance of East 88th Street, a guard is sitting behind a desk. He gets up and verifies her name on the list that is on his desk, before him. Then he shows her to the elevator. She must go through a metal detector to get to the elevators.

Once on the eighth floor, she is immediately greeted by Mrs. Charter. "Welcome! So good of you to come at such short notice. We are looking for a cleaner to start immediately." They walk down a dimly lit, narrow corridor to Mrs. Charter's modest office.

By the end of their forty-minute interview, Mrs. Charter smiles and gets up. "Let me show you the house. Dr. Glenmore and Mrs. Christel are at their weekend residence in Martha's Vineyard. That's really their preferred residence. They also stay there during the week, whenever possible." Saskia walks around, trying to match the rooms, corridors, and stairways with the floorplan on Eli's computer. She asks questions about the routines of Dr. Glenmore and Mrs. Christel. By the end of the tour,

Mrs. Charter and Saskia find themselves back on the eighth floor in front of the elevator. "Right! If you want the job, and you can start next Monday, it's yours! The rate is fourteen dollars an hour, and there is a three-month trial period to start with, during which you can resign or be laid off with immediate notice."

Saskia lights up. "Perfect! And thank you so much. I am so happy that you've given me a chance. What time do I start Monday? Eight?"

Once back in the Harlem apartment, Saskia conceives a plan with Eli for how to go about the theft of the diamond. "There is a guard right inside the staff entrance, and a metal detector that all staff have to walk through before getting to the elevators," Saskia explains.

Eli looks contemplative. "Right. That rules out a lot of the equipment. Maybe I can find substitutes for the equipment that won't trigger the metal detector."

Saskia and Eli spend the whole weekend going through the floorplan; they agree, at least in theory, where to put the listening devices, room sensors, and cameras—that is, if Eli finds a way for Saskia to get such devices past the metal detector. "You should also plan to smuggle in a loaded firearm that can be hidden and retrieved. Just in case you need it," Eli says.

Saskia reflects, "But how do I get a firearm through the metal detector?" Eli reassures her there are hard plastic firearms after that will pass through the metal detector undetected—although they can't be used more than once or twice. He will try to get hold of such a gun, as well as the other devices that will also have to pass through it.

Monday morning, Saskia steps out, feeling up to the challenge of familiarizing herself with her new job, new colleagues, superiors, and surroundings. To her relief, it is Rita who shows her what will be expected of her, and what the household routines are. She almost feels that she knows Rita, even though she's only known for ten minutes longer than everybody else in the household. Saskia thanks Rita for making the contact. Rita is happy to have what seems to be a new ally on the staff.

Days pass; Saskia is settling into her job, and winning over her new colleagues, including Mrs. Charter, who politely nods to her when they pass each other on the top floor corridors. In the kitchen, Mrs. Charter asks her how she's doing. If there is anything she needs. Saskia smiles and declines, reassuring Mrs. Charter that she is the right person for the job.

After about a week, Saskia is so comfortable in her new job that she has a bit of time to spare. She uses that time to sneak around the top floor of the house and places the sensors and listening devices that will help her pull off the theft. On a couple of occasions, she engages in small talk with Mrs. Christel, who seems kind but extremely timid and private. Because she is very beautiful, her shyness is usually misinterpreted as an almost intimidating arrogance. Obviously, Dr. Glenmore never misinterpreted Christel's shyness for arrogance. Consequently, he was able to sweep her off her feet ahead of plenty of young, ambitious men who were less self-assured. These men let their insecurities get the better of them, and convinced themselves that Christel is too remote, too arrogant and inapproachable. However, Christel is just a shy woman. She is also kind and intelligent. Dr. Glenmore could see this as clear as daylight, because he did not put stumbling blocks in the way of his own pursuit. After Christel married the self-assured Dr. Glenmore, the young, ambitious men added "gold-digger" to the list of Christel's misunderstood characteristics.

Another thing Saskia notices is that Christel is depressed, bewildered, and distracted. Marrying into vast wealth has certainly not seemed to make her happy, Saskia thinks. She can't believe that Christel has always been so helpless—even though, she acknowledges that a lot of powerful men seem to be attracted to helpless women. *Maybe she grew into this peculiar state of mind through the encouragement of her husband. It is a way for him to keep her in his shackles,* Saskia thinks.

One day, she sees Christel's personal assistant (who doubles as her maid) blend some powder into Christel's morning juice. The personal assistant *cum* maid, called Sophia, is herself a young woman. Sophia has solid schooling and a higher education. In fact, Saskia wonders why she is working as a personal assistant and maid, but then she thinks of her own de-route. Sophia is from St. Louis, where her expansive family still resides. Sophia's job includes waking up Christel and reading aloud the day's program, which often includes socializing with Dr.

Glenmore's business associates and their wives. "Sophia, it is your job to know what I am doing, and what is the most appropriate attire for each occasion," Christel insists. "The worst thing that can happen is that I turn up in attire that makes my husband and myself look like a fool." Sophia wants nothing more than to make a fool of Christel. She resents Christel's privileges, believing that Christel is totally undeserving of them. In fact, she resents Christel. Even though she has often gone as far as she could in making a fool of Christel, Sophia has always made sure not to cross the line of mockery that would get her fired.

Saskia sees Sophia dropping the powder into Christel's morning juice again and again. Sophia altogether stops trying to conceal to Saskia what she is doing, prompting Saskia to ask her. "What is that powder, you are giving Christel every morning?"

Sophia confidently and casually responds, "It is part of Mrs. Christel's long array of daily supplements, including her Xanax and Prozac. Not that they make a damn bit of difference. She is in tatters anyway!"

The subsequent day, Saskia takes a sample of the white powder, when no one is watching. She brings it back to Eli for analysis. Eli confirms her fear. The powder is cocaine mixed with benzodiazepines. "No wonder Mrs. Christel is in tatters!" Saskia concludes, upset. She feels sorry for Christel. Nevertheless, Saskia is thinking how best to use her newly discovered intel to further her own cause: the theft of the diamond. "Should I tell Christel what Sophia is up to?" she asks Eli. He gets up and clears the table after dinner. By strict orders of sub-level 3, he does everything in the apartment.

"Saskia must focus *only* on stealing the diamond!" Eli was told by one of the leaders of sub-level 3 before leaving the underground. This supposedly justifies why he must do everything in the apartment. Eli doesn't know what Saskia should do with her intel.

Still pondering, he replies, "On the other hand, telling Christel of Sophia's betrayal doesn't necessarily get you closer to stealing the diamond."

After sleeping on the matter—because talking to Eli hasn't gotten her closer to a resolution—Saskia thinks that her best option is to use her newfound intel to blackmail Sophia into giving her the code of the safe. The safe, installed in Christel's bedroom during the early days of their marriage, is entirely dedicated to Christel's ever-expanding collection of expensive jewelry.

As part of her duties, Sophia is in charge of keeping Christel's clothes, bags, shoes, and jewelry tidily organized in her private rooms. Nevertheless, Saskia cannot be sure Sophia has access to the code of the safe. Saskia hopes that if Sophia knows the code, she will willingly part with it when faced with the threat of exposing her drug scam to Dr. Glenmore and Christel.

Saskia has no time to waste. The theft must be executed the subsequent week. In preparation of the break-in of the safe, she has already installed detector-proof listening devices and sensors in Christel's bedroom, dressing room, and corridor. With the code, she can open the safe quickly and quietly rather than using explosives, as Eli originally proposed. Before walking out of the apartment door that morning, Saskia tells Eli of her plan and asks him to get her an exact replica of the 18-carat diamond in case she has a chance to quietly open the safe with the code and swap the real diamond for a fake without being noticed. That would buy her time. Eli knows a dealer in the diamond district near Rockefeller Center who also sells fake diamonds made of cubic zirconia. Apparently, some men propose with fake diamonds! These men either do not want to go through with their marriage proposals, or they do propose only to sure that the woman of their desire stays a bit longer.

That morning, Saskia confronts Sophia when they are alone in the kitchen. "I know what you are doing," Saskia says with a piercing gaze into Sophia's eyes.

Momentarily, Sophia looks upset, then answers, "I make little secret out of giving Mrs. Christel *all* the meds she needs to get through her day. It is hardly a secret." Sophia knows she is audacious. She hopes Saskia doesn't know the exact nature of the white powder. The two women look at each other. Like in a staring contest, no one dares to blink.

Saskia says, "I mean, I *know* what the white powder is. It is cocaine and benzodiazepines. I am sure you are not supposed to give *that* to Mrs. Christel."

Sophia almost stutters, "Dr. Glenmore and I have an understanding that Mrs. Christel needs her meds. *All* of her meds!" Saskia is shocked. Can this really be?

Can it really be true that Dr. Glenmore is secretly drugging his young wife? Why? Maybe he wants to get rid of her. But then, if Dr. Glenmore wants to rid himself of his young wife, why is *Sophia* drugging Christel? Something doesn't add up.

Saskia says, "Listen, I am not here to stir things up."

Saskia tries to calm down Sophia, who replies, "It sure seems like you are here to stir things up! Don't you think?"

Saskia leans against the kitchen countertop as she continues, "I have a particular request. If I get what I am looking for, you can go about your business uninterrupted. To be honest, I don't much care what happens in this household."

Full of anticipation, Sophia asks the obvious question: "And what *do* you want?"

Saskia replies, "I want the code to Mrs. Christel's jewelry safe. You have that, right?"

Sophia shakes her head. "No. Only the head of security has that. He passes it on to the guard on duty, who is the only one allowed to open and close the safe. The code is changed, daily. They don't trust anyone else but the head of security and the guard on duty with the code."

Saskia is taken aback. Then she says, "Look. I don't care how you get the code. Just get it! And then I will do whatever I need to do and disappear out of your life. You will never see me again."

Sophia, who slowly starts to realize that she will probably go to jail if her crime is uncovered, looks at her with fluttering eyes and says, "I will try to see what I can do. Okay?"

Saskia replies, "Actually that is not okay. I *need* the code next week. Thursday? Friday? The code that is valid that day. Otherwise, I will go straight to Mrs. Christel. And by the way, I don't believe Dr. Glenmore approves of your drugging his wife. He probably thinks you are giving her something to calm her nerves. But how could he condone your filling her with cocaine and benzodiazepines!"

Saskia gets up and turns around to leave while asking insistently, "Thursday?" Sophia nods in reluctant acceptance and lowers her gaze. Saskia walks off.

Saskia feels terrible to be letting Sophia get away with drugging Christel. She might even kill her. When Christel returns from her morning run, Saskia looks at her with compassion and sadness. Christel is naturally upbeat and full of life. Life that is being squeezed out of her day by day. By the late afternoon, Christel is just an empty shell who submissively follows the instructions of Sophia, Mrs. Charter, Dr. Glenmore's butler, Dr. Glenmore himself—and anyone else, for that matter.

Saskia talks with Eli over dinner that evening. "Maybe I can leave an anonymous note for Christel before I leave?"

Eli looks at her, tilting his head while saying, "I don't think so! Look, get the bloody diamond and leave these people to kill themselves and each other. It is not our problem." Eli reflects, "Anyway, you need to continue going back to work *after* you have stolen the diamond. Even if they don't realize immediately that the diamond has been swapped for a fake, you'll draw unwanted attention to yourself if you suddenly stop coming to work." Saskia nods her head. "Yeah, I know. But as soon as I have the diamond necklace, I will hand in my resignation."

The subsequent day, Saskia asks Sophia if Christel takes something before going to bed. "She takes a sleeping pill, especially if she has been drinking at dinner," Sophia confirms. While cleaning Christel's bathroom, Saskia opens the medical cupboard in Christel's bathroom, takes out six sleeping pills and pops them in a sachet, which she pockets in her apron. "Make some *strong* sleeping pills that look exactly like these pills!" she commands Eli when she returns to the apartment that evening. They both know they are running out of time.

Thursday morning arrives and Saskia is hitting the pavement for 1067 Fifth Avenue with anticipation. She is waiting for Sophia in the kitchen. Sophia is late. *Damn her, if she just stays away and disappears!* Saskia thinks while pacing the kitchen floor. Suddenly, the door opens, and Sophia and Rita enter, chatting loudly. Saskia makes eye contact with Sophia and goes about some mundane tasks in the kitchen.

Once Rita leaves, Saskia turns to Sophia. "And?"

Sophia replies, "Don't worry, I sneaked a peek at the new code when the guard opened the safe this morning. I told the guard that I needed to prepare Christel's attire while she was out on her run. With Christel out, the guard and I were the only ones in her room, and I could easily distract him and see the code he entered to open the safe. Yes, I think, I got it right."

Saskia flushes. "I think it's is not good enough. It had better be the right code. It had better work..."

Sophia replies, "I will try to confirm the code again this evening before dinner. I will choose Christel's jewelry for dinner. When the security guard enters the code to return what she is wearing now into the safe and take out the jewelry I've selected for dinner, I will try to confirm that the code I have is right." Saskia looks slightly panicked, when she says, "Don't give her the diamond necklace tonight. Just don't!"

Sophia looks as if she's just had a revelation. She nods her head in assent.

Saskia is weighing the best time to steal the diamond: when Christel is out for dinner, or when she is fast asleep? She decides on the former, the best time is when Dr. Glenmore and Christel are out for dinner, which, she hopes, will offer Saskia the opportunity to access Christel's bedroom alone.

The household of Dr. Glenmore employs so much staff that Saskia cannot be certain that she is the only maid turning down Christel's room for the night. It's not impossible that another maid or servant might suddenly walk in on her. She must keep more options open, just in case. Thus, to be on the safe side, when cleaning Christel's bathroom that morning, Saskia swaps Christel's sleeping pill for Eli's stronger version—hoping Christel will ask for them in the evening before going to bed, and thus be in deep sleep, if, for whatever reason, Saskia must wait until then to reach into the safe.

"Good news!" Sophia confirms the code after she has finished dressing Christel for dinner.

While Sophia is putting on her coat to leave, Saskia repeats the code for reassurance and asks, "Remember. If you say anything to anyone, I will tell Mrs. Christel, Dr. Glenmore, and the police, if necessary, about what you've been giving Mrs. Christel. I have evidence. In any event, I have nothing to lose."

"Nor do I!" Sophia says loudly, and walks out of the door.

That evening, while Dr. Glenmore and Mrs. Christel are out at one of their dinner parties, Saskia calmly enters Christel's bedroom to turn it over for the night and steal the diamond. On an earlier occasion, Saskia had hit the fake diamond in the light panels out in the corridor, adjacent to Christel's rooms. She retrieved it earlier in the day as she dusted the panels in the corridor. The fake diamond is in her apron, wrapped in a cleaning cloth.

After finishing her duties in Christel's room, Saskia remains there, silent, waiting for Eli to send a message that the coast is clear. Despite having faith in Eli's surveillance system, all her senses are on high alert. She listens carefully to hear if anyone is out in the corridor or in the adjacent dressing room. Suddenly, Eli's text ticks in. "Clear! Go!"

She goes about her theft with a calmness that almost frightens her. Entering the code. It works! Looking in the many jewelry cases for the diamond. "There it is!" She replaces it with the fake one. No one will notice, and by the time they do, she will be far gone. She walks out of the bedroom with the real diamond in her apron, wrapped, as the fake was, in the cleaning cloth. Once downstairs, she carefully puts her rags in her bag. Only if she acts in a suspicious manner will she draw attention to herself. She is trying to swallow her rising anxiety and stay calm.

"That was so easy!" she exclaims, once back in the apartment with Eli.

"Well," he says. "You planned it well. And it was a truly smart move to get a job there." Later in the evening, Annona comes to collect the diamond. Saskia reluctantly hands it over.

"The leaders have promised that I will advance to sublevel 2 and live with my children, right?" she says, while clutching the diamond in her right hand.

Annona nods. "They are very pleased with the way you went about this assignment," Annona says and continues, "And they keep their word. Otherwise, it will soon be known that they cannot be trusted. You see? We cannot risk mutiny." Saskia is in no position to bargain. She must have faith, and offer her trust to Kate and Annona. Annona is on her way out of the door when she turns around to say, "Remember—if you do not turn up for work tomorrow and the days that follow, you will bring suspicion upon yourself. You can resign from your job, now, but you have to stay for however long you decide with Mrs. Charter. And think up some plausible excuse as to why you have to leave!"

Saskia dreads going back to work the following morning. She just wants to disappear. Crawl under a rock. Sophia looks at her somewhat surprised when she sees Saskia walking into the kitchen that morning. "Oh! It's you?" she asks.

"Why would I not be me?" Saskia says in a dry tone of voice. Later, Sophia corners her in the stock room to hear if she managed to steal the diamond. "Mind your own business!" Saskia says, annoyed. "You do what you must. I will do the same." When Saskia offers her resignation later that day, Sophia interprets behind the gesture a mission successfully completed. Mrs. Charter pleads with Saskia to stay until a replacement is found. Finally, Saskia agrees to stay this week and the subsequent week out. She feels that if she rushes her departure, she'll unnecessarily draws suspicion upon herself. She'd like to disappear into the underground and never resurface again.

On her second to last day of work, there arises a terrible commotion. Mrs. Charter sits in the kitchen, crying. Dr. Glenmore's butler is comforting her. Saskia looks confused and turns to Rita. "What is going on? What happened?" Saskia feels cold sweat running down her spine. She is careful not to speak a word for fear of putting her foot in her mouth and divulging incrimination information. "It's Mrs. Christel..." Rita says through the tears in her eyes.

"Yes?" Saskia begs. "What is it?"

"She jumped out of her bedroom window last night."

Rita holds her hands to her eyes as she starts sobbing. "Oh, my God," Saskia sits down. "Oh, my God. What a terrible thing to have happened."

After the whole household has settled into a state of shock, the police turn up in the kitchen. A police detective named Cliff Benson is leading the inquiry. "We'll treat this as a suicide, but we still need to speak to each and every one of you to rule out any foul play," detective Benson warns them. Saskia feels like running. Fleeing. Getting out of the building. She is suffocating. She can't breathe. Sophia walks across the room piercing Saskia's eyes with a stare as cold as ice. Saskia tries to calm her nerves.

In that moment, Dr. Glenmore makes his entrance in the kitchen yelling, "There you are! You sure took your time. My wife did *not* commit suicide! My wife did *not* commit suicide!"

Benson walks toward him. "Dr. Glenmore. I am leading this investigation. Can we go somewhere private to talk?" The two men exit, while a swarm of policemen and women dressed in civil attire and uniform stay behind in the kitchen.

A female officer turns around to address the room. "I will need to talk to each one of you. One by one. Please be patient."

The female officer is Claudia Brady. She is an assistant criminal investigator who reports to Benson. *What a fucking mess!* Saskia thinks to herself. *This is such a fucking mess!* Some time has passed since the interviews began. Brady then waves for Saskia to follow her upstairs.

"You! Come with me!" she commands. This is not Saskia's first encounter with the police. Back in Baychester, the police were constantly stopping people in the streets to body search them for firearms and drugs. Harassment and interrogation had become commonplace. Once the factory closed, these efforts intensified; naturally, this inflamed a deep hatred between the citizens of Baychester and the police. Saskia hates the police. She hates Brady.

After going through all the introductory questions regarding Saskia's job when she started work at the Glenmore's, Brady asks her where she lives. Saskia tries to maintain a steady gaze. She knows that if her eyes nervously search around the room, Brady will know that she is searching for an answer and become suspicious of her. "West 117th Street," Saskia replies calmly, while freefalling inside. No, she did not notice anything out of the ordinary.

"Really?" Brady looks at her with disbelief.

"Nothing?" No, Saskia assured her, she did not notice anything out of the ordinary.

As soon as Saskia is alone in the staff cloakroom, she calls Eli. She knows that a text message will be retrievable by the police. "Christel jumped out of the window last night, and the place is crawling with police. I was just interrogated by a detective." After some hesitation, Saskia says, "I had to give them our address. I didn't have the bandwidth to come up with a plausible lie on the spot!"

Eli is quiet at the other end of the phone. Then he says, "Okay. You need to clear Dr. Glenmore's place of all the devices you installed. Shit! What a mess! Get the gun! Get the gun!"

They are both in a panic. Saskia panics. "I can't. I just told you. The place is crawling with police."

Eli insists, "Saskia, you have to! The devices and gun are not traceable back to us, but they will provoke a million questions from the police. That won't do anyone any good."

Eli says, "I guess, I will go back into the underground with all my stuff. You should remain in the apartment on your own until further notice. Now that you have told the police where you live, you can't just evaporate. Your sudden disappearance will just arouse suspicion. But what if they look you up here?" Eli pauses, then he exclaims, "Shit! I will get hold of Annona."

Saskia frantically tries to remember where she installed devices and gun, but she is in such a state of panic that her brain has shut down. In her head, she had till the end of next week to get all her stuff. Now she needs to do everything in a hurry and do so during a full-blown panic attack, with the place packed to the brim with police, staff, and people everywhere.

She goes upstairs with her cleaning trolley and acts as if she is cleaning. Once upstairs, she swaps the cleaning trolly for a laundry trolly. She dumps the loaded gun, sensors, and listening devices into the bottom of the laundry basket. But did she get it all?

As Saskia heads back to the apartment in Harlem that evening, she thinks of Christel. *We are our circumstances. Maybe poor Christel was just not cut out for this world.*

And what a tragedy to have such a nemesis as Sophia worming her way into her body and soul, slowly killing her. Saskia isn't sure she understands Sophia's motive; perhaps it was simply jealousy and hatred toward Christel—someone Sophia believed had everything, but deserved nothing. Saskia thinks, *Maybe, it is for the better that she is no longer*... Deep inside, she knows that this is just a pathetic effort to assuage her own guilt for doing nothing. The fact is that Saskia and others in the Dr. Glenmore household did not want to acknowledge and deal with the profound unhappiness of Christel, including her excess self-medication. *Maybe I am not the only one who knows what Sophia was up to*, she thinks, while getting dizzy with the ramifications of what that means.

Annona is waiting for her when she walks through the door of West 117th Street. "What do you want now?" Saskia snaps, annoyed at the sight of Annona. "I am tired. Exhausted. And you know what? I'm fucking sad. Sad that Christel was pushed over the edge by that sicko Sophia! And that I didn't do anything to stop it!"

Annona looks at her and says, "This has nothing to do with you. You just keep your mouth shut and work your last days at the Glenmore's. Then you walk right back into the underground through the door on Lexington Avenue. Remember to bring all your shit with you. Don't leave anything behind. We will get rid of this apartment and erase all traces of us so that the police will not be able to find us. You ratted us out to the police by giving them this address. What a total disaster!"

Saskia looks surprised. "Precisely because I have given the police this address, I *can't* just disappear! Not even after I stop working at the Glenmore's. I have to stay here till things have calmed down."

Annona says impatiently, "These are my orders. If the police come here looking for you, you will *not* be here. That's all. The leaders don't trust that you won't talk. Spill the beans! You are summoned to the underground as soon as your employment terminates."

Saskia drags her feet to 1067 Fifth Avenue, the next morning. She gets there late. The house is in a solemn state of sorrow. Engulfed in grief, Dr. Glenmore is sitting in his office, staring blankly into the air. The police are still wandering around, picking out staff and family members for interrogation. They have effectively taken over the four top floors of 1067 Fifth Avenue.

After saying goodbye for the last time, Saskia cries all the way back to Harlem. Once in the apartment of West 117th Street, she packs everything and clears the place. Before she leaves, three men appear. They don't look at her, nor speak a word. They are going through the whole apartment, removing its contents and disinfecting everything.

Walking out of the door, Saskia contemplates how the underground seems peculiarly well-organized, well-resourced and equipped. *This is not just a community of homeless...* she reflects, *But what is it, then?* Once on the other side of the door on Lexington Avenue, she is greeted by the female leader of sub-level 3, Kate, who did most of the talking when Saskia was handed her assignment.

Annona is also there. "You did a phenomenal job!" Kate says.

As they walk the long way back to the vast plant floor at sub-level 2, Saskia thinks, she sees Sophia out of the corner of her eye, passing them. She decides not to say anything. She is too tired to deal with this now. But the more she *thinks* she knows, the less she actually knows of this peculiar underground society.

Once at sub-level 2, she is shown to her own new room. When she wakes up the following morning, daylight, of sorts, is shining on her face. Her room is in a sidewalk vault. A large bed is placed right beneath the glass prisms set into the concrete sidewalk above. Multiple prisms are set into steel-reinforced bars at different angles to collect and spread daylight throughout the room. When she lies in the soft bed with plenty of quilts and pillows, she can look up on the shadows of New Yorkers busily going about their daily errands. A new day. A new world.

Chapter Three

Saskia finds more freedom at sub-level 2 than she had previously experienced in the underground. The theft of the 18-carat diamond is highly appreciated by Kate, Annona, and others managing her life in the underground. They have come to recognize that, despite not perfecting any of the combat techniques, Saskia is clever, meticulous, and—most importantly—relentless in her approach. Saskia asks for some time off with Ava and Max. "Just three days to hang out with my kids. Without the constant pressure of performing. Please!" she pleads with Kate.

Kate has a rigidity about her. She is unbending in her ways, which makes her seem emotionally cold and distant. On the other hand, it makes sense. Most of the people in the underground have emotional scars on their souls that have rendered them reserved. They tend to shy away from deeper, more meaningful human relationships. Saskia wonders if Kate has any kids of her own. But, most of all, Saskia wonders how Kate ended up in the underground. She doesn't seem like someone who could have once lost her way and become homeless. Rather, Kate's manners and accent suggest that she has come from considerable social standing. Only those with a good education speak the way she does. Saskia doubts that Kate will ever really understand what it means to live like an outcast—leading

Saskia to altogether question Kate's right to be a leader in this hidden world of theirs

Kate looks at Saskia with a stern, calculated look. Then she says, "You deserve some days off with your children. I will give you a three-day pass for the subway and rail so that you can get away from here. Take your kids out of the city and get some fresh air. I will also give you a couple hundred dollars."

Saskia feels her eyes watering up. "Thank you!" she whispers.

Kate looks down, as she says, "You can leave tomorrow. Skyman is coming tomorrow morning to pick up the diamond, and we want to showcase you to him. You don't need to say anything. Just meet him."

Saskia sighs for a short second with disappointment and then says, "Of course, I will stay through tomorrow's meeting and complete my assignment. We will leave as soon after that as we can." Saskia hurries away to prevent Kate from piling any more tasks on her.

She is looking for Ava and Max. She can't wait to share the good news with them. "We leave tomorrow morning after the meeting! Let's take the train to the end of the line and see where it takes us," Saskia says. Ava and Max are excited until Max mentions that his combat unit has an upcoming tournament. "But you can miss that, Max. I cleared it with Kate. We are all allowed to go away together for three days," Saskia says, with hope in her voice.

"But I don't want to miss the tournament!" Max replies. Saskia feels she is losing her children to the underground. In the end, after some persuasion, they all decide they will leave first thing the next day. Saskia is relieved and excited.

Before falling asleep, Saskia is lying in bed looking up at the commotion on the street. She feels exhausted and weak. Her body is collapsing after months of hard labor, stress, and anxiety. Early next morning, a sudden, hard knock on the door wakes her with a jolt. She sits up in bed, still half asleep. Kate is almost yelling. "Saskia, are you coming? Skyman is here!" Saskia appears in the doorway, still drunk with sleep. Kate looks at her, displeased. "Could you please man yourself up a bit? Skyman is very important to 'the cause.'" Saskia waddles along after Kate to the meeting room at the end of the plant floor. On the opposite end of the conference table sits the legendary Skyman. His earthling name is Mr. Skylar, but down here, he just goes by Skyman.

The room is dark, and Saskia skews her eyes to get a closer look at him. He has dark hair and eyes, and olive skin. Kate shoves her gently forward with a hand on her back, making Saskia feel that she is some kind of prized animal on show. Skyman stays seated. Saskia walks all the way in front of him until he mutters, "Thank you. Well done!" He gives her a brown envelope. "This is your bonus for a job successfully completed. I hope you will do more jobs like this for us. And for 'the cause'!" Saskia just nods while holding the envelope. She feels a warmth permeating her body. Blood is racing to her head, bringing color to her cheeks. She is unable to utter a word. She just stands there for a while, looking at Skyman. She has never seen a man who is so calmly collected and in charge. He is kind and assertive.

Kate intervenes to prevent the moment from becoming even more awkward for Saskia. "We are all very grateful, Saskia, as I already told you." Saskia is still standing there, frozen in front of Skyman. She is numb. "Okay," Kate continues. "Let me take you back to your room. You are probably busy preparing for your trip."

Later, in her room, Saskia comes back to her senses and counts all of her money. "What the fuck! I have four thousand two hundred dollars! Wow!" She is beyond excited. Never before has she had so much money of her own. Her money was always treated as her husband's, and her husband always managed to squander most of it. At least, that's what happened after he lost his job, which was when they needed money most. During the last year, her husband's mismanagement left them hanging out to dry. Now, with more than four thousand dollars in her hands, she is wondering if the time has come to leave the underground. *Maybe we should just leave and never come back.* Her mind is racing. On the other hand, she is positively in love with this mystery man, Skyman, as he is called. She wants to get to know him.

Later that morning, Annona shows them the way to Atmosphere Station. They walk through a labyrinth of back alleys. Saskia is surprised by the endlessness of the underground. It just goes on and on. She never seems to encounter its outer boundaries. Suddenly, Annona stops in front of a rusty metal door. "I will not go beyond this door.

On the other side, you find Atmosphere Station. Any of the trains leaving from there will take you far out of the city. Just stay on the train till you reach the end of the line." Ava and Max cannot contain their excitement as they jump up and down. Annona smiles before she turns around, and walks the long way back.

Atmosphere Station. What the hell is that! Saskia thinks to herself, while carefully opening the door. On the other side of the door, the station is packed with people who all seem to be going on some kind of excursion. They wear their finest Sunday clothes and have with them small suitcases, picnic baskets, and bikes. There is a happy, humming noise. As the train arrives, everybody peacefully lines up along the floor indications by the train doors. Upon arrival, the train seems to be empty. "Wonder where it comes from?" Ava contemplates aloud.

Shortly after, Atmosphere Station is empty, and the train is full to the brim. The train is one of those old subway trains, entirely covered in shinning silver metal. It has a large American flag on both sides of each car. As soon as they board, the train seems to gather speed quickly. It races pass all stations at an immense velocity. Still, when Saskia looks around at the other passengers, everybody seems happy and totally at ease.

"No reason to worry," she tells herself with little effect. She grabs the hands of Ava and Max, who are squirming in their seats with excitement. At some point during their travels, Saskia wonders if all these people come from the settlement in the underground. All of them boarded at Atmosphere Station, which doesn't seem like a regular subway station.

The train slows down somewhat as it starts ascending from the underground, up the height of seven floors toward the sun at the end of the tunnel. As they approach it, the passengers gasp in reverence and awe. Daylight! When they reach the surface, the whole car spontaneously breaks into applause. The sun touches their faces and hands. Ava and Max are playfully dancing their small fingers against the bright sun.

"End of the line! End of the line!" the muffled voice yells from the loudspeakers. The train is busting with joy. People are chatting and laughing as they get off the train at Ocean Station. The station platform is raised high above a breathtakingly beautiful landscape of fields of wildflowers. In the far distance, they can see the ocean, its surface reflecting the glittering sun, as if casting each of its rays back into the universe. An infinite stretch of pearly white sand separates the ocean from the fields. Saskia is unable to move at the sight of its beauty. "I have never seen anything so magnificent before in my whole life!" she exclaims. Ava and Max tug at her hands. "Come on!" Soon the landscape is dotted with thousands of people busting with joy, just like themselves.

Saskia and the kids sit on a bench on the beach promenade. They're eating ice-cream! They haven't had ice-cream for years. Nor have they sat on a bench *doing nothing*, just the three of them, since they entered the underground. Saskia turns around to see where all the people have gone. Along the beach promenade, there are motels and hotels bidding everyone welcome with open doors. Saskia decides that they should be prudent with their money, since she is still contemplating making a run from the underground, in which case her money must extend well into the future. "We should go and check into a motel before all the motels are full," she says while getting up. "After all, so very many people arrived on the train today." They enter a pale pink establishment, where an elderly man invites them in from behind a dated wooden counter with beautifully carved ornaments. "Would it be possible to get a large room for the three of us?" They are shown to a beautiful spacious room that resembles her room on West 117th Street in Harlem. The relentless sun has given it the same look of wear and tear.

On the second day, they feel well rested but somewhat restless in this static time pocket of joy and happiness. Saskia proposes that they visit the large, white hotel sitting on the edge of a protruding cliff that overhangs the pearly white beach and glittering ocean. This luxury hotel is entirely white such that the reflected light of the sun almost hurts the eyes of the beholder. Ava insists they take English high tea in the luxury hotel. "I have always dreamt of taking tea like a real English lady," she says with begging eyes.

Once inside the hotel, they can hardly believe their eyes. The place is swarming with beautiful people, who seem to do nothing but look beautiful. There is a new breed of dandies about town. Youngsters who aimlessly drift around town to be seen with and by the likeminded. Youngsters whose bases of existence stem from staging and capturing themselves in different social contexts, ideally in close connection to wealth and power. They are stargazer cons or just simply stargazers presenting themselves in swanky settings with glittering names. These social media youngsters spend their entire existence contemplating what to wear, where to go for dinner, and with whom to be seen. Their only pursuits are sex, enjoyment, and riches.

The cleverest of the self-staged luminaries and fabulists cherry pick their bios, thereby assembling a kaleidoscope of achievements from across the world. These bios look impressive, but are nearly impossible to fact-check. One of the principal challenges faced by these luminaries and fabulists is that it is almost impossible to erase their modest backgrounds on the internet. Internet searches reveal their true origins that, though nothing to be ashamed of, present an awkward clash with their new personas. Yet, the more successful of these individuals have access to media companies that have the ability to wash and wax the public image of anyone. This is not some run-of-the-mill search engine optimization, but data hydrology at its finest. Some of these media companies even provide titles of royals and nobles, doctorates and professorships, pageantry, and ancestry. All at a cost. Thus, in some twisted way, it is the democratizing of inheritance and labored achievements. Everybody should be able to attain whatever they desire with a simple click on the computer.

These self-staged luminaries and fabulists collude with the offspring of the wealthy—for whom there is no need to go to such trouble: their pedigree secures and shelters them from a life that entails any type of aspiration and sustained, laborious effort. The social media youngsters seem to exist only for the amusement of these wealthy offspring. "How did all these youngsters earn the right to live in such excess?" Saskia asks herself aloud, while taking in the splendid sight in full.

The social media youngsters recast their identities on the internet. In most cases, these new identities are entirely fictive. However, they miraculously become real as soon as people in their cyber vicinity respond to their fictive identities—whereby said identities are reinforced and bolstered. In this way, a new breed of entirely self-staged personas sees the light of day and are idolized by their massive internet following. Followers who, like themselves, come from modest backgrounds, aspire to one day create and showcase new imaginary online identities, just as their idols have done. With fame, small and big screen opportunities emerge. Thus, today, it is possible to become something through nothing more than skillful smoke and mirrors. Pure illusion. These luminaries and fabulists create new parallel realities in which their fanciful purports on the internet make the diligent and honest worker's life seem mundane, shallow, and meaningless.

They sit there, the three of them, in the middle of the spectacle. They hardly utter a word to each other until Max says, "I actually prefer the underground. I miss the underground." Saskia feels a heavy weight pressing her down. Secretly, she had been contemplating asking her children to leave the underground with her.

She argues in vain. "But this world is no more unreal than the underground. Both these worlds are strangely choreographed. They are not real."

Ava looks at her. "Both worlds are entirely real, Mum. If they are not real, how can we be sitting here in flesh and blood?"

Saskia replies, "Yes, you are right. Both worlds are real. But each is also at one extreme of the continuum. There is a middle ground somewhere. I hope. Or maybe that middle ground has disappeared... Maybe the world, now, consists only of the casted and the outcasts. The rich and the poor. No middle ground. No middle class. What a strange world!"

Somewhere deep inside of her, a little burning flame was lit the moment she saw Skyman. Yes, she wants to leave the underground and its endless trials and tribulations. But now that her children seem to want to go back to the underground, she feels that flame being nurtured by hope. Yet, hope is a dangerous thing for a woman like Saskia to have, as she does not possess the right to live her own life as she chooses. That right was taken away from her and her children when they entered the underground.

Life does not consist of a series of choices. Life is the reality of the choices we have made. Saskia's choices are solely based on survival. She is constantly fighting against the storms that are raising hell in her life. To the outside observer, one could argue that she has made a series of bad choices, but those who really know the nature of life at the bottom understand the narrow spectrum of choices that are necessary to survive.

The following morning, they head back to the underground. "We are leaving the beautiful, bright light behind for a trip down the hell hole," Saskia thinks aloud. Her children hush her, as they are entering a crowd of passengers all heading back to the underground. The train descends further and further down into the underground, passing unused stations and vacated tunnels. She feels how the air is getting thinner and thinner. Depleted of oxygen. Her head is spinning.

Saskia yearns to depart, yet she remains. It's not iron bars that confine her, nor is it the boundless uncertainty beyond the underground that restrains her. Instead, it's the intangible psychological barriers erected by the underground that seem insurmountable. If she were to leave the underground, where would she even venture?

A few days after their return, Saskia is again summoned to the meeting room at the end of the plant floor. She drags her feet trying to postpone, as long as possible, the delivery of the next ordeal. She opens the door, and her heart jumps as she recognizes the silhouette of Skyman at the opposite end of the conference table. She knows he does not live in the underground, and she wonders why he has come back.

Kate delivers the next assignment. "Welcome Saskia!" she starts. "We have a new assignment for you…

We need you to steal the crown of Nefertiti, the daughter of Egyptian Pharoah Akhenaten, who lived in the fourteenth century B.C. She later became Queen. She is one of the most prominent women in history! You like that, right?"

Saskia looks at the leaders in both, astonishment and resignation, as she says, "Where do I find this crown?"

Kate is forcefully calm. "In the Met. The Metropolitan Museum. But we have the entire floorplan and everything you need, just like last time."

Saskia pulls a chair out and sits down, uninvited, besides the table. "This really is an impossible assignment! And why do you need this particular crown?"

Kate looks around the table to see if she is allowed to divulge such information. Suddenly, Skyman gets up. Saskia had almost forgotten he was there. "You don't need to know that. But I have a perfect replica of the crown that you can come and pick up once you are near the time of the steal. Like last time, you'll swap the original one for a fake. That is a good strategy!" With those words, Skyman exits the room, while saying, "You can get my address from Kate." Saskia's flame sparks with the prospect of visiting Skyman.

Saskia returns to her room. She will soon, once again, ascend the underground and go live in the city to study and plan her theft. She will again work with Eli. Before she leaves the underground, she wants to spend time with her kids. "Let's go up and out and have some lunch," she says in an upbeat voice to Ava and Max.

They emerge from the hidden door on Lexington Avenue. It is a beautiful spring day. New York has shifting temperatures, but the cloudless, blue sky remains intact, all year round. They make a turn down Madison Avenue, which has more concentrated wealth than anywhere else in Manhattan. "Look!" Ava exclaims. "Look at the deep cracks in the street!" Max and Saskia stop up and look down.

"These are cave-ins. Deep cracks between the sidewalk and the road proper. Cave-ins," Saskia explains.

Max and Ava stare at the cracks, when Max says, "But you can almost see down into the underground. If the cracks get much deeper and wider, our world will be revealed to the earthlings!"

Saskia looks at the cracks. "I think we have another, even bigger problem... If the cave-ins extend all the way along both sides of the avenue, Madison Avenue will simply collapse into the hell hole! You see, there is no solid ground below Madison Avenue, because the underground just keeps expanding up and out. The underground hollows out the land upon which the city is sitting. What a mess!"

Ava concludes, "We should tell Annona and Kate about this. They need to send some people up here to inspect the damage."

The cave-ins are demonstrative of the buzz and busyness going on below ground. The fact that such deep wedges are driven into Madison Avenue is also demonstrative of the lack of activity occurring above ground, triggered by record low levels of the city coffers.

Previously, the city reaped the taxes of a vast middle class. However, over the past decade, the middle class has withered—and whatever is left of it has abandoned New York due to the skyrocketing costs of living. The middle class is now living far out of the big city, working remotely and trying to make ends meet. Thus, the city now relies on taxes paid by wealthy New Yorkers, which, in any case, are insufficient, since the wealthy generally avoid paying taxes. Consequently, decay is creeping up on the city. Streets, bridges, and buildings are collapsing.

In stark contrast to the apathy of the city, the underground refuses to stay under wraps for much longer. Its cause can no longer be contained within this society of abundance and decadence. During the coming months, while Saskia is living in an apartment with Eli, raids and looting of the luxury stores, lined as pearls on a silk thread along Madison Avenue, become more and more frequent. Saskia wonders if it is the people of the underground causing havoc above ground. She discusses it with Eli over dinner, but as they are both living in total isolation from the underground, they have no way of knowing if the city is indeed falling apart.

In response to the raids and looting, the luxury stores vacate the ground floors and occupy the buildings' upper floors, leaving the street levels idle and ghostlike. This is reinforced by the stores' wealthy clientele avoiding the streets altogether for fear of the savages roaming the streets. The wealthy clientele arrives via chauffeur-driven vehicles or choppers that land on the rooftops of the buildings of the luxury stores. The separation between the wealthy and the poor is thereby reinforced. Now, they never need to encounter each other, ever again. All the while, the city is collapsing.

Saskia is taking her time to plan the theft of the crown of Nefertiti. She refuses to work on such a difficult task under the pressure of the tight deadline, as she did last time. Eli explains that since the underground has detailed knowledge and documentation of hidden tunnels, passages, and doors, the best way to access the Met is from *below*. The Met itself has a network of passageways and storage rooms below ground. "We just keep looking till we find a hole in the Met's vast building. This is not a closed loop. Dirty water must exit. Fresh air must enter. Artifacts enter and exit. Somewhere there will be an open door for you to creep through," Eli reassures her. Eli hacks the plans of different utility companies, including the water and electricity companies. He is meticulously trying to integrate the numerous maps he now has to make one master plan of the underground below the Met. They agree that while Eli studies the plans, Saskia should descend into the underground below the Met and familiarize herself with its layout. She will do her own search for a door that opens into the Met.

Wandering around the underground, Saskia is venturing beyond the perimeters of Eli's map in her search for an entry to the Met. Maybe she will find the secret door into the Met before Eli, she thinks. Down below, she encounters places that her own community of outcasts have yet to discover. She feels like she is adventuring into unchartered space to uncover stars untouched by human beings. She wonders if maybe communities other than her own exist in the underground, possibly further ahead.

One day, she pulls the handle of what looks like an unassuming door that she believes might lead to yet another maze of tunnels, passageways, stairs, and small confinements in the underground. To her utter surprise, the door opens into a dry storage room. The room is packed to the brim with shelves, boxes, and cradles. The room is pitch dark. The air is dirt-dry, almost suffocating. The lack of oxygen makes the room claustrophobic, and she is fighting to catch her breath. She edges her way past the shelves, stacked cases, and cradles toward the distant outline of a door that reveals light on the other side. Next to the door, there is a light switch.

She turns on the switch and finds herself in a dim light. Dust has settled on the floor. Fresh footmarks on the floor traces her path from the peculiar secret door to the exit door by the light switch. Carefully, Saskia opens the exit door leading to the outside world of the earthlings, and takes a first step into a bright, wide tunnel dedicated to shuttle carts. A blue line on the floor separates the shuttle carts going in both directions. For a moment, Saskia is almost unable to contain her excitement, as she believes to have found the secret entry door to the Met they have been looking for, for days and weeks.

Yet, shortly after entering the tunnel, the stale smell of anesthesia creeps up on her. The horrendous smell of hospital. This stark reminder of our own mortality is the faithful companion of hospitals. Saskia cringes. In a split second, she realizes that there must be surveillance cameras in the tunnel. She turns around and hurries back through the door to the dry storage room. Leaving the light in the storage room on, she vanishes the world of life and death back into the eternal underground.

The minute she closes the door behind her, she hears the door from the tunnel to the storage room being kicked open. Agitated male voices argue. She holds her breath, trying to listen what they are saying. "Where did she go?" one man asks, and continues, "I saw her on the surveillance camera. She can't just vanish into thin air."

The other man says, "Are you sure you saw a person on the camera? Seriously." The two men walk clumsily around the shelves, boxes, and cradles. "Watch out, man! This shit is not properly stacked. It'll collapse if you push it."

The first man then says in a resigned tone of voice, "Oh, let's just go. This is a waste of time. I am sure I saw someone, but maybe it was a nurse who went back up."

The second man looks at him. "You know very well that NO ONE unauthorized is supposed to be here at this time of night and when they conduct the procedures on the scum migrants! NO ONE! So, if someone is here, we need to find them and shut them up!"

The first man says, "I think, I saw someone. But how can that person just vanish? I mean, I *think*, I saw someone…"

The second man looks annoyed. "Let's just go back up. We are not supposed to leave our posts and go on some fucking wild goose chase in the basement."

Saskia hurries back up the underground, while trying to trace her route in her head. Yet so many other things are crowding her mind. *What were those men talking about? What scum migrants? What is that place?* she thinks. Once, back on the street, Saskia reflects that maybe it is best not to tell Eli or *anyone*, for that matter, about her expedition. *I obviously put my foot in it. I was not supposed to be there, and I almost got caught.* With no further ado, she decides to keep her discovery secret. She also decides that she will go back to the hospital to find out more about what is going on.

A couple of days later, she seizes the opportunity to return to the hospital. This time, she chooses to go back during regular working hours, hoping that the hospital will be busy. That will allow her to blend in with the hustle and bustle. Once Saskia enters the small storage room, she takes her time to go through the boxes. She is looking for a plausible disguise. She finds some white trousers and a doctor's lab coat. She takes off her own trousers and puts on the uniform. She also finds a holder for an identity card which she puts on in reverse. She stashes some pens in her pocket. She pockets a reflex hammer that she thinks could come in handy.

Fully disguised, Saskia opens the door to the shuttle tunnel. Carts are zipping pass her. "You can't walk here!" a driver of a cart yells.

"Sorry! Sorry!" Saskia says, while jumping to the side.

The man in the next cart over stops. "Where are you going? Let me take you, so you are not yelled at again," he says with a crooked smile.

"Just take me to the nearest stairway," Saskia casually replies as if she knows what she is talking about.

"You are new?" the man asks.

Saskia would rather not make small talk, but she must reply so as to avoid suspicion. "Yes. I was sent down to the storage room to pick up something and lost my way. It is massive down here!" she replies.

"I know. It takes a while to get used to. The hospital has eight hundred employees. Pretty big for a highly specialized private hospital. I have been here for four years. I still get lost," he says to comfort her. Saskia is dying to ask what the specialization of the hospital is, but that would blow her cover.

She is moving up the stairs, while reading and mentally logging the different departments on each floor: transplant coordination, laboratory, transplant medicine, ICU, transplant surgery, and so on. *Okay, the hospital specializes in organ transplant,* she thinks, and in that second, her gut feeling tells her that the "scum migrants" are used and abused for illegal organ transplants. She knocks the gut feeling out of her head, as we so often do when we are unable to deal with the consequences of reality. She tells herself that this cannot be true. Mocking herself, she concludes that she has been watching too many crime movies.

Now, Saskia finds herself at a crossroads: does she pursue the truth knowing that it may reveal something that she would rather not know? Or does she suppress her gut feeling and the unresolved matter of the scum immigrants and crawl back into the hole she came out of? She doesn't know. She is still trying to convince herself that her gut feeling is wrong. This gives her the peace of mind she needs to crawl back into her hole. But, then, why would her mind flee if it has nothing to flee from? Suddenly, she is overwhelmed by sleep and hunger. "Canteen," it reads on the wall. She walks toward the canteen. *At least I can get a decent meal, while I am here,* she thinks.

An avalanche of white coats swarms toward the canteen. She piles her tray to the brim. "You are hungry," the driver of her cart says with a smile. He is suddenly standing next to her in the queue to the counter.

"Yes, yes," she is looking down, trying to avoid making conversation with him.

At the counter, the cashier looks at her impatiently. "Card?"

"Oh... I forgot my card," Saskia replies.

"Well—no card, no food."

The driver intervenes, "Let me get this for you."

She is stuck with him. They sit down at the end of one of the long tables. "Seriously, have you already lost your card?" he asks once they are seated.

"I have," Saskia says in a dry voice.

"They are going to whip your ass!" he says, laughing while continuing, "Listen, I know a guy in facility management who can help you. But promise you don't tell anyone. Who do you work for?"

Saskia is panicking, as she says, "Samantha!" He looks strangely at her. Then he says, "Oh, Samantha Williams?"

"Yes!" Saskia says with a sigh of relief.

"Look, I need to be in Section H in thirty minutes. If we hurry up, we can drop by Rob right after lunch. Rob is the guy in facility management who can help you."

Saskia says, "Yes please. Thank you!"

They make a bit of small talk walking over to facility management. "How are things going over at Section G?" he asks and looks at her. "That is where Samantha's ward is, right?"

"Yes, yes." Saskia nods.

Rob, at facility management, is busy. "Do you have time to wait?" he asks. The driver of the cart starts pacing around nervously. "I need to leave you. By the way, my name is Miguel. If you want, we are a couple of colleagues meeting at the bar across the street around six. Will I see you then?" Saskia is trying to focus on Rob and getting her identity card.

To quietly hush up Miguel, she replies without looking at him, "Sure. Probably."

After fifteen minutes of anxiously waiting, Rob returns to the reception area, where Saskia is sitting alone waiting. "So, who are the doctors working with Mrs. Williams?" Rob asks casually while they are walking across the open office space.

"Dr. Patel and Dr. Rodriguez are often there, I think. But I am new, so I don't know everybody's names. It is a bit overwhelming," Saskia answers, trying to remain calm.

"Right. Well, give me your name and personnel number, and I will get you a new card. But it stays between us…"

Saskia follows Rob to his desk. "I will look you up in the system."

In that moment, Rob's phone rings. He needs to go and tell his boss something important, he says. He gets up. Saskia is frantically looking through some miscellaneous papers lying on Rob's desk, trying to find a name and personnel number that she can recycle.

"Elisabeth Taylor!" Saskia exclaims, when he comes back. She has put the paperwork of Elisabeth Taylor in her pocket. "I don't remember my number, but you can look me up."

"There you are!" Rob says. "I am sorry for keeping you waiting. We are pretty busy. There's construction going on in the basement. Building some new high security operating theatres. We need to oversee the work, compliance rules, security, and so on. It is such a mess!"

Shortly thereafter, Saskia walks off with an identity card. But she decides that she'd be pushing her luck to meet with her fictive colleagues for an after-work drink. She returns to her apartment just in time for dinner. "Another fruitless day!" she sighs to Eli.

"Did you have any luck finding an entry door?"

"Nope!"

With an identity card, Saskia decides to enter the hospital through the main entrance. She knows she needs to snoop around to find out what is going on. And she needs to move fast before her true identity is revealed.

Once in the hospital, she spends most of her time in the basement trying to find the "scum migrants"—if they're still there. She often sees Miguel in the basement, driving his cart around the maze of clinically lit tunnels. "Do they do operations in the basement?" Saskia asks Miguel during lunch.

He looks up at her, straight into her eyes, with a serious look. "Funny you should ask... I know that there are some operating theatres in the basement, but they are shut off, so that no one can enter. But I know that the ORs are being used, because the cleaners come every day and bring out trash, including blood-soaked tissue, the kind used during operations. I have never been in there. Only rarely does anyone go in or out. Other than the cleaners, of course," Miguel says. Before Miguel gets suspicious and clams up, Saskia manages to deduce approximately where in the basement the sealed off operating theatres must be.

It is a balancing act. On the one hand, she must push to get the information she is looking for. On the other hand, she must not expose herself to unnecessary danger. Saskia leaves after lunch. Knowing where to look, she still needs to get past the locks and security guards to enter the sealed off area, where the operating theatres are. She wonders where the scum migrants are kept. Maybe in the sealed off operating theatres? Maybe that's why Rob from facility management talked of high-level security. To keep *them* in, and *outsiders* out. Maybe the fact that they're still under construction will mean that she'll find some kind of gap or opening to crawl through.

She decides she must include Eli in her mission. It is too complex for her to do on her own. "I have a strong suspicion that the exclusive private hospital, Langmore, which specializes in organ transplants, is conducting some shady business with illegal migrants."

Eli looks disinterested as he looks up from his plate. "That is not our mission. It is not our problem…"

Saskia is quick on her toes when she says, "Is it not our mission, 'the cause,' to help those at the bottom of the pecking order, at the bottom of society? We can grow the number of people supporting the cause if we try to help them! Draft some people who truly support the cause. They will owe their lives and loyalty to us, and to *THE CAUSE*, if we save them from fucking organ transplantation! From death! We should call out the private hospital capitalizing on these people." In fact, Saskia is not certain she has connected the dots correctly, but she is trying to quickly think up a plausible narrative that helps convince Eli to help her.

Still looking disinterested, Eli looks into her eyes. "You don't even know what the cause is! It is not about helping those at the bottom of society. Do you think we are stealing 18-carat diamonds and Nefertiti's crown to feed ourselves?" Eli pauses and answers his question himself. "No! We are stealing for the rich, who then finance *their* rebellion to tumble society's old establishment. Like a phoenix, these high net value individuals who finance us will sweep in to create a new societal order—with themselves at the pinnacle of society." Saskia looks at Eli in utter astonishment.

Eli nods his head in a resigning manner and says, "Come on, Saskia. You are not stupid. We, the outcasts, homeless, downtrodden, and discarded of this unjust society, are (of course) only too happy to help, because we only look at the immediate rewards, the tumbling of this establishment, while the rich people financing us have the long view. In the meantime, while working as helpful fools, we get a bed, food, life skills, medical care, and some kind of protection and community. We are all used as cannon fodder. You and I are just fortunate enough to use our brains in the process, and not get our hands dirty. But your children *are* getting their hands dirty. You know that!"

Saskia turns her head away as she feels tears start to come. "I honestly thought that we, Kate, Annona, and the men and women sitting around the conference table were *heading* a rebellion. I thought *we* were doing it. Not just doing the bidding of some wealthy individuals. I don't know what to think anymore." Saskia gets up to leave the kitchen and go to her room, where she stays for the rest of the evening.

When Saskia was a small girl, she grew up with perpetual violence from her cunningly psychopathic father, who was able to beat and break his five children without their mother ever intervening. Saskia has since ceased to try to understand if her mother knew of the violence, if she lived in denial, if she, too, feared the father, or if it was some strange conflation of all of the above. Of course, Saskia recognized all too well that she was reliving her dreadful childhood when her husband started becoming violent. There was something inside of her that almost expected her to eventually return to the nightmares of her childhood. There was something predictable in the unpredictable violence that made her beatings feel like a long-awaited homecoming. There was something strangely comforting in this homecoming.

The violence of her marriage rekindled her oppressive, all-consuming childhood fear of her father. In some ways, she was propelled into her childhood as she groveled and crawled along the floor panels under the heavy beatings of her husband, who had an instinct for inflicting terror. A "new old" emerged everyday as she felt how easily she slipped into being permanently on guard.

Violence is all-consuming. It is not the physical wounds that are the deepest. It is the mental decomposition that results from the beatings that cut the deepest. These wounds may never heal, because the suspicion, distrust, and fear will never go away. They don't leave room for any other emotions. When she was not contemplating what mood her husband would be in when she got home, and what she could do to mellow his mood and protect her children, she was at her wits' end to try to understand how she ended up repeating the tragedies of her childhood and forcing her own children to grow up with the same unpredictability and permeating fear that she grew up with.

Nevertheless, Saskia would probably never have survived her recent fall to the bottom of society had she not already been in the hell hole before. Deep inside her, she knew she had survived once and would, consequently, survive again. *Something good did come out of all this misery,* she thinks to herself whenever she reflects on her childhood. She learned something incredibly valuable: how to mobilize her subconsciousness in her sleep. As a child, when she went to bed, blue and yellow from her beatings, she felt engulfed with rage and hatred. Yet, during the night, this rage morphed into an inner strength and the will to survive.

In her later years, she consciously activated her subconsciousness by posing challenges before shutting her eyes. How do I pay that bill? How do I rid myself of my violent husband? In the morning, or sometimes after several mornings, a solution presented itself. Still half asleep, she would scribble it down on a piece of paper next to her bed. "Mix fentanyl with coke to create a lethal cocktail." This is precisely what she did when desperation seized her mind and faced with her husband's beatings, drinking and squandering their little money away. Before going to bed that night, she asks herself how she can help the migrants. Maybe a solution will present itself during the night.

The next morning, Saskia probes Eli again. "The only help I need from you is to access the plans of the basement. A guy from facility management told me that they are building new operating theatres there. Maybe we can access the building plans online. They must have filed for a building permit, one would think… I wonder if you can deactivate the security system, just for a short while. Then I could slip in and check out the place."

Eli looks at her with suspicion. "Are you talking to some guy at facility management in the Langmore Hospital? I am telling you... We need to focus on the crown of Nefertiti and the Met, Saskia. Not the Langmore Hospital and some illegal migrants gone rogue."

Saskia looks at him. "Listen, as long as we are still looking for an entry to the Met, and I *know* that this hospital, that prides itself with being saintly, is doing all these things, I will pursue this till the end. It doesn't even need to take that long."

Eli shakes his head. "And I suppose, you want me to keep it secret from Kate and Annona that we are chasing this assignment now?"

Saskia looks at him with pleading eyes and releases a frail. "Yes, please."

That evening, Saskia enters the Langmore Hospital through the main entrance. She has gained a certain casual confidence in her demeanor, enabling her to hide in plain sight. In her chest pocket, she has a drawing of the plan for the basement. She learned that at exactly two o'clock at night, the security system is shut off for just ten minutes. This will enable her to enter the highly secured section, still under construction, in the basement. "You need to move in and out, fast. No lingering," Eli tells her. She hopes that her gut feeling does not let her down. In her head, she visualizes how she enters the sealed off section and rapidly proceeds to the smaller rooms along the long corridor, where she thinks the post- and pre-operation patients are. She wants to save the migrants.

Saskia hides in a mechanical room opposite the main door that leads into the sealed-off section. She hears a murmuring from medical staff as the main door opens and closes. If she is detected, she has decided that she will say that she has come to see Dr. Hinnemann, who is the chief medical doctor of the Langmore Hospital. He specializes in pancreas transplants. She suspects that he, too, is culpable, as he is one of the founding partners of the hospital.

Saskia gets worried when a commotion ensues in the tunnel. "Fuck all those people in there…" She calls Eli to tell him that it may not be possible to get in and out in just ten minutes.

"Look, if the systems are down for longer than ten minutes, they will sound the alarm. I am sure. Then you are really screwed!" While Saskia is sitting in the mechanical room, she thinks that maybe she can sneak out and enter the sealed off area by following some of the other nurses. That way, she does not necessarily have to be out again within ten minutes.

But no nurses arrive. So, at precisely two o'clock, Saskia sneaks out of hiding and crosses the brightly-lit tunnel, entering the sealed-off area in the basement. She is able to open the door without sounding the alarm. She sends Eli her gratitude. But she had barely made one step through the door before she was stopped by a guard. "What are you doing here?"

Saskia feels a flush of warm blood racing to her head. "I need to deliver an urgent message to Dr. Hinnemann."

The guard waves his hand. "Give it to me. I will pass it on to him. You are not authorized to be down here."

Saskia musters all her courage and insists, "No. It is a personal message that I was asked to deliver in person. I am Dr. Hinnemann's new assistant nurse."

The guard looks at her identity card and then at her. He waves his hand for her to pass, while saying, "He is in theater three, but hurry up. They are just about to start the operation."

Saskia walks through the glass door. Momentarily, she sighs with relief. In her mind, she is trying to recall the image of the building plan from Eli's computer. She is retracing the way she must take. "Second left, first right... Through two doors and across the Post-Anesthesia Care Unit..."

"Stop!" a nurse yells. "This is the recovery room. You can't just walk in here." But Saskia is already out of the door again. She is walking down the narrow corridor with small rooms. She feels the nurse following her, so she decides to slip into one of the rooms.

A young boy looks up at her. He starts crying when he sees her. "No! Please don't!" he begs.

Saskia tries to comfort him. "Don't cry. Don't cry!" But he won't stop. She hides in the bathroom as the nurse opens the door.

"Did you see a nurse coming in here?" she asks.

The boy continues to cry and plead for his life. The nurse shakes her head in annoyance, slams the door, and leaves.

Saskia sneaks out of the bathroom. She takes a picture of the boy before he can hold up both his hands to cover his face. She leaves the room. She enters the next room. Takes a photo. Leaves and enters the next room. After entering seven rooms and taking photos of the patients, she decides to haul ass down the corridor. Following the exit signs, she leaves through a different door than the one she entered. The alarm goes off. Saskia runs down the tunnel. She takes a sharp turn around the corner, where Miguel suddenly appears in his cart.

"Get in!" he insists.

"Take me to section E," she says, trying to catch her breath. Miguel doesn't ask any questions, but zips around the next corner toward section E. Saskia turns around to send a look of gratitude to Miguel before she enters the dry storage room that she frequented the first time she entered the hospital. Miguel looks perplexed, but there is no time to explain.

A hot storm is raging the following morning. The kind of storms that foretell of a massive thunder in the making. "You need to go to the hospital today like you do all days," Eli insists. "You know that is how it works. If you suddenly stay away, it will raise suspicion. You also went back to work the day after you stole the diamond. Staying away is precisely what has the potential to give you away."

Saskia mumbles, "So many people saw me yesterday. I am absolutely not going back!"

At breakfast, Saskia explains that she will give up the case of the Langmore Hospital if Eli helps her assembly all the information, including plans and photos, to make a compelling case for the police to investigate.

"The police!" Eli exclaims. "We don't trust the police. Have you lost your mind!" Saskia doesn't know what to do with all the information, but she knows, she cannot continue to pursue the case any further herself. She needs to focus on the Met.

"We give the information to Investigator Brady. She worked on the Christel case, and she seems trustworthy. Anyway, she is the only person in the police that I know," Saskia reasons to herself that morning.

Eli is beaming. While pointing at the map, he says, "I think I found a way into the Met through the old cistern system. We can start preparing the raid on the Met now!"

Saskia is exhausted. "Let's finish this first. Please!"

Eli opens an empty hardcover paper box and starts throwing all the papers in it. "I will gather all the intel in this box. You can deliver the box to Brady. After that, case closed! Do you get it? Case closed!"

Saskia gets a bike courier to pick up the box in front of the magazine stand in the middle of Penn Station. The box reads: POLICE, ASSISTANT CRIMINAL INVESTIGATOR CLAUDIA BRADY, MIDTOWN PRECINCT SOUTH.

Chapter Four

Taking a rest from her relentless search for the entry to the Met, Saskia sits on the edge of a water basin eating her lunch while watching a rat swim across to the other side. The cisterns are like a cathedral with consecutive columns continuing infinitely into the unknown underworld. She thinks there must be many more communities like theirs living in this vast underworld.

As she is sitting there contemplating, Saskia can't help but think of the youngsters, women and men she saw in the basement of Langmore Hospital. She smiles at how happy they will become when the police rescue them. "Don't get your hopes up," Eli says. "This is the police we are talking about. They probably already know what is going on. They are choosing to turn a blind eye, as the hospital's benefactors are amongst some of the wealthiest and more influential people in New York. Don't get your hopes up."

To find the entry of the Met, Saskia needs to walk and crawl for almost two hours all the way through the underground and to the back of the cisterns. Eli explains, "The entry door is probably hidden. But it is there! Keep looking…" Eli found the door into the Met on the electricity company's map. Therefore, Saskia should look out for clues associated with the electricity, such as the thundering lightening sign on a door. She should also watch out that she doesn't get electrified in the process of breaking in.

The underground is littered with idle passageways, tunnels, stairs, and doors leading nowhere. After five days of attempting the long journey underground and opening countless doors in the process, Saskia finally opens a door to a cylinder-shaped room with vertical tunnel extending high above her and with walls plastered in cables. Some of the cables extend freely from somewhere high above. She carefully examines the cables to confirm their recent use.

The cylinder is dry and warm, and at the very top, rays of light shimmer through the cracks of some kind of grid. If she listens very carefully, she thinks, she can hear the humming sound of people talking at low voice. Convinced that the cylinder is the entry to the Met they've been looking for, Saskia asks Eli, "How am I going to climb up the cylinder when I have nothing to hold on to? I can't use a cable as a rope. The cables won't hold me."

Eli proposes, he enters the Met and locates the door from inside the Met. "If I can find the door at the Met, we'll know exactly where you arrive in the Met. I can also fix a rope to the ceiling of the cylinder that you can climb up," he says.

Eli walks around the Met with his eyes fixated on the electricity company's map. For a moment, he reflects on how lucky he is that most of his work can be done from behind his computer in a safe place far away. He only rarely ventures out in public. Once close to the place, where the door supposedly is located, he stops to orient himself. In front of him is a craftly carved wooden door painted in high gloss white. Eli pulls the door handle. To his surprise, the door is unlocked. Eli opens it onto a small passageway connecting two large exhibition rooms. Once inside the passageway, he finds himself alone and can carefully pry open the door to the electricity cupboard. Inside, there is a metal grid serving as a floorboard in the cylinder.

Eli cautiously places his foot onto the grid, pressing it to see if it is securely fixed. *Damn!* he thinks when he realizes it is fixed. Small holes in the grid allow him to peek at cables extending further below into the underground. Attempting to lift the grid, he realizes it is tightly held by hinges along the edges. He rassles the grid, frees the hinges and lifts the grid. He tries not to make any noise. The grid goes unhinged on one side only allowing him to open it like a ledge. He looks down into a deep, dark hole leading to the underground. Eli throws a rope down the cylinder, securing it at the ceiling. "I hope you're fit because the climb up is going to take a lot of strength," he says, smiling. Saskia increases her training.

While Saskia is preparing for her raid of the Met, police investigator Brady is summoned to the reception, where a parcel is waiting for her, they say. She walks down the dusty cement stairway, where the large, single-glazed windows in the dated building are hazy from years of persistent oxidization. The world outside appears as in a haze.

Brady is trying hard to fit in. In fact, since she joined the force four years ago, she has been trying to fit in.

Unlike most of her peers, Brady has a university degree and prior career. She successfully managed to work her way up the frauds department of a large insurance company until one day, she realized, only working with insurance frauds her entire life would not be fulfilling. That day, she resigned and applied to the police to go into criminal investigation. Brady, with prior experience, secured an entry-level position as an assistant criminal investigator reporting directly to Benson, unlike her peers who must work their way up from street cops. Her colleagues have since stopped making spiteful jokes about her lack of street patrolling experience, which allows her to still see the good in people.

It is when Brady is totally absorbed by some intricate crime that she is in her right element and most at ease. All the time spent making small talk in the kitchen, walking to the parking lot, having lunch in the canteen, and picking up a parcel is spent forcefully trying to fit in. She nods politely at the colleagues passing her on her way to the reception area. She has somewhat succeeded in attaining the acceptance of her superiors by acknowledging the line of command and working the hierarchy to her advantage. Nevertheless, she has not, yet, succeeded in winning over her peers who are at best indifferent to her. Every time, her peers talk in police jargon, joke, and laugh, she is reminded of how different she is from everybody else. As she walks down the stairway, she thinks that indifference is probably the best thing she can hope for from her peers.

The only colleague, who Brady exchanges words with beyond work matters, is Lizzy. Lizzy is very pretty. She is also younger and of lower rank than Brady. Brady expects that Lizzy is trying to befriend her under some wrongly judged assumption that Brady can help her, maybe even help her advance. Brady sometimes unintentionally sneers at her male colleagues who objectify and ogle Lizzy, when they pass her in the corridors or on the stairways. No matter the breadth and depth of mandatory diversity, inclusion, and sexual harassment prevention courses, Lizzy's male colleagues still make her feel uncomfortable and insecure. Brady recognizes that Lizzy is quite a quick thinker with a logical mind that enables her to read patterns, and connections faster than anyone of her colleagues. Yet, apparently, Lizzy is not smart enough to understand why she does not and will never fit into the force. A riddle that haunts Lizzy, and that she is seemingly unable to solve.

By the time, Brady calls Lizzy to join her in the meeting room and go through the content of the parcel with her, Brady has altogether decided not to involve any of her other colleagues. Still, she knows that the choice of Lizzy as her principal collaborator on this case isolates her even further from her colleagues.

The papers of the parcel are mumbled jumbled together. The compilation of evidence reveals hasty recklessness, they think.

It is the kind of hasty recklessness that makes many police officers feel superior. In fact, police officers often feel superior when they are able to point out the obvious mistakes made by their fellow human beings who have surrendered to the inhumane pressures of everyday life.

But neither Brady nor Lizzy use this opportunity to elevate themselves at the expense of the anonymous sender of the parcel. "Where did you get this information from?" Lizzy asks while reclining into her chair. She is surprised.

"It was delivered by courier. We can find the courier and trace our way back to the sender." Brady reflects and continues, "But then again... the person, who sent this material wants to be anonymous, so he has hardly sent it from his home address." The two women decide to organize and categorize the information and subsequently draft up a memo that they will present to Benson.

Brady carefully lays out the maps, photos, and notes of the parcel. The hand-drawn map that previously lived in Saskia's chest pocket bears marks of sweat. Yet, after trying to run a DNA analysis, they discover that Saskia's DNA is not on file with the police, who cannot put the sweat marks to any productive use. They are totally taken aback by the gravity of the crime spread out on the table in front of them. They cannot help but think of the potential praise and advancement in the wake of solving such a huge crime.

"Where did you get this?" is predictably the first thing Benson asks. Brady is wondering why he does not, at all, look pleased. In fact, Benson looks upset. Brady is mystified by Benson's response. Benson gets up and starts pacing the room, as he says, "It is unfortunate that you have received all this information, because Sullivan and Davis investigated this case a couple of years ago. The case was closed over six months ago, when the commissioner of Midtown decided there were no grounds for upholding the charges against the management and board of Langmore Hospital. You see... We already investigated and shut down this case. The case is closed!" Both Brady and Lizzy look at Benson in total bewilderment. Brady says, "Okay. I get it. But with this new and substantial evidence, we have good reasons for reopening the case?"

Benson nervously shakes his head in agitation. "Yay, yay, yay. You can say that! You can say that! It is easy for you to say. But we were reprimanded by the top. You understand *the top*! For investigating a dead-end case and in the process getting on the nerves of some of the wealthiest and most influential people in New York. The chief was even involved in the case at some point." Benson sits down, as he continues in a lower tone of voice, "I really don't know how I am going to convince the deputy inspector and maybe even the commissioner to reopen the case with all the mayhem it entails." After a while of silence, Benson gets up and says, "Leave it with me. I will talk to the deputy inspector, and we will decide what to do. I will get back to you. But please be patient!" Brady and Lizzy get up, as they sense their stay has come to an end.

"We cannot just leave the case at this," Lizzy insists as they walk back to the meeting room. "It is outrageous!" she continues.

Brady is quiet. "I am as disappointed as you. I really didn't expect this. Who are these guys anyway? Sullivan and Davis... Do you know them?" Brady asks Lizzy, who nods "no." Once back in the meeting room, they carefully assemble the information in folders. "What should we do?" Brady asks.

Lizzy reflects, "There must be a case file somewhere that we can access. If it is a shut case, the file will be in the basement with Brett. I know him well, because when I first started in the force, I spent months as a runner, picking up files in the basement, amongst other shitty jobs!"

Brady looks at her watch. "Shit! I have to run. I promised to visit my parents. My mother has long been ill, and she just got diagnosed. I must go. I promised to be home by five for early dinner."

Brady starts picking up her personal stuff as she says, "Look, if you have time later this evening, come to my place. Say nine? See if you can pick up the old case file at Brett's before you leave the station and bring it along with all the other information we have. Then we can go over it tonight at my place."

Lizzy looks excited until she says, "What about your husband?"

Brady answers, while scribbling her address, "What husband? Do I see you later?"

Saskia must brace herself with patience regarding the liberation of the Langmore Hospital patients. While Brady and Lizzy take action on an investigation that management seems unwilling to pursue, and they are unwilling to let go, Saskia walks past Langmore every day to check if there is any commotion resulting from a police raid. Still, there are no signs of such commotion. She goes back into the cisterns, disappointed, and angry at the world. When she thinks of the injustice of this world, she contemplates never resurfacing the cisterns again. She is disillusioned with the world above. However, increasingly, she is losing hope for the world below as well. 'The cause' seems nothing else but an excuse to mobilize the underworld in the service of the overlords of the world above.

By the time, Saskia climbs the rope in the cylinder, it has been hanging there for four days. Saskia is nervous. She is trying to calm herself by asking what the worst thing is that can happen. Of course, the worst thing that can happen is that she is caught, but whether she is a captive of the underworld or a captive of the overworld hardly makes any difference at this point, she reasons. On the other hand, she knows that if she succeeds, she will gain legendary status in the underground as a master thief known for her cunningness and tenaciousness. Maybe she will even advance to sub-level 3. She smiles to herself at the prospect of advancing until she thinks of leaving her children behind at sub-level 2. Nevertheless, the thought of getting closer to Skyman warms her.

In her backpack, she has the replica of the crown that Skyman gave her. She went to his apartment three days ago to pick up the replica. Kate passed the address to Eli and instructed her to be there at exactly seven o'clock the following evening. "Skyman will be waiting for you, personally, to give you the replica and share with you any intel he has," was the message from Kate. Saskia is almost more nervous going to see Skyman than she is climbing up the cylinder to the Met.

The day she goes to see Skyman, she bounces off to 111 West 57th Street. She walks through the grand door of the skyscraper and into an immense hallway, where the doorman has noted her name in his book and shows her the way to the elevators. She proceeds up to the 72nd floor, where Lee, the butler, dressed in relatively casual attire, greets her and shows her to the living room. "Mr. Skylar is on his way. He is running a bit late. He apologizes. Can I get something for you to drink, while you wait?" Lee asks. Saskia hasn't had alcohol in over a year, since entering the underground. For a second, she thinks that Lee may not realize who she is or where she comes from. It is a pleasant relief to be mistaken for a common earthling for once. *Maybe he thinks, I am a normal person living a normal life*, Saskia contemplates, while asking for a gin & tonic.

"Nolet's?" Lee asks. Saskia nods accepting, even though, she doesn't know what he means.

She sits on the luscious, white couch where a fur blanket is nonchalantly thrown over the armrest. The expansive view from the 72nd floor is breathtaking overlooking Central Park and New York City. From the sky, the world below seems undauntingly small and insignificant. Up here in the heavens, nothing can touch you. Nothing can harm you. You are closer to God than to mere mortals and their ridiculous feelings of resentment and jealousy. You are God! Indeed, Skyman is a kind of God of the underworld. It is not just Saskia who is in awe over his persona and presence. *Everybody* in the underground stops up and takes a step back when Skyman effortlessly walks through in the underground. Skyman feels equally at home amongst the scum of the underworld as he does amongst the scum of the overworld. He intuitively navigates hell and the heavens with equal ease. There is some commotion when Skyman finally arrives about an hour late. The butler Lee and a maid rush to the vast high ceilinged entry hall with the gold and crystal chandelier and the round table reflecting the light of the chandelier in its highly polished black vanish. On the table, there is a cornucopia of fresh delicately scented flowers. All along the edges of the hall, on the walls, dimly lit works of art tell a tale of sumptuous wealth. It is not just Saskia, but anyone entering this sealed off world of astronomical wealth who ask themselves, how this one individual could amass such riches in just one lifetime.

In the underground, Skyman looks tall. Nevertheless, here in the sky, standing in his hall, he looks small. When Saskia sees the slightness of his persona, she reflects on what terrible things could possibly have happened to this Skyman for him to so singleheartedly dedicate his entire life to amassing wealth. *Who hurt him so much as to make him so eager to gain riches?* Saskia asks herself, while standing in the doorway with her drink observing him. *Is he driven by revenge? Who is he taking revenge on?*

"Sorry, sorry…" Skyman says modestly as he walks toward Saskia.

She turns around and goes back to her seat on the couch. "Not to worry!" she says and continues. "It is not the worst place in the world to be stuck waiting."

Skyman smiles. "I am ravenous! Can I offer you something to eat? I must eat," he insists. Skyman speaks in a slightly undefinable dialect. His language is sophisticated, but Saskia can detect some kind of dialect, which she is entirely unable to place.

By the time, they walk into the dining room, they have already exchanged several stories about their sorry lives. They talk with eagerness and excitement. It is difficult to tell if this eagerness and excitement make them open their hearts, or if they opened their hearts first and subsequently became overly eager and excited. There is a euphoria, which runs like an almost violent energy around, through and between them. It is impossible to contain their draw toward each other.

By the time, Saskia passes the pile of pebble stones on the pedestal that they both laugh at, while Skyman painstakingly explains that it is a highly priced piece of art, she is totally smitten. It is probably too early to tell if she is actually in love. But smitten, she is, for sure. They are on their way upstairs to the bedrooms. As she lies in Skyman's humongous bed overlooking Central Park, she mutters something about becoming emotionally attached to a man once she has sex with him. Something about him not hurting her vulnerable feelings now that she is giving herself to him. Nevertheless, flushed with excitement, she is unsure if she can formulate any coherent sentence at this point. She is unsure if he hears her. Inch by inch he penetrates her defenses, and she lets down her guard.

She doesn't want to fall asleep. The moment is too precious. *Every second of this moment must be savored, not just slept away,* she thinks. But eventually, during some unspecific second, she falls into deep sleep in the strong arms of Skyman.

They are woken by Lee at six a.m., when Lee pushes the bottom by the door and the curtains automatically draw to reveal their close proximity to the morning sun. "We will take breakfast in the dining room," Skyman grunts into his pillow. Lee nods. Saskia thinks this morning ritual is a strange intrusion of Lee on his privacy. But she guesses that rich people resign on privacy to gain the comforts of having servants around them to do their every bidding. She thinks that she would not be willing to make such a sacrifice. She cherishes the early morning moments when she is laying in her bed, alone, beneath the glass prisms looking up at the world above.

Before Lee leaves the bedroom, he places a small, silver tray with a glass of water and a pill on the nightstand next to Saskia.

"What is that?" Saskia says in a surprised tone of voice.

Skyman, still talking into his pillow, mumbles, "It is a pill of regret."

Saskia is wide awake now. "What is hell is that?" she says trying to conceal her sadness that is maybe morphing into regret.

Skyman senses her distress and gets up on his elbows. "It is a pill to prevent you from getting pregnant. It is for your own protection," he says.

Saskia feels her throat narrowing, tears pressing. The pill symbolizes the briefness and shallowness of the moment they shared, indicating that their relationship will never extend beyond a fleeting moment. She doesn't want to get pregnant; she doesn't. But she also doesn't want him to manhandle her into not getting pregnant. With the pill, he takes charge of a decision that should be hers. Additionally, there is something strangely automated about Butler Lee entering with the tray, making her wonder, *How many women have been here before me? How many women have taken this pill before me?*

Saskia gets up swinging her legs around and sits on the edge of the bed with her back turned to Skyman. She feels like taking her hands to her eyes and weeping. But she doesn't. Instead, she takes the tray and walks into the bathroom to start getting ready. It is the second last day of preparation before the theft at the Met.

She is reunited with Skyman at breakfast in the splendid dining room. On the table, sits the replica. Saskia almost gasps for air at the splendid sight of the replica of the crown. The dining table sits fourteen people, but Saskia and Skyman are sitting next to each other at one end of the table. Saskia presumes that Skyman is normally sitting at that end of the table, alone. "Did you take the pill?" he insists.

"Yes." She is determined not to spoil this moment and ruin what flourished between them the night before. There is a moment of awkward silence, in which Skyman contemplates if Saskia is telling the truth. He wishes he had *seen* her taking the pill. Normally, he insists on seeing the women take the pill of regret the day after, but Saskia went into the bathroom with the tray and locked the door. He went to one of the guest bathrooms.

At breakfast, Saskia's mind is racing with ways to break the awkwardness between them; ways of reviving the euphoria of last night. In the clear light of day, things are different than in the dark of night. In dark of night, maybe partially hiding in the dark, we let our guard down and show our true self. Now, in the daylight, unable to hide in the dark, both Skyman and Saskia can see each other more clearly.

Still trying to break the awkwardness between them, Saskia asks, "What do you do for a living?"

Skyman contemplatively replies, "Oh... It is complicated." He looks at Saskia and realizes she is disappointed by his answer, and he decides to elaborate. "I have developed a certain kind of technology, a chip, that traces the whereabouts of people, which is inserted under the skin. The chip also enables simple communication and transactions through the force of the mind. All of the people, and their communications and transactions are kept secret from governments rendering the opportunity to create an alternative society operating on a high-tech grid that is inaccessible to the authorities. The idea is to create a pioneering antiestablishment society, such as we are growing in the underground. An alternative to the nation state. The idea is to demolish the nation state. We do this with force, and by growing a parallel society that operates on a different grid to the traditional one overseen by corrupt and delinquent government, their officials, and institutions."

Saskia is hardly listening to what he says, but she is pleasantly surprised that he is willing to engage with her and tell her about his work. Skyman continues, "You know, wars are not won by the most valiant and fearless.

They're not even won by the one with the biggest and best-trained army. Wars are won by the one with the most sophisticated technology. With this chip, we can amass and connect a large following of people, who can break free from the shackles of this oppressive society. With this chip, new connectivity, and communication, we can rise to the challenge of starting a new, better, and more just society. That is what we are doing in the underground. That is why the people down there must sever all their ties to the existing society." Skyman looks her in the eyes with compassion, as he senses that she is not listening. It's not that Saskia is stupid; she has just given up hoping and fighting for a better society. All she wants now is for her and her kids to have a decent life. Big thoughts about a big society, she left in her hopeful youth. Skyman takes her hand and kisses it. In that moment, the flame of hope flares up inside Saskia.

Saskia leaves Skyman's residence that morning with a glimpse of hope for a relationship with a man she has fallen totally and completely in love with. As she walks along the busy morning streets, she thinks why human beings make relationships so incredibly difficult when they are in fact the single most important thing in our lives. Relationships equip children with the mental robustness to confront life with all its challenges. Relationships give us unrivaled depth and meaning in life. People with no or scarce relationships suffer mental illness and die prematurely. No one will suffer mental illness or die prematurely for the lack of money. Most importantly, no one gets any happier for having more money than they need to lead a good life. Yet, in New York, the pursuit of money, often at the expense of meaningful relationships, takes precedence over everything else.

Now, considering how important relationships are, why can Saskia not just say out loud to Skyman that she is totally and completely in love with him? Why does she have to engage in a cat and mouse game? Play hide and seek? Century old rules of courtship are proscribed to us since the dawn of the Abrahamic religions, in which the woman must take a passive receiving role. Such proscription creates the perfect storm for conflict and misunderstandings, from anything from unintentional rapes to overlooked love and devotion that could in fact render the absolute happiness of two people.

As soon as she walks through the door of the apartment, Saskia is woken up by reality. "Where were you!" Eli yells. "You don't understand... I was nervous for you. I thought something had happened to you. I mean, you go *looking* for trouble. Don't you! Also, I thought, you might have defected. What the fuck, Saskia!" Eli is almost breaking into a sweat, as he says, "I didn't even dare to use your phone, because I was scared Kate and Annona would find out that you had gone rogue the day before the raid!"

Saskia has never seen him like this before. Eli *is* calmness. He *is* tranquility. Except for now. Saskia is totally taken aback. "I slept with someone," she blurts out as if it is the most normal thing in this world.

Eli looks at her with suspicion. "Seriously. Did you sleep with Skyman?" he asks. She wants to deny, but she feels the truth is written on her forehead. There is no point in denying it. "You can get into serious trouble if Kate and Annona find out that you are sleeping with Skyman," Eli says.

"Well, they won't find out. Will they?" Saskia asks in a sharp tone of voice.

Eli nods no and says, "We have no time to waste. Let's go over the plan again. Then you can go for a run and relax, if you can relax in that crazy fuck of a head."

Saskia feels claustrophobic suffocation going through the plan of the theft again, but through persistent lifelong hardship she has learned to control her thoughts and emotions. She is certainly in control of her demeanor. She has totally internalized the plan of the theft. Going over it again and again only agitates her at this stage. She knows that a slow run in Central Park is what she needs the most.

While she is out running, she receives a text on the secured phone, the underground has given her. No one, except Eli, Kate and Annona, has the number to that phone. It is only used for emergencies.

Good luck with tomorrow! the message reads from an unknown sender.

She thinks it must be from Skyman. She smiles until she realizes that he is the one who is making her go through this whole ordeal. And for what? For some centuries-old pile of metal. He is in fact making her risk her freedom and life to get this artifact. The artifact means more to him than she does.

The next morning, she puts on skintight clothing that allows her to move up through the forest of cables in the cylinder without getting stuck. She has some loosely fitted lightweight clothes in her streamlined and seamless rucksack that allow her to blend in with the other visitors of the museum. She knows the way through the tangle of passageways, stairs, and tunnels in the underground by heart even though she doesn't have her heart with her today.

She passes the catacomb, not understanding where it stems from. The catacomb is next to the cathedral of the cistern. It is the graveyard to the cathedral. The only true religion of the underworld is death. The catacomb is a daunting reminder of our mortality and the somber bleakness of our lives. Racing around above ground to amass recognition, wealth, gratitude, love, and what else in the short time we exist, to then end up below ground having your bones picked on by roundworms and rats till all traces of our sorry existence have completely vanished.

Almost effortlessly, she climbs up the rope dangling from the top of the cylinder. She lifts the grid slightly more to press herself through the opening. Placing a knee at the edge, she can barely open the door. She pushes herself forward onto the fine parquet floor in the passageway. Here, she puts on her disguise. She sneaks out of the door into a massive exhibition room bathed in light from the glass dome in the ceiling. She must make the steal during plain daylight because Eli cannot find a way to tamper with the security system. During the day, security is kept at a minimum to offer the public free passage to the past.

Still, Eli manages to shut off the cameras of the room where the crown of Nefertiti thrones. He also manages to turn off the security sensors of the glass case displaying the crown. But there is always the risk that a vigilant guard starts wondering why the cameras in the room of Nefertiti crown are not showing and raises the alarm. She must move fast. She enters the room where the crown is displayed. After working herself up into a panic attack, she runs up to the guard overseeing the crown and yells that her daughter has fainted in the room next door. "There is not enough air in here. It is totally unacceptable and dangerous!" she yells. Visitors start flowing into the room next door to glare at the supposed incident. People like watching other people suffer, because it reminds of how well they are doing themselves.

While the guard and visitors run into the room next door, Saskia walks determined toward the glass case where the crown is. She opens the case and lifts out the crown. She takes out the replica from her rucksack and places it in the display case. The few people still in the room, while Saskia steals the crown, are astonished. For the most part of the theft, they just stand still and observe. Finishing her theft, Saskia starts moving in high pace toward the passageway and her exit back into the underground.

It takes quite a while before someone runs to fetch a guard. "But the crown is right there!" the guard says, when he reemerges in the room. After him, two more guards enter the room and unanimously agree while pointing at the crown. "The crown is right there!" There is total chaos with everybody talking over each other. Talking all at once, the visitors, who saw the theft, try to explain that the glass case contains a replica of the crown. After repeating himself several times, he manages to cut through the overlapping talk, to deliver his revelation. The three guards quiet. They stand still for a short second. Then they run toward an alarm button on the wall.

The alarm is sounded when Saskia can see the door to the passageway connecting the two exhibition rooms. If she doesn't encounter a guard now, she will probably make it to the cylinder, she thinks. She is running with the crown in her rucksack. She hopes it doesn't break.

Suddenly out of nowhere, two men block her passage in the door. She decides that the element of surprise is her only weapon, as she pushes through between them with all her force. One of them turns around, grabs her and holds her in a firm grip. She wriggles out of his grip by twisting her body—a trick she learned in combat training in the underground. Before she knows it, she is throwing herself into the cylinder barely holding onto the rope. She is hauled down the cylinder desperately trying to hold on to something. She feels deep cuts slice through her flesh. She wants to scream from the excruciating pain, but everything is going so fast. She reaches the bottom of the cylinder with a hard bump. Once she regains her consciousness, she hears voices of two guards above. They are too big to make it down the cylinder. She runs through the cathedral of the cistern and its graveyard until she is out of breath and collapses on the soiled moist ground. She doesn't know for how long she is laying in the dirt, but it is long enough for her to be soaked and wet, when she wakes up.

By the time she reaches the world above, she is at a breaking point. To her surprise, there are no police in the streets, even though, she can hear sirens in the far distance. She picks up the pace using the last ounce of energy left in her. When she walks through the door to the apartment, she doesn't say a word. She puts the crown on the kitchen table and walks into her room where she collapses on the bed.

Eli follows her. "You did it! Again! You are unbelievable!" She is pleased until she realizes the hell hole will just keep throwing trials and tribulations at her until she either breaks, is caught, or killed. She is spinning on a downward spiral.

Back in the meeting room at sub-level 2, Saskia is reluctant to hand over the crown to Skyman. She feels that he is no more deserving of the crown than her. *Why must he have it?* she thinks to herself. *I am the one that stole it! It should be mine.* In fact, she doesn't want the crown. Instead, she feels the kind of entitlement that comes from sleeping with someone and then subsequently irrationally thinking you are on par with that person, just because you shared an intimate moment.

Skyman is still holding out his right hand waiting for Saskia to hand over her bounty.

"Saskia?" Kate says in a stern voice. "Give him the crown!" Now that Skyman has taken possession of the crown, the only redeeming thing, Saskia can think of, is that her and Skyman may continue seeing each other. She has a relationship with a man she is in awe of and in love with in return for stealing stuff for him, she justifies.

Perhaps their relationship may even cement into something more than the occasional one-night fling.

Surely, he must be pleased with her. She smiles. After all, no one else would risk their freedom, even their life, for this thing he obviously values very highly. Saskia, still feeling entitled, wrongly presumes she has a choice in the matter. She does not. She and her children belong to the underground. The endless trials and tribulations are part of their contract.

"Don't think life is fair!" Annona is trying to teach Saskia a life lesson. But Annona does not know that Skyman came down from his pedestal and into bed with her. She does not know that they made love. If she knew that, she would say, "Don't be delusional!"

*

When Brady and Lizzy finally obtain the warrant to search the basement of Langmore Hospital, suspicion arises beyond the organ transplants of illegal migrants. The esteemed founder of the Langmore Hospital and highly acknowledged organ transplant specialist Dr. Hinnemann conducts all operations in the sealed off theaters in the basement himself. He has the assistance of two people. There are also nurses let into the sealed off area in the basement, but they do not know the full extent of the clandestine operation.

One of Dr. Hinnemann's faithful helpers is a warden, Milo, who assists Dr. Hinnemann during surgery, despite not having any formal medical credentials. Milo came to the U.S. when his parents fled the Bosnian civil war after losing their two oldest sons. Thus, when Milo was just nine years old, his parents, adamant Milo should not also die on the altar of human misunderstanding and indifference, fled with their youngest son.

Years of struggle followed in the Land of Opportunities that grants no opportunities for those at the bottom of society. In pre-war Bosnia, Milo had started school at four, and subsequently, during the war, he was homeschooled by his highly educated parents. Despite solid schooling and a deepfelt eagerness to learn, Milo found himself struggling with a new language, new norms, and peculiar rules. After a few months, when Milo somewhat mastered the language enough to follow the classes, a broken public school system led to him unlearning everything he had learned leaving him worse off than he was before he attended American public school. By the time, Milo left public school at sixteen, having successfully unlearned everything, he could not do simple calculations, read, nor write. At this point, his brain was a mishmash of conflict and confusion. Additionally, there is no need for unskilled manual labor in this land, as such labor had been replaced by automation, robotics, and AI. Even Milo's job as a warden was being replaced by autonomous vehicles and other robotics taking over the basement.

In the meantime, his father, who was himself an esteemed medical doctor in the public hospital University Clinical Center Sarajevo, struggled with depression at the loss of his sons, his broader family, home, and everything else. Coming to the U.S. at the age of fifty-six with nothing to prove his life's worth, seemed almost unbearable to his parents. Depression and despair made it impossible for Milo's father to take the U.S. medical license. Subsequently, only odd jobs as a driver, builder, and janitor were available.

Milo was proud and happy when he got the job as warden in Langmore Hospital. But his father did not share his excitement, as he had hoped his son would pursue a medical career of his own in this Land of Opportunity. In fact, his father thought that Milo becoming a warden was a sign of Milo's disregard and downright ungrateful for the hardship endured by his parents to bring Milo to the Land of Opportunity. When Dr. Hinnemann acknowledged Milo and invited him to help at the operations, Milo found the long-awaited recognition of a father. Milo is Dr. Hinnemann's faithful accomplice. In fact, Milo is eternally grateful to Dr. Hinnemann for granting him the opportunity to assist him in operations.

The other accomplice is nurse Miss Jane, who mainly oversees pre- and post-operation patient care. Miss Jane is also scarred on her soul having grown up with a sadistically incestuous father. Now, Dr. Hinnemann's sadism seems like a welcomed homecoming to something entirely recognizable. After twenty years of faithful service, Miss Jane still harbors sexual fantasies of Dr. Hinnemann raping her on the operating table. There are a couple of other nurses on duty in the basement. They report to Miss Jane. Their generous pay refrain them from asking any difficult questions.

No doubt, when Dr. Hinnemann removes organs, sometimes even vital organs, from the illegal migrants, he is first and foremost driven by mere greed, as his wealthy and desperate New York clients pay him generously to obtain organs that are critical to their survival, the survival of their spouse or children. Nevertheless, when Dr. Hinnemann strangles his migrant patients, he is first and foremost driven by sadism. In fact, to get full satisfaction, and ultimately ejaculation, Dr. Hinnemann must see his patients fully recovered, and then strangle them.

Unlike presented in popular media, strangulation takes several minutes during which time the life and death of the victim is entirely in the hands of the strangler. Thus, the motivation of Dr. Hinnemann to become a doctor and a killer is identical: he gets excited, even sexually aroused, from having the life and death of someone defenseless in his hands. It is unknown why and how Dr. Hinnemann obtained his psychological composition, but undoubtedly, he has demons of his own to fight.

During the police raid of the basement of Langmore Hospital, social workers and medical staff help the migrant patients into safety and care. Nevertheless, most of the migrants resist their rescue, as they are more concerned with getting deported than they are with losing their organs. Over the coming days and weeks, a narrative unravels, in which the migrants explain that they were lured with a free passage to the U.S. by middlemen in cities along the Mexican border, such as Ciudad Juárez and Tijuana. With or without their consent, the migrants were then ferried in minibuses across the U.S. to New York arriving at night, in the basement parking lot of the Langmore Hospital, from where they were hurtled to their hospital beds in the basement by guards. They unanimously explain that they thought their operation was legal and occurred under the watchful eyes of the U.S. authorities. Brady and Lizzy agree that the whole criminal operation is so complex, yet systemized, that some authorities must have known and turned a blind eye. "Fresh organs for dying New Yorkers don't just suddenly appear out of nowhere!" Lizzy argues.

Brady and Lizzy's suspicions of even more sinister things going on at the Langmore Hospital are confirmed when they talk to two different migrants who both, independently, insist one child and a spouse vanished from one day to another after the operation was successfully accomplished.

In one incident, Miss Jane nursed eleven-year-old Carmen back to full recovery. Carmen was a happy girl, who was, luckily, hospitalized together with her father. She hardly understood why she was in the hospital and kept asking her father if she was ill. Her father explained her, to the best of his ability, the operation Carmen would undergo in the coming days.

To Brady and Lizzy, the father explains how the whole thing started, when they met a woman and two men in Tijuana, where their little family of five had waited for almost three months to make the crossing to the U.S. Desperate, and out of sorts and hope, the father and mother listened attentively as a local woman and two men explained that they would smuggle them across the border and give them all the fake documents they needed to get by, all free of charge, if the father or mother would donate a kidney at a highly specialized hospital. As the journey from Escuintla, Guatemala, to Tijuana, Mexico, had depleted their inadequate traveling funds, they had no other choice but to accept the offer. Their only alternative was to throw themselves across the barbed wire at night with the risk of getting shot, as so many others had. Such a suicide plan would not work with three young children in tow. In the end, the father decided that he, and not his wife, would donate his kidney for the safe crossing and future of his family.

Once on the U.S. side, well-nourished men twice the size of the Guatemalans greeted them. They took a hard look at all the five of them, took some blood samples and decided then and there that Carmen was the only one they could use. Realizing that the men would take Carmen from them regardless of whether they wanted it or not, the father pleaded on his knees to be allowed to follow his little girl to the hospital. To be allowed to stay by her side. The men thought about what would happen to the young girl *after* the operation. With no parents, social services would get involved and from there... who knows! They allowed the father to tag along.

After an emotional parting, the mother and two youngest children were left in Albuquerque, from which they had to make their own way northward for the reunion of the little family. Having only limited communication, the father and mother were anxious they should not lose each other for good, as so many illegal migrants do, when crossing into no man's land. Even though, none of them received any of the promised fake documents that would prevent them from being deported if captured by the U.S. authorities, they gave their most-prized possession to the men.

In this way, Carmen became the unknowing and unwilling savior of the whole family. "We are so proud of you," he told her in a tearful voice, as she rolled into the operating theatre. Carmen felt proud.

In the end, Dr. Hinnemann removed a significant portion of Carmen's little liver. While Carmen sacrificed her liver for her family, Mrs. López had sacrificed hers to alcohol. Mr. López, a wealthy businessman, had established a successful logistics company specializing in transport from Southern to Northern states and cities, including New York. He is a close business associate of Dr. Hinnemann, having assisted Dr. Hinnemann in trafficking illegal migrants for organ transplants on several occasions.

Mr. López convinces himself that he is helping these people toward a brighter future, but deep down, he suspects that Dr. Hinnemann's operations are more sinister than he wishes to know. Nevertheless, he is willing to suppress his gut feeling when the day arrives that he himself needs to ask Dr. Hinnemann for a favor. Mr. López thanks God for his collaboration with Dr. Hinnemann.

Mr. and Mrs. López were once illegal migrants themselves, during a different era when it was still possible to climb socially upward in U.S. society. They arrived in the States at the age of twenty, and together, they built their family and business. Despite their achievements, Mr. López had rarely been home the past twenty years, often under the pretense of working late. In reality, he engaged in a series of thriving affairs, one lasting almost ten years. Growing extremely tired and resentful of his mentally unstable wife, Mr. López feels enormous guilt and remorse when his wife drinks herself into unconsciousness. Perhaps it is precisely because he wished his wife dead on so many occasions that he now feels guilty and is willing to do almost anything in his power to get her back on her own two feet. This seems almost impossible, as Mrs. López hasn't stood on her feet since she stopped struggling for survival and took up boozing.

Once Mrs. López ceased struggling for her family's survival, she became lonely, bored, and self-absorbed, leading to her drinking herself into oblivion and, eventually, death. Her liver is giving in to her drinking. This is where Carmen, or rather Carmen's liver, comes into the picture.

Dr. Hinnemann does not see his migrant patients till they are in general anesthesia laying on his operating table. He has no feelings toward his numbed patients, but his professional pride induces him to successfully complete the transplantation without losing the life of the patient. Already a couple of minutes into Carmen's operation, Dr. Hinnemann notices that he is sexually aroused by the lifeless little girl. This is why he comes to her room late the evening after she has fully recovered from the successful operation. "I need to give her a full medical check before I can sign her out tomorrow," he explains to Carmen's father. Before the father knows it, Carmen is rolled back into the operating theatre on the pretense that something is terribly wrong.

Once in the operating theatre, Carmen feels Dr. Hinnemann's hands around her neck. Her small hands clench onto Dr. Hinnemann's wrists idlily trying to remove his hands from her neck. Her body is free floating midair. Within three long minutes, Carmen's body wriggles in violent jerks, as she grasps for air. This is when Dr. Hinnemann feels his body letting go and releases himself. He makes a large groan the moment Carmen stops to struggle.

*

Brady sees Saskia watching, as she and Lizzy come out of the hospital with Dr. Hinnemann, who is taken into questioning. At first, Brady cannot recall from where she recognizes Saskia. But she knows their acquittance must be work related because Brady doesn't have a life beyond work. When Brady walks within a couple of feet from Saskia, she suddenly recalls talking to Saskia as the cleaner at the Glenmore's. Before she can properly connect the dots, Brady instantly and instinctively gets a feeling that somehow Saskia is involved as she asks herself if Saskia is the one who sent her all the evidence on the Langmore case.

This is Brady's first thought, but she continues to reason that it is too much of a coincidence that Saskia should both be present at the unraveling of Christel's death and now at Dr. Hinnemann's crime scene. Additionally,

Brady is too busy to pursue the thought further. After all, whatever Saskia's involvement may be, it is a good thing, Brady reasons, as without the evidence, she would not have been able to nail Dr. Hinnemann.

As the two women get eye contact, Brady's gut feeling is confirmed. Brady almost feels like nodding in acknowledgement of Saskia's help, as she passes her on her way to see Inspector Benson, who arrives just in time to oversee the grand finale of the raid.

Chapter Five

There is standing applause as Brady and Lizzy walk through Midtown Precinct South. The synthetic, gray, wall-to-wall carpet that was recently installed as part of a broader effort to refurbish the run-down police station is still static. The smell of plastic from the cheap carpet and furniture gives workers a headache if they stay in the office all day. Sparks of electricity leave a trail behind Brady and Lizzy as they glide across the department of criminal investigation.

Even though, Brady would like to return the hugs of her colleagues, most of whom she has never spoken to before, she stops as each human touch results in the massive static electrification of both parties. Her colleagues interpret this as a rejection of their newly found friendliness. Most of them understand why Brady does not just readily accept their embrace, claps on her shoulder and handshakes. After all, for years, they have rejected her and socially excluded her from their group. The same goes for Lizzy.

It is peculiar that the individuals who are not part of socially constructed groups are usually the ones to drive change. Groupthink smothers the senses, preventing individuals from keeping an open mind and thinking in critical ways. Yet, on the other hand, we all need social recognition like we need the air to breathe. It is a catch-22. Socially constructed groups are precisely constructed around shared perceptions and thinking. Yet, such group thinking reinforces already established ideas about the world. When new ideas are floated in an existing group, it is important *who* floats the idea. To a lesser extent, it is important *what* the idea is. This explains why strong groups, such as political parties, for instance, rarely come up with any innovative ideas. It is simply not important what the idea is in order for it to gain momentum. Therefore, if you find yourself in a socially constructed group, which is the case for most of us, it's essential to introduce your idea and seek the support of the group's leader. This will enable you to eliminate hostility to your idea *before* floating it with your group.

In fact, what most often happens is that the leader steals and presents the idea as his own invention, while your silent participation wins you the respect of the leader. In turn, with the respect of the leader, you attain the respect of the group. It is a sad and sorry spectacle that goes on and on, day in and out. To a large extent, it explains why we keep on doing the same things despite knowing that we are heading straight for the hell hole.

Socially constructed groups and their innate groupthink explain the large and destructive path dependencies that roll across the globe like uncontrollable tsunamis, such as continued wars, resource depletion, and natural disasters. Each and every one of those can be traced back to groupthink and its inherent inability to see more viable alternative paths forward.

In Midtown Precinct South, all and every one of the existing socially constructed groups would have refrained from pursuing the Langmore Hospital and its highly esteemed founder and medical doctor, Dr. Hinnemann. They would have followed orders and stepped down. Thus, with socially constructed groups and groupthink, meaningful ideas, actions, and paths are left undeterred, while meaningless ideas, actions, and paths are, at best, left intact and, at worst, pursued.

Brady sits at her desk. There are different colored post-its stuck on the screen with greetings and congratulations as is customary for colleagues to do when someone makes an important arrest or solves a big case. She barely sits down before a young police assistant rapidly approaches her desk. "Benson is asking for you." He points toward Benson's office with an open door.

As Brady walks closer to the open door, she can hear Benson moaning and groaning inside the small, dark, gray-in-gray shaded office. Of course, people at Benson's level have windows in their offices. Afterall, they spend most of their lives in their offices. Yet Benson repeatedly broke his blinds in one of his many rage fits. Facility management finally gave up fixing the blinds. Now the blinds permanently block all daylight from entering Benson's office. Dust has settled on the bookshelves behind Benson. Some of the selves have given in to the heavy weight of paper, folders, and books piled up over the years.

In many ways, walking into Benson's office is like traveling back in time. The office is a time pocket of the late nineteen nineties. After months of procrastination, Benson finally resisted altogether having his carpet and furniture refurbished, because he could not overcome sorting out the enormity of stuff built up with the passage of time. He had to tackle his mess for the builders to do their work.

Brady wonders why Benson is in such a bad mood. "Close the door!" he commands in a harsh tone of voice that reveals years of exhaustion accumulated in his mind and body. Benson is seated and points to the chair opposite his desk. Brady sits down. "Did I not tell you *not* to proceed with the investigation of the Langmore Hospital?" Benson is agitated shifting around on his chair nervously.

"Oh... yes, but you see what they were up to?" Brady is confused. She continues, "You see they steal organs of defenseless and desperate migrants. Granted, most of these migrants weren't supposed to be in the country in the first place, but still... That hardly justifies stealing their organs. Langmore Hospital is at the epicenter of both illegal organ harvesting *and* human trafficking. We have even found out that some migrants may have disappeared altogether after their organs were removed!" Brady looks intensively at Benson. She is trying to see if she can understand what is going on by reading his expression.

Faced with the prospect of death, most individuals would go to great lengths to save themselves and their loved ones. Thus, these accessories to crime have taken a sharp turn on their life journey to save themselves or a loved one. In the process, they manipulate the course of their destiny, or, maybe, destiny is what meets them, when they take that sharp turn. Their choice is simple: either you die, or you become an accomplice to crime.

Benson shakes his head over and over again. Then he says, "I really don't know how to tell you this, Brady, but Dr. Hinnemann also saved the lives of many, many Americans, many of whom would have been left to die if he had not stepped in to safe them. Most of his business, the great majority, is totally legal! If we close down this side *geschäft* of his that you so skillfully discovered, we also lose the legal business of saving American lives."

The desperation in Benson's eyes is startling. Benson continues, "Loads of people, some of whom are very powerful, will be against this case unfolding in the courts. Some people will get prosecuted for being accessory to these crimes, some of whom are innocent bystanders who wanted to save their own lives or that of their child or spouse. Other people are now destined to die instead of getting the organ transplant they are scheduled for." Brady cannot believe her ears. She is sitting in total silence observing Benson, who is sweating and shifting in his chair.

Very often, people like Benson and Brady start their careers in the police, because they want to protect people and society. Their motivations are noble and admirable. In the world of noble and admirable motivations, the narrative and reality are simple black and white. Yet, with time, some of them realize that things are not that simple. People are not either good or evil. Life is not simple. Society is not just. From this, in many ways, saner position of less noble and admirable motivations, they are easily convinced that certain things and people are best left unchanged to preserve society. With time, they convince themselves to sacrifice their principles and morals for the greater good: the preservation of society. In this realm of reasoning, they convince themselves it is okay to target a particular group of people, who is statistically overrepresented in crime. Such a targeted approach allows the police maximum impact with minimal effort. Yet, if one group is targeted, it naturally follows that more criminal behavior will be revealed within that group, since criminal behavior is everywhere in society, but goes undetected most places and amongst the groups in society that fly under the radar of the police. Also, if you feel that you are persistently targeted by the police, you may fall into a pattern of negative thinking. In fact, most people would probably fall into a negative thinking pattern in that life circumstance. Thus, you may think that whether you are a law obedient citizen or a criminal has no impact on the outcome as you are going to jail regardless, because that is what the police want.

Another tendency, in the wake of realizing that certain groups are targeted by the police, is the counter swing, in which the police now eagerly pursue individuals, who precisely fall *outside* the groups overrepresented in crime statistics. This is done to demonstrate that the police are precisely *not* targeting certain groups in society. Yet, like the justice exercised by the courts, there is nothing black and white about policing. It is all about human beings, their motivations, perceptions, and beliefs. Afterall, we are all just human beings.

In this case, Benson is weighing the pros and cons and trying, as best he can, to explain these to Brady. The pros of the arrest and prosecution of Dr. Hinnemann and the Langmore Hospital are that the police have identified and apprehended criminals who fall outside the groups overrepresented in crime statistics. In this way, Dr. Hinnemann and the Langmore Hospital serve to illustrate that the police are precisely *not* targeting certain groups in society. As such, Dr. Hinnemann and the Langmore Hospital become ideal scapegoats.

Another advantage is that the arrest has ripple effects; the human trafficking organizations working with the Langmore Hospital are suddenly on shaky ground. These effects may even extend further to include sex and drug trafficking, as well as other crimes such as money laundering and terrorism. Once you start scratching one surface, you may uncover a whole disarray of people and places involved.

Nevertheless, Americans receive organ transplants not only from illegal migrants but also from other Americans. In this way, the Langmore Hospital aids people in desperate need of a new organ to survive. In cases where no suitable organ is available through legal channels, individuals with power and wealth may resort to purchasing an organ from an unknown source. Their guilt is dampened by Dr. Hinnemann's convincing argument that their riches can help these poor souls to a betterment of their pitiful existence.

Thus, the arrest and prosecution of Dr. Hinnemann and the Langmore Hospital disrupt the foundation upon which society is built. The police and courts are not in the business of whacking society out of sync. In fact, the police and the courts are precisely in the business of protecting the society we live in. The problem is that this requires society to be just because what is the point of protecting an unjust society?

Some may argue that, in fact, the police and courts are precisely preventing a just society by protecting the status quo. This protection of status quo and therefore an unjust society is precisely what unravels when Bracy and Lizzy start their investigation of Dr. Hinnemann and the Langmore Hospital.

During the following days, the entirety of the crime reveals itself in the media. Firstly, there are numerous non-governmental organizations that start arguing in the media. One organization advocates for the human rights of migrants, also illegal migrants. Another organization discusses how the American health system has reached breaking point, when so many people must literally fight with their lives to get an organ transplant. Yet another organization argues that this testifies to the deep cutting social inequities that exist in this unjust society. Wealthy people can skip the line and get whatever they need as long as they have the money to pay for it. Big law firms and their lawyers are bolstering their defenses getting ready for combat. The fight of the Langmore Hospital is likely to whack society out of sync. At least for a moment.

Brady and Lizzy try to stay on the narrow script and playbook they have written for this investigation. They are going through endless arrests and interrogations. They cross-examine staff, current and former patients, the wealthy and powerful individuals who stepped forward to tell their story to the newspapers, and lastly the illegal migrants, who were saved in the raid. Brady and Lizzy also talk to the non-governmental organizations that are all extremely eager to present their view of events to the police in order to help justify their existence.

Dr. Hinnemann has been provided with a team of exceptional lawyers by Mr. Marlowe, one of New York's wealthiest residents, who boldly grants an interview to the New York Times, which lands on its Sunday cover. In the interview, Mr. Marlowe rages over the U.S. public health system. In particular, he is disillusioned with the New York City health system. He argues that the city is spending all its money on mental illness diagnosing and treatments that never seem to cure anyone. In fact, the number of mentally ill people is only ever going up. Mr. Marlowe presents solid numbers documenting that mental illness of the poorest segment of the population, the middle class, and upper class continuously rise. He points toward the ever-increasing number of mentally ill roaming around the streets in the city, whereby he triggers deeply ingrained fear of many New Yorkers. The city is no longer safe! It is dangerous to walk its streets, even at daytime. People are getting more and more scared.

This is just one of several examples that Mr. Marlowe mentions in his argument that public funds for healthcare are being misplaced and misused in an attempt to treat and cure diseases that only ever seem to get worst. In this city context, people must take things into their own hands! As this case of organ donation and transplantation is illustrative of. Mr. Marlowe's wife, who is still very ill, had one of the covert operations performed by Dr. Hinnemann. The operation did not cure her, but, at least, it postponed her eminent death.

It is in the wake of this article; Mr. Marlowe starts what looks like a crowdfunding exercise amongst the wealthiest New Yorkers to cover the exorbitant lawyers' fees of Dr. Hinnemann and the Langmore Hospital. Subsequently, all crowd funders become suspects in the investigation of the Langmore Hospital. Within days, Brady and Lizzy are overwhelmed by the breadth and depth of the investigation, leaving them exhausted. Brady asks Benson for assistance in the form of more investigators and police officers. A request that Benson reluctantly grants.

Mr. Marlowe materializes an illegal migrant from Nicaragua, Mr. González, who donated his organ and, in return, received a sizeable amount of money from the hospital, for which Mr. and Mrs. González are eternally grateful.

In yet another case, a Hispanic migrant himself, Mr. Ramirez, steps forward to tell that his son received a kidney from a young boy at the Langmore Hospital during an operation that was privately funded, but not covert, as it took place at the broad daylight in the hospital proper. However, as the operation was privately funded operation, Mr. Ramirez explains, he had to mortgage their home to the hilt. With COVID, Mr. Ramirez lost his job, and consequently, he could no longer pay the mortgage. The family lost their home, but they would do it all over again to save their son. Yet another tale of human misery and another nail in the public healthcare's coffin.

In reality, what is happening is that two significant factions are emerging in New York and elsewhere across several large and mid-sized cities in the United States. On the one hand, there are affluent New Yorkers, individuals like Dr. Glenmore, Dr. Hinnemann, Mr. Marlowe, and other long-established families within the city, those wealth and privilege have grown with each generation, as over time, property and stock prices rise. These old families thrive on the status quo, which keeps, in a gridlock, their privileges and wealth. They are protected by the police and courts through systems and structures that they themselves meticulously constructed over several generations through meddling with politics. Politicians are all too eager to sell out on their principals and beliefs in return of funding for their campaigns that will get them closer to power. Many of the politicians reason that without power, they will never be able to achieve any change, at all. Ergo, it is better to compromise your principals and beliefs and get some power rather than being completely sidelined from the game due to the lack of funding. Status quo prevails.

The other faction consists of up-and-coming individuals, such as Skyman and other supporters and backers of the underground. These individuals, who wear casual clothes and walk in a swanky laid-back way, want a revolution that will shake the foundation of society to the extent that the old affluent families lose their footing, privileges, wealth, and influence. The underground is the tool by which this revolution is possible. Nevertheless, the growth and mobilization of the underground, and similar communities across other large and mid-sized cities in the United States, is only possible due to the desperation and despair of the majority of the population that is free falling into deep poverty. At best, outcasts, like Saskia and her children, will find new highly appreciated roles in the revolutionary guard and the new society taking shape. At worst, they will end their lives prematurely as cannon feed. There is nothing more noble about the motivations of the new breed of wealth than there is about their predecessors' motivations. At the end of day, all both factions want is a free runway to amass privileges, wealth, and political influence.

Brady and Lizzy have reached the point on their to-do list that concerns questioning Milo. During the raid, he was briefly questioned, but at that time, it was unclear how much he knew and contributed to the crime. Lizzy calls Milo on a windy Thursday afternoon to summon him to the police station the following day. Milo seems utterly surprised and extremely confused on the phone. He repeatedly says that he does not understand how he can contribute to the investigation. When Lizzy hangs up, she too is somewhat confused. "Milo Kovačević seemed totally confused. Perplexed even. Does he not understand the magnitude of what he has been involved in?"

The subsequent day, Milo enters Midtown Precinct South with two lawyers, who turn out to come from the same law firm as Dr. Hinnemann's. Thus, it is fair to suspect that Mr. Marlowe and his associates are also funding the legal representation of Milo Kovačević. Later, it is revealed that they also fund the legal representation of Miss Jane. Milo seems better prepared than he was on the phone, but he still comes across as somewhat disoriented. "Did you operate on the migrants together with Dr. Hinnemann?" Brady says in a commanding voice.

"Yes," Milo replies. "But I thought nothing wrong of this. I was told we were helping both the migrants and the patients waiting for new organs. Dr. Hinnemann is a well-respected man in his field. Why should I suspect him of any wrongdoing?"

Brady and Lizzy leave Milo and his lawyers in the interrogating room for about half an hour, while they discuss the strange revelations revealed during the questioning. "It is hard to believe that he is totally unaware of criminal aspect of the operations," Lizzy says and continues, "After all, he must have wondered why the migrants were in the basement as opposed to in the hospital proper."

When they ask Milo to clarify this, he replies, "Well, Dr. Hinnemann explained that the American patients do not want to be confronted by their donors and especially not the migrant donors. Sometimes Dr. Hinnemann would take a donor migrant to meet a recipient patient if the patient requested it. That usually meant that the donor came back exhilarated with joy after having received a large amount of money in gratitude from the patient."

When asked why the operations took place at night, Milo explains that they did not always occur at night and that Dr. Hinnemann is a busy man, so operations must take place whenever the doctor has time, regardless the time of day, or night. Milo's lawyers point out that operations also take place at night in other hospitals across the city. "That is not an indication of anything else but a busy schedule that requires the medical teams to work around the clock."

People are different. Brady knows she cannot judge everybody by the same standards. For instance, she herself is intelligent, but her intelligence is of a particular sort: the kind of intelligence you attain on the streets when confronted with many different people of different walks of life. Some people are naïve, like Milo. Nevertheless, such naivety may stem from not having been raised by American parents, who have a natural understanding of the cultural norms and behavior. In fact, Milo's parents have a distorted view on America, which they have passed on to their somewhat gullible son. Other people are scholarly intelligent. They can solve complex and complicated problems. Yet, they may blind to anyone doing anything wrong, least of all themselves.

Brady is willing to entertain that someone, who has grown up in a different culture may not read the warning signs like everybody else. Her job is particularly complex due to the multitude of cultures coexisting in the city. On a daily basis, she is confronted with culturally defined peculiarities that make her stop up and reflect. "Well, did you never question the fact that you were helping out, as the only one, during operations? You have no medical credentials," Brady inquires.

Milo answers, "I did! But first of all, I only handed Dr. Hinnemann the tools he needed to conduct the operation. Secondly, Dr. Hinnemann explained that I was doing such a great job that there was no reason to change anything." In the end, Milo and Miss Jane are also charged. It is up to the courts, biased by societal norms and speculation, to decide their destiny.

Benson walks rapidly pass Brady's desk with his head bowed. He has a particular walk, where he looks as if he is in a daze and about to give up on life, while moving very fast. "In my office!" he commands. Brady gets up swiftly and follows him. "Okay, I am assigning Sullivan and Davis to your case. We have so many complaints from wealthy donors to the city and police. Also, complaints from the mayor. I am sick of it. Sick of it! They think, you are working too slow and that you are questioning too many people, many of whom have nothing to do with the whole thing! I mean, why are you questioning all funders of the defendants' legal teams? Many of them have never even set foot in the hospital! And why are you questioning patients who have received organs that were legally attained? You are casting your net too widely. It is jeopardizing the whole investigation. You will never finish this way."

Benson sits down in a resigned manner, while he continues, "All the while, the whole city is in turmoil with a million NGOs fighting in the press every day." Even though, Benson is annoyed with Brady for being so persistent, he looks at her with compassion as their eyes catch each other. He appreciates she still has the purity of soul and resolution of mind that he once possessed.

Brady also sits down in a resigned manner and exclaims, "Sullivan and Davis! You can't be serious? They had the case before us, and nothing came of it. Nothing! That doesn't exactly speak for anything but their failure to investigate altogether. Does it?"

Benson shakes his head. "You can say that. You can. But they know the case. The alternative is to assign more juniors, which only seems to complicate and prolong everything. Sullivan and Davis know that case very well, and I have spoken with them about the gravity of the crimes investigated at the hospital. You are all on the same page."

Brady gets up as she says, "You already spoke to them? Before discussing this with *me*?"

Brady leaves Benson's office slamming the door behind her. However, the scene doesn't have the desired effect, as the door is made of cheap, thin plastic that only *pretends* to be wood. It makes no noise as Brady slams it, as it can only close slowly. That annoys Brady even more. She walks straight to her chair, picks up her jacket and leaves the office. Lizzy is looking at her, while asking, "Where are you going? What's wrong? What did Benson say?" Brady is gone.

Benson observes from the opening of his office door, as Sullivan and Davis enter the large office space dedicated to the Langmore Hospital investigation. They hold a stack of brown cardboard boxes with their own material on the case that has not been part of the investigation till now. Sullivan and Davis make sure to appear defiant and accessible as they approach Brady and Lizzy. Brady is struggling to conceal her anger, as she forces herself to say, "Welcome to the Langmore investigation!" She turns around to address her team colleagues who have ceased working. Brady continues, "Please welcome Sullivan and Davis to our investigation. They worked on this case a couple of years back and are very familiar with the case and the people involved." She sits down, while Lizzy shows them to their desks. Brady catches Benson's eyes through the door opening. He looks somewhat pleased. He is attempting to read Brady. *Is she being genuinely forthcoming or just pretending? How do the team respond to her welcome?* Benson's mind is racing.

*

At some point during the early days of the investigation, Sullivan is summoned to meet Mr. Marlowe's handler. He dutifully meets this contact at the Queens Public Library, far from the usual paths of Sullivan and his colleagues. Their meeting takes place in the crime section on the ground floor, under "M." Sullivan knows who he is looking for—a nondescript, stocky, short elderly man with a New York Times under his arm.

Straight to the point, the handler asks, "How can we make this Langmore investigation disappear?" Sullivan doesn't appreciate that Mr. Marlowe has him in a tight spot. Sullivan's accelerated career at Midtown Precinct South owes much to Mr. Marlowe and his close friendship with the Deputy Commissioner of Midtown Manhattan NYPD. Sullivan isn't sure if the Deputy Commissioner owes Mr. Marlowe a favor, but what matters is that Sullivan owes Mr. Marlowe.

Mr. Marlowe is a powerful man with connections at the top of the force, and now Sullivan has no choice but to carry out Mr. Marlowe's every bidding. "I can't make this investigation disappear on my own, like I did last time. If you want me to shut down the investigation, you need to get Brady, Claudia Brady, the assistant criminal investigator, removed. She is an overambitious, self-righteous bitch, who thinks she knows better. She thinks, she is elevated above all of us."

The man nods. "Okay, let me look into it. but if I get her removed, then I expect you to shut down the investigation ASAP." He turns around to leave. "I'll be in touch."

*

After some trying days of getting settled into a new everyday, where Sullivan and Davis challenge the baseline perceptions that Brady and Lizzy so strenuously constructed, Benson calls Brady to his office. "I requested the commissioner to promote you based on your recent break-through and success in this investigation." He looks at her pleased, not least pleased with himself. Brady is too surprised to truly appreciate the news. Benson continues,

"I hope you appreciate how difficult it is to get someone promoted extraordinarily. As you know, we have procedures, once a year, for promotions and bonuses. I managed to get you promoted, skipping the regular procedure and based entirely on your merits in the Langmore investigation. It is a huge recognition. I hope you realize that!"

Brady puts her right hand on the back of the chair opposite Benson, as she says, "Yes. Yes. I really appreciate it. What am I then?"

Benson looks delighted. "Criminal investigator!"

Brady is content, but not thrilled. Her rise in ranks is taking several years longer than that of most of her peers. Till today, she was an assistant criminal investigator for almost six years. She completed all the mandatory courses two years ago! She worked on several cases, including three homicides. In her mind, she should have been promoted to criminal investigator at least two years ago! Nevertheless, she values that Benson is finally in her corner. That he took on the bureaucracy for her sake. Afterall, it is not his fault that the system is so archaic and rigid, Brady reasons.

Sullivan and Davis are already criminal investigators, and Sullivan has twice acted as chief investigator in cases relating human trafficking and drug smuggling. In fact, many of her team members worked with Sullivan before and have started referring to Sullivan on the Langmore investigation instead of referring to her. Brady gets unnerved and bids her lower lip, when this happens, especially when it happens right before her eyes. She wants to put her foot down, assert herself, but she also doesn't want to come across as petty, small minded and controlling. So far, she lets these incidents pass.

Benson gets up and walks into the investigation room. Brady tags along. They are twelve people working fulltime on the investigation now. "Listen up, folks! I want to share with you some great news. Brady has just been promoted to criminal investigator. You should all be proud of this. It is in recognition of all your great work that your leader gets promoted. Especially, since it is an extraordinary promotion. Out of the ordinary annually round of evaluations, promotions and bonuses." Her team gets up and claps. For a moment there, Brady feels happy and proud. She feels recognized and included.

They are three months into endless interrogations, when Lizzy asks to speak with Brady in private. "I get the sense that Sullivan is reporting directly to Benson. He is bypassing you," Lizzy says.

Brady doesn't know how to respond. She and Lizzy are close. Brady trusts her. Still, for the past three months, since Sullivan and Davis were assigned to the investigation, they have both been so emerged in work that they have slipped apart. Whenever they are finally able to leave the station at nine or ten in the evening, the last thing on their minds is to meet up socializing or to talk through the investigation. In this way, the early days when they met after work at Brady's and worked secretly on the investigation are over. The "us against the world" is over. Now, they are both embroiled in office politics, which has reached new heights since Sullivan and Davis joined their team. Brady feels that she and Lizzy must deliver results before Sullivan and Davis can. The two teams are racing against each other and time.

"What do you mean that Sullivan is going straight to Benson?" Brady asks concerned.

"Well, I am not sure, but there have been several occasions where I have seen Sullivan enter or exit Benson's office. I also overheard a vivid argument between them yesterday. I mean, what is the reason for Sullivan to go see Benson on so many occasions? If it is once or twice, it can be an administrative matter. But if it is several times a week, it seems strange. Don't you think?" Lizzy looks at her. Brady gets nervous. She is singularly focused on the case, and therefore, she has not noticed the growing resistance to her tactics of investigation, little less Sullivan's behind-the-scenes maneuvering.

Benson repeatedly tells Brady that she is questioning too many people, and the investigation is taking too long. "You are losing time, valuable time, on trivialities!" he insists, as he continues, "You need a clear strategy and then you must pursue that strategy. You can't still, three months into the investigation, keep all your options open. I know, it is difficult, when you make a choice, you choose *not* to pursue something else, but that is the way it is. A good investigator can almost intuitively see what path to pursue, Brady."

Benson speaking to her in a condescending manner, which Brady hates. She maintains, "But I have made a choice! My choice is that this case is much bigger than we originally anticipated. It is bigger than we can even comprehend. Don't you see! Wealthy New Yorkers have invested in the Langmore Hospital. They have received services, and some of those services have been acquired illegally. We need to understand to what extent these individuals are involved. Have they knowingly financed illegal operations? Who is involved in the trafficking? Do the crimes extend beyond the trafficking of illegal migrants? These individuals have either money or life at stake. Dr. Hinnemann's rocketing career was only possible through the support of these people. And they, in turn, have played, and maybe even paid, the politicians, mayor, maybe even the top of the New York police to allow this to continue. Otherwise, how do you explain that so many organs enter the flow of organ donations out of nowhere!"

Brady looks at Benson, while opening her arms in a confrontational manner. Benson shakes his head, as he says, "I have told you many times, you are your own worst enemy, Brady. You are good. You are a good investigator. No question about that! And you have good intentions, but you won't go far pissing all over the people who want to help you. Will you?"

*

After about a week, Sullivan receives a new message summoning him to the Queens Public Library. It is difficult for him to conceal his nervousness, as he leaves the station in the early afternoon. He takes the M line toward Queens. At the library, he greets the handler at the crime section, again. He looks around to make sure nobody sees and hands Sullivan a brown wrapper. "Open it when you are home. It incriminates this Brady woman. She materialized a witness to testify that Mr. Carlson started a fire in the engine room of a large building complex that he owned in order to claim the insurance. This was back in 2008. Turns out the witness, the *only* witness, that Brady could stamp up was her cousin who just happened to be at the scene, but otherwise lives in Hicksville Kentucky. I am sure that will get her fired. It got her fired from the insurance company, anyway." After telegraphing the material in the wrapper, the handler turns to leave without a word.

It is as expected; Sullivan has been spying on her. She was either too naïve, stupid or busy to realize this. Sullivan is younger than her and despite having been on force fewer years than Brady, he knows how to play the game of politics. He wants to get ahead. He is doing and saying all the right things. Recently he married a pretty woman in her late twenties, who is a teacher. His wife mistakenly thinks that being a woman, being feminine, means being complacent and submissive. Sullivan thinks she is somewhat boring, but she fits well into his own self-image and that of those higher up in society who he aspires to become. In fact, most, if not all, of us internalize flattery. Our socialization occurs in response to other's flattery that we crave so much. It is this imaginary socially constructed self-image that we end up enacting and even worshipping. We become obsessed with our own self esteem.

Benson did *not* ask Sullivan to spy on Brady. In fact, he feels uncomfortable when Sullivan sullies Brady. Benson says on a couple of occasions that he wished Sullivan and Brady would work as a team. "You can achieve amazing things if you work together. You really complement each other," he says, in vain. Sullivan is not going to tie himself to the deadweight Brady. He tells himself he will not sink with her. He thinks she is on a personal vendetta to vindicate New York of influential people.

"She is a communist. A communist. I'm telling you," Sullivan tells Davis one evening at a bar after work. They are both fed up with "heedlessly running around interrogating everybody to no apparent end."

Lizzy is concerned when she says, "I mean, Sullivan is held in high regards by the management. He can totally torpedo you. If he is going behind your back to spy, report and detriment you, you don't know what could happen." Brady reflects on what Lizzy says, but, in reality, her mind is on the imminent interrogation of Mr. Marlowe, who is scheduled to come into the station later that afternoon. "Brady! Do you hear what I am saying?" Lizzy insists.

"Of course, I do, but to be honest, I do not have time for office politics. *That* is a waste of time. Anyway, Benson has my back."

Lizzy looks at her. "I am sure he has your back, but he also has Sullivan's back. Sullivan has made a pretty impressive career. Management is watching him. They are also watching over him. All I am saying to you is, you need to be careful, Brady."

On their way to the interrogation room, Brady and Lizzy bump into Sullivan and Davis. Sullivan says in a loud voice, "Hold on! Don't go into the interrogation room!" Brady and Lizzy stop right in front of the door behind which Mr. Marlowe and his highflyer lawyers are waiting.

"What!" Brady says annoyed.

Sullivan replies, "We have been instructed to do the interrogation of Mr. Marlowe. We know him through our own investigation. I dealt with him before."

Brady is totally perplexed and at loss with what to do, but she maintains her cool and controlled façade, when she says, "This is *my* investigation. I am leading this investigation. And I am leading the questioning of Mr. Marlowe!"

Sullivan walks in front of the door to the interrogation room blocking Brady and Lizzy's entry. "You have to take this up with Benson. We have strict instructions. All we are doing is following instructions," Sullivan pauses and continues is a soft voice, "Brady, I am not your enemy, and I don't want to have this argument with you. I will give you a detailed briefing of the questioning afterward." With that Sullivan opens the door to the interrogation room with a "Hallo gentleman!" He is already in the room, before Brady can even object. She is furious. Fuming, she walks to her desk, grabs her jacket and leaves before Lizzy gets back to their office.

As anticipated, a significant number of the affluent New Yorkers have either received services or invested in the Langmore Hospital. Some of them, like Mr. Marlowe, have done both. Knowingly or unknowingly, they have become involved in the illicit enterprise. Brady, Lizzy and their team are now faced with the task of determining the extent and magnitude of this criminal activity and their involvement. They still have a long way to go, but at least they are on the right track.

Brady asks Benson to participate in the next team meeting, where they will take stock of how far they have come and plan what to do next. After the meeting, Benson looks jittery and agitated, as he asks her to his office. "I have received some alarming reports of how you are totally out of control in some of these interrogations! I have been told that you turn off the recording gear to scold at possible witnesses, victims and other people. But most of all, I received this anonymous parcel evidencing that you fiddled with the case, you worked on, while you worked at Nationwide to deny the insurance claim of the owner of a building complex. The only witness to the alleged arson turned out to be your cousin! Did you lose your mind? The end, Brady, does not justify the means!" He is flushed and angry. "Brady, for fuck sake! What is going on? Is this true?"

Brady looks confused. "I don't know what you are talking about. What reports? What evidence? I left Nationwide with an excellent recommendation. You know that!" Benson replies. "Never you mind the reports! Is there any truth to this accusation that you materialized a witness? Is there?"

Brady replies, "No! Of course not! Who do you take me for!" Benson sits down. He is thinking. He waves for her to leave.

Now, Brady is getting worried. She asks Lizzy if she has any news on Sullivan and his frequent visits to Benson's office. Lizzy confirms that the meetings persist, but she doesn't know what Sullivan and Benson are talking about. A few days later, two imposing men in dark suits from internal affairs come to Brady's desk and ask her to follow them. Her heart is pounding. Her palms are sweaty. She is too shocked to take in the response of her team, who are all watching as she is taken away. She is mortified thinking of the embarrassment of being escorted out of the office by two officers from internal affairs like a regular criminal. Sullivan conveniently takes over the investigation.

For the next many weeks, maybe months, Brady spends all her time defending herself. Recordings of her tempered interrogations, whistleblower denouncements and personal accounts all go toward totally undermining her person and good work. She is fighting an unwinnable battle against a system built to protect the very people who built it. She is treated like an infectious disease that must be removed from the body of police. Benson is nowhere to be found. He has sunk into the ground and left her to sink. After several months, maybe a year, of defending herself, she is laid off with no further ado. In fact, she is blacklisted from working in public office for the subsequent ten years and charged a hefty fine. The men from internal affairs explain that she is lucky not to go to jail. She is totally baffled. She walks away perplexed and crushed. She never speaks a word to any of her colleagues again, including to Lizzy.

They ask Brady to clear her desk. She asks to do so over the weekend to avoid prying eyes and questions of her colleagues. When Brady puts the photograph of her mother into the crate, she is overwhelmed by grief and sorrow. Her mother would have supported her. Her mother would have understood her. She leans over the desk sobbing. She doesn't know what to do now. Where to go. She is exhausted and deflated after years of defending herself, to no end. She knows her temper gets the better of her. She knows she speaks her mind. But this! This is too much.

From the initial shock of the internal affairs officers picking her up till the day she is clearing out her desk, a new reality creep up on her. She thought, her society was ruled by justice. That her job was to enforce the law that laid the foundation of a just society. She even thought that justice was somehow objective and measurable. Black or white. Now she feels first-hand what injustice feels like. What it feels like to be wrongly convicted. To be pursued and prosecuted by people who have the state apparatus on their side.

She thinks that some of her team members must have sided with Sullivan and Davis and might mistakenly believe her to be culpable. "It's not their fault," she reassures herself. Before experiencing the upheaval that shattered her perception of reality, she would probably have thought the same of someone like her.

Thus, some of her team, especially the more junior members, think that you can only be prosecuted and convicted, if you have indeed done a criminal offense. "There is no smoke without a fire," they tell each other over lunch in the large and brightly lit canteen in the basement of Midtown Precinct South. But that is not true, is it? In fact, it is a whole series of fortuitous events that led to Brady being picked up and tossed out with a hefty charge and crime to her name. These events count Sullivan and Davis's dislike of her. They wanted to get rid of her to clear the way for their own advancement. Taking over and solving the case is an important landmark in anyone's career. Additionally, from the very beginning, Sullivan and Davis disagreed with Brady's tactics of the investigation. "But they didn't make any headway when they led the case two years ago!" Brady reasons with herself. She thinks that maybe Sullivan believed that there was only room for one of them at the top of this investigation.

In the days after leaving the police, a clearer, more frightening picture emerges. Sullivan and Davis didn't make any headway in the Langmore investigation because they didn't, and still don't, want to. They are, in fact, protecting the very people that Brady and Lizzy were pursuing and prosecuting. The scariest bit about the whole thing is that management also don't want to pursue these affluent New Yorkers either. Ergo, it is convenient for management that Sullivan and Davis protect, in the name of the law, these individuals who clear the covers of the newspapers to speak for society, donate to charity and the police, and socialize with the chief commander and others at the top echelon of the force and society. These individuals play a finger in forming the laws shaping society through political mingling and meddling. As a result, laws, rules, and regulations favor those at the top of society. The police and other institutions of society are the result of decades and even centuries of pilling laws, rules, and regulations on top of each other. New laws, rules, and regulations call for new systems and structures. In the end, impenetrable multi-layered institutions become the vanguards of society. At best, these institutions should be teared down and destroyed, which would enable a fresh start mirroring the current state of affairs. Nevertheless, that is unlikely to happen, as it would make the pillars upon which these individuals stand crumble. Instead, society with its myriad of institutional vanguards forms a ring around the privileged class when the laws created to protect them backfire, as happens when Brady and Lizzy charge affluent New Yorkers. Consequently, Brady and Lizzy have been discarded and replaced with Sullivan and Davis, the ringleaders of societal indifference and ineptitude. All the while, Brady's former team members and other colleagues are the gullible idiots tagging along this enterprise with lethal consequences.

Over the course of the next days, Brady contemplates engaging a lawyer to open a liability case against the police. She knows Sullivan instigated the whole thing, helped by Davis and a couple of team members; gullible idiots, whom she is now able to identify. She feels they should all be held accountable. But the whole thing seems bigger than her. She doesn't know where to start and where to end. Instead, she continues her own investigation of the Langmore Hospital to get justice and reveal how Sullivan and Davis are themselves contaminated and corrupted.

During her questioning by internal affairs, she asked multiple times, why Sullivan and Davis stopped investigating the Langmore Hospital back when they led the case. "There are so obviously several crimes taking place at the hospital. Either Sullivan and Davis are stupid, which I don't think, or they somehow stand to benefit from *not* investigating the Langmore Hospital," she insists. Regardless, the officers from internal affairs maintain this has nothing to do with the case raised against *her*. A counterattack against someone else will not vindicate her, they explain.

In the subsequent weeks, Brady faces her father, when she resigns the lease on her apartment and moves back into her childhood home to save whatever money, she doesn't have. Her father is mortified to hear that she has been convicted of serious malpractice and blacklisted from public office. Her mother would have been, too, if she had survived cancer. Nevertheless, one morning over breakfast, he explains that he has mortgaged the family home to finance her fine and set her up in an undefined future endeavor. "So, you have a shot at a fresh start. That is what your mother would have wanted," her father says looking at her lovingly. Brady is grateful and cries with relief. She is an only child. Her father so wants her to make him proud.

That morning their conversation drifts, as it so often does, when they are together. Her father reflects, "If you think about it; what is the point of saddling felons with a fine or expense to the courts and lawyers so exorbitant that they can impossibly pay it? It just doesn't make sense. It only serves to keep the downtrodden down. Felons become slaves to the legal and prison systems, even after they have served their sentences." Her father continues, "That is precisely why criminals keep doing crime after they have been released from jail. They come out of jail with a criminal record, so no one wants to hire them. On top of that, they must repay this exorbitant fine or expense to the courts, lawyers, and prison system. With no chance of getting a job with a criminal record, the only way to survive and repay the state is to return to crime." Brady has never thought of that before. It is all part of her awakening to a new reality.

Starting from scratch, Brady rents a dinky office. It is basically one room, with a shared toilet in the corridor. A cheap plastic shower cabin is sitting on top of the worn linoleum floor in the shared toilet. The building is dedicated entirely to small business offices, but for the past years, more and more people have moved into the offices. Brady even stumbles across a couple of single mums with young children living on her floor. It is peculiar that the poorest population segment in most societies across the world is single mothers with children. Keeping women in poverty is yet another way for society to keep everybody in their place. Hence, being a single mum should *not* be financially rewarding. Only families are rewarded with accessible mortgages, tax breaks, and other financial incentives. The landlord doesn't seem to mind that people live in the office building. Brady wonders if he doesn't mind because he wants to help these helpless people, or if he wants to earn money on their misery. In the end, she decides it doesn't matter either way. The building is located on the corner of the 8th Avenue and West 37th Street, in the Garment District on Manhattan. It is a district that has undergone substantial transformation over the past decade. It used to be a thriving semi-manufacturing trading hub. However, when garment manufacturers left the district in the nineteen sixties and seventies, it descended into a derelict slum.

In recent years, Brady's new neighborhood has become a quasi-commercial, quasi-residential area. This transformation is primarily enabled by the High Line pedestrian trail, a couple of streets over, that has driven gentrification of the entire area. Even though, the ripple effect of this gentrification has not quite reached the office building of Brady, it has lifted the immediate neighborhood out of the most derelict slum. Today, there are a few trendy hotels and hostels, decent residential buildings, and newly refurbished office buildings. Yet, Brady wonders why property owners bother refurbishing office buildings, when there seems to be little or no use for office space in a city that already offers an abundance of offices, many of which are empty post COVID.

People are simply fed-up commuting for hours to go to and from a city office in order to do their work. Additionally, as property prices skyrocketed in New York coupled with the decline of real wages, the office working middle- and upper-class fled the city resulting in even longer commutes to and from work. As a consequence, now post COVID, this office working population is refusing altogether to commute every day into the mayhem of the city to work when they can do the same work from home. In this milieu, flexibility is what is called for. Luckily, Brady's landlord possesses plenty of flexibility, as she too moves into her office to save money she still doesn't have.

From the outside, the building on the corner of the 8th Avenue and West 37th Street has a beautiful Classical Revival facade dating back to the late nineteenth, early twentieth century. However, inside, it is dated and in decay. Several rounds of more or less successful refurbishing have left its interiors shambolic. The floor of the main entrance is almost intact with an intricate marble design, high marble panels, a large solid mahogany entrance door and connecting door to the stairway and retrofitted elevators. Residents of the building, or maybe rather their children, have carved symbols and names into the mahogany doors. The steps of the stairway are covered in beige linoleum that has turned black and gray through wear and tear. The icon works railing of the stairway is missing several bars. An old elevator in the middle of the stairway is left unused. It will one day fall from the top floor to the ground, when the rope suspending it finally gives in. Three solid silver elevators were installed in the mid nineteen sixties. They are entirely foreign to the rest of the building.

Once up on the 5th floor, where Brady's office-cum-bedroom is located, the linoleum nightmare continues. The wooden panels lining the corridor walls are partially missing, revealing layers of paint and wallpaper, some of which dates back a century. The door to Brady's office is paper thin. It has a smoky glass window that lets the daylight filter into the otherwise dark corridor. Inside the office, there are three large windows, also with paper thin glass. One of the windows contains an air conditioner.

After Brady starts living in the office, she buys a microwave, a kettle, and a sofa bed. She places an ad in The Village Voice that reads, *"Former New York criminal investigator offers private eye and investigation to private customers. Specialization: criminal cases. Price: $150/hour."* She settles behind her desk and waits for the phone to ring.

Chapter Six

Saskia is summoned to the conference room. Annona fetches her in her room. Kate and the four men and women, all in the same simple gray buttoned up uniform that Kate also, today, wears, silence their lively chatter, as Saskia enters the room. Kate gets up and walks toward Saskia, who has stopped right inside the door. She embraces Saskia, which Saskia is totally taken aback by. Ignoring Saskia's somewhat off-putting reaction, Kate directly proceeds to introduce an elderly man with white hair, icy blue eyes, and a jovial attitude.

His name is Mr. Sind. He looks powerful and distinguished, despite or maybe even because of his cheerfulness, which elevates him above the people destined to live in the hell hole. They rarely possess cheerfulness. In fact, Saskia has noticed that the only people in the underground, who share the lighthearted cheerfulness of Mr. Sind are the ones, who have lived in the underground most their lives, like her children, or those who have propelled straight into a somewhat comfortable life at sub-level 3 without having gone through the hardship that earns you the right to advance. Mr. Sind belongs to the latter category of cheerful people. He has little or no knowledge of the dark side of the underground. By now, Saskia has gotten so used to the unfairness and injustice of life above ground that she doesn't question for a second this pattern repeating itself below ground. Nevertheless, like above ground, the underground praises itself with pursuing a just cause for the outcasts of society.

Mr. Sind is almost threatening as he bounces over to Saskia. He reaches his right hand out, smiles and says, "We want to show our gratitude for your excellent work by offering you to advance to sub-level 3. We think, you are ready!" Saskia is astonished. Mr. Sind pulls out a chair for Saskia and continues, "Sorry, it is not fair to spring such news on you," Mr. Sind pauses before picking up a white envelope from the pile of papers laying on the table. "We have a bonus for you. You must have grown accustomed to getting bonuses. I can tell you; it is not normal to get two bonuses within such short period of time, but you have excelled yourself. We recognize that."

Mr. Sind hands Saskia the white envelope that contains eight thousand dollars. Saskia is lost for words, but quickly regains her wit. "Well, when you are summoned, you come. Regardless the matter..." she goes on. "I am really happy to hear that I have been summoned for praise this time. You never know..." The men and women share a clever laugh.

Kate looks satisfied, as she turns around to address the four men and women. "It was such a rocky start for Saskia, because she didn't fit into any of the combat categories. She literary broke the mold. She is one of the best! You solved *two cases* in the span of one."

Saskia suddenly starts wondering. She turns to Annona, who standing behind her and asks, "What two cases?"

Kate intervenes, "Well, Skyman informed me that you played a pivotal role in the downfall of the Langmore Hospital. This was an assignment, you took on independently and on top of the assignment you were already tasked with, which you *also* completed per excellence." Kate smiles. Saskia gets the clear sense that, as Kate's prodigy, Kate benefits directly from her achievements. Kate continues, "You know that dismantling the establishment is a critical aspect of 'the cause'? The Langmore Hospital is part of that establishment. The old wealthy families of New York think they are above everybody else. They think they can get away with murder, literally!"

Saskia's mind is drifting. She hardly listens to what Kate is saying. Instead, her mind is racing with the question of how Skyman can have revealed her role in the Langmore case without divulging their relationship. *Shit! It is definitely against all rules to have a relationship with Skyman. Eli told me so!* Saskia thinks. The last thing Saskia wants is for Kate to have leverage over her that she can use, in the future, for extortion. She wants to ask Kate what else Skyman shared, but she knows that the current circumstances are neither suitable nor appropriate for revealing the truth.

After a short while, Saskia starts wondering what it means to be at sub-level 3. She knows that at this level decisions are made. Still, she finds it incredible that she should be offering advice to anyone, little less deciding anything concerning the cause. Saskia fires off a succession of questions she is thinking of, aloud. "What does it mean to progress to sub-level 3? I mean... what will my role and responsibilities be? And will I live there? Will my children come and live with me?" Saskia gets anxious at the thought of leaving Ava and Max at sub-level 2. She has just gotten used to seeing them occasionally when they are all three off duties. The thought of not seeing them regularly makes her stomach ache.

Whenever she gets these thoughts, she thinks of Becky, who lost her son to the underground. In hindsight, Saskia thinks that the mental illness of Becky was precipitated by the loss of her son. Saskia is worried that she might suffer the same destiny if she loses her children. Kate puts a hand on her shoulder. "Now, now... There is no reason to get all worked up. Your children will not advance, but you are always allowed to visit them at sub-level 2. You can move freely across all 3 sub-levels, as you please."

With no further ado, Kate and the four men and women simultaneously get up and leave the room. Saskia is left in the meeting room with Annona, and all her unanswered questions. Annona congratulates her on her advancement, "You have made such an impressive ascent, Saskia. Remember to be proud of yourself."

Saskia restates her concerns that are becoming more and more real. She finally says, "Thank you, but right now, I am just worried about Ava and Max. What am I going to do?"

Annona tries to console her. "Look, before you know it, they will join you at sub-level 3. They are smart kids, and they are doing really great."

Saskia remains unassured, as she asks, "Can't you ask Kate, if I can advance, but stay living here at sub-level 2 with my kids? They are too young for me to just leave them. It is bad enough that days pass where we don't see each other. Still, whenever I am not living above while on some assignment, at sub-level 2, we live right next to each other. Max crawls into my bed at night when he has nightmares."

The next morning, Hammer returns out of nowhere. Suddenly he is standing in the doorway to her room taking up the entire frame with his large and muscular body. Saskia thinks that his body looks like it could pop if you took a needle to it. She remembers him from when he escorted her from sub-level 1 to 2. It seems that Hammer is the gofer of the leaders. Saskia tries to make some light conversation, while she frantically runs around the room stuffing her things into her duffel bag and a large black garbage bag that she drags along the floor. Hammer doesn't speak a word. *Maybe he is deaf,* Saskia thinks. *That would be clever, to have a deaf gofer, who cannot eardrop on the leaders' conversations.* As it turns out Hammer is deaf. But even if he could speak, Saskia senses that he would not. Deafness serves Hammer well as an armor behind which he hides his thoughts and emotions. His best commentaries are silent.

Hammer picks up her large black garbage bag, swings it across his shoulder, and onto his back. With his left hand, he grabs her duffel bag. The whole maneuverer is entirely effortless. They walk along a narrow corridor next to the meeting room toward a solid iron door neatly painted in a greenish gray color. All doors in the underground are nondescript, almost invisible. Hammer opens the door and lets Saskia walk through it first. On the other side, a long tunnel, bathed in light, emerges. With its vaulted ceiling, it looks like a deserted train tunnel. It contains no tracks. They walk for almost an hour. Throughout their walk, the tunnels, corridors, and stairways are almost clinically clean and bathed in light. Saskia senses that no expense is spared at this sub-level. It sets her mind racing. *How can the underground steal so much electricity and water without anyone above ground getting suspicious? Maybe the leaders of the underground are in fact collaborating with the leaders above ground, like Skyman, who lives in both worlds.* The lines between below and above ground are becoming blurred the closer Saskia gets to the underground's summit.

Finally, they descend a broad thoroughfare with loads of chatty people all walking toward the gateway at the far end of the thoroughfare. Saskia thinks that about fifty people are walking along the thoroughfare with Hammer and her. She hasn't seen so many good-looking people before, ever. They all wear the same buttoned up gray uniform, as Kate, Mr. Sind, and the others in the meeting room. It makes them look genderless. They are polite, calm, and smiling. Saskia suddenly realizes that part of the reason why they speak in low voices and walk in this controlled manner is that they are much older than inhabitants of sub-level 2. They have the experience that comes with age and a demeanor permeated by self-control. The erratic and feverish attitude of the youngsters of sub-level 2 stayed at sub-level 2. This is a new world on several levels.

Walking through the broad gateway at the bottom of the expansive thoroughfare, they enter a large hall. One long side of the hall is covered in massive floor-to-ceiling windows in frosted glass. Saskia finds herself momentarily breathless, caught between a sense of awe with the magnificent sight and fright at the sight of the windows exposing their hidden universe to the outside world. Through the windows, earthlings can peer in and observe the heart of their operation. She halts.

Suddenly, Kate appears right in front of Saskia with her arms wide open. "Welcome, welcome, my darling Saskia!" she exclaims, as she grabs Saskia's right arm and drags her along. Hammer follows, still carrying Saskia's stuff. Once Saskia regains her senses, she whispers to Kate, "What is this place? And how can you have windows to the outside world?"

Kate turns around. "My dear! This place is dug deep into the trenches of a rail grave. The windows turn to the tracks. No one comes down here. In any event, they cannot see us through the frosted glass, can they? This place is so inauspicious that no one questions it." Inauspicious is the last word Saskia would use to describe this place.

Kate seems more at ease at sub-level 3. She left her stern attitude and controlled appearance at sub-level 2, at least for now. Saskia follows Kate to the far end of the large hall, where some leaders of sub-level 3 are gathered. She recognizes Mr. Sind and one of the women from the meeting room, the other day, at sub-level 2. Saskia nods politely to both. She continues to stand behind the leaders, as they to take turns to ascend the podium and address the crowds. At some point, Kate walks up on the podium. During her talk, she bids Saskia welcome. While turning around and opening her right arm and pointing her hand toward Saskia, Kate induces the cheerful clapping of the crowds.

Once, Kate is standing next to her again, Saskia asks in a low voice, "Do you think, I could stay living in my old room at sub-level 2? I want to live near my children."

Kate looks astonished as she replies, "Nobody wants to stay at sub-level 2 if they are promoted to sub-level 3. What nonsense is that! Stop getting all worked up about these things. You have made it, Saskia. You have arrived!"

Saskia insists, "But my children. I need to be close to my children. I would rather decline on the opportunity to advance altogether than move away from them."

Kate is looking straight ahead while shaking her head. "I heard you. If you insist, I will discuss it with the other leaders before I can give you a definite answer. But it is not a wise move on your part to start your life at sub-level 3 with special requests. We don't want to bend *even* more rules for you, Saskia. We bent the rules when we let you advance to sub-level 2 without perfecting any combat skills. Now you want us to bend the rules again." Kate walks away. She is moderately annoyed with Saskia.

After the gathering in the large hall, Hammer shows Saskia to her new room. He drops all her stuff in the middle of the room. Her room has a lot of amenities, such as a fancy coffee maker and what looks like a futuristic air fryer. Saskia even has her own bathroom. A built-in cupboard. And a bed inserted into the wall, like an alcove. You can draw a curtain to create a kind of cave for sleeping. The room has an air conditioner, television, and radio. All the furniture is made-to-measure integrated into the cubical room. All furniture is the same greenish gray color as the sub-level 3 uniforms. The walls are high-gloss off-white.

Saskia would happily sacrifice all of it for her old room at sub-level 2, and its prisms inserted into the pavement above. She felt better connected with the outside world from her old room at sub-level 2 than from her new cubical room at sub-level 3. Her old room was less coiffured, clinicalm and sterile than this one. Her new room has no windows. It has all the amenities of modern life, yet it is lifeless. It is an air-tight cubical squeezing the life out of her. All the cells along the corridor are identical. She feels like they are bees crammed into each their little cell in the beehive. They are all tiny anonymous bees working away for the queen bee.

There are three things that characterize her advancement in the underground. The first thing is the further she advances, the closer she gets to the light. Specifically, all the natural light flooding the large hall, but also the synthetic light bathing the corridors and cells at sub-level 3. This closeness to light symbolizes a closeness to the summit of their settlement. At sub-level 2, there is no daylight, apart from in her beloved room. Sub-level 1 is hidden far below in the underground, maybe six to eight flights below ground. It is impossible to get daylight and sufficient electricity that far below ground. Now, at sub-level 3, there is a window in the large hall to the outside world. The line dividing "us and them" is paper thin consisting of just one single glazed frosted window. They are dangerously close to the real world.

The second characteristic is the uniformity of the sub-level 3 people, who all wear the same simple gray buttoned-up suit. At sub-level 1, the homeless people wore their own racks. At sub-level 2, people were offered clothes that fit, were clean, and in a good state. The cloth is probably second-hand, but it made sub-level 2 members able to do their job in combat and move in society above without drawing attention to themselves.

This place is uniform, devoid of any personal touches. The space of sub-level 3 is highly optimized granting, in its small space, all the conveniences of modern life, but these conveniences are fake luxuries. They are, in fact, installed to keep sub-level 3 inhabitants occupied and complacent. For instance, the television and radio only have one channel that is turning and twisting reality to align with the cause. Instead of forming her own opinions with the lay of the land, she is now spoon-fed the so-called truth.

This is how parallel worlds are crafted by manipulating the minds of their followers through distortion of the truths. In reality, it is not much different from what happens in the world above where politicians deceive populations about the true motivations behind their actions. The disillusionment and disappointment with the deceit, lies, and corruption in society push people to embrace parallel worlds, like the underground. In this way, both the parallel world, such as the underground, and the world above distort the truth and reality.

The third and last characteristic of sub-level 3 is the rigor of life. Saskia feels that life at sub-level 3 resembles life in prison, even though, she doesn't know first-hand what prison life is like. At sub-level 1, they were free to ascend whenever they wanted. They could come and go as they pleased, as long as no earthling saw them enter or exit. If none of the hopeless homeless had any food, there was no food that day. Lucky, and his helpers Trish and Trash, tried to introduce some system to the madness, but they never insisted and rarely succeeded.

At sub-level 2, rigorous physical training within the combat categories and specific tasks shapes each day. Sub-level 2 contains uniform rules and regulations and meticulous systems and structures. Now, Saskia feels that control has subtly shifted from the bodies, at sub-level 2, to the minds, at sub-level 3.

She realizes that the homeless people at sub-level 1 only serve as an entry point funneling followers deeper into the underground, first as fighters and later as truly incarnated followers taking orders from somewhere higher up the chain of command. What began as a rebellious and chaotic community of outcasts at sub-level 1 has evolved into a community more rigid and regimented than even the world above. Everything is stacked, numbered, and contained at sub-level 3.

Mr. Sind politely knocks on Saskia's door and enters before she has time to respond. Saskia wonders why Mr. Sind, rather than Kate, comes to her cell to bid her welcome. She believes that Kate is probably fed up with her and her ingratitude in insisting not to be separated from her children. Mr. Sind's previous upbeat cheerfulness is somewhat dialed down revealing a glimpse of his true persona. "How do you like your new quarters?" he says expecting to receive her gratitude.

"Yes, they are very nice, but I would rather stay at sub-level 2 with my children," Saskia swiftly replies.

Mr. Sind looks at her inquisitively. "I understand that. I really do! Kate told me that you requested to go back to live at sub-level 2. But it is just not possible. However, you can earn your right to spend weekends and go away on vacations with your children. That is how we do things in the underground. You understand?"

Saskia sighs and sits down with her shoulders slumbered, while thinking, *Earn your right! This is endless!*

During their conversation, Saskia is puzzled by Mr. Sind's behavior. He showers her with compliments at any given opportunity. She modestly accepts his compliments. Yet, after a while, the whole situation becomes uncomfortable for her. But she has nowhere to go. This is her room, her cubicle, that he is trespassing. At one point in their conversation, Mr. Sind says, "Oh, America is so great!"

Saskia replies, full of spite, "Why do you say that? It is not even true!"

Mr. Sind sits down uninvited and starts laughing, while he says, "Well, if you think about, the fact that we have this parallel society, hidden settlement, is emblematic of the differences in opinions that coexist in this country. Do you know, I have lived in many different countries. In some countries, people are not allowed to access information from other parts of the world freely. They are only fed with the information their government releases. In other countries... And you will be surprised to learn that here I am talking about the Nordic countries, Denmark, Sweden and so on, the great majority, if not all, information comes from the state funded mass media outlets. In these places, populations are cleverly led to believe that they have access to diverse information, but in reality, only a small percentage ventures beyond the state funded media. What these two types of society have in common is, for instance, that when the government goes to war, the enemy is painted uncritically evil by the media. When the prime minister wants to achieve something, even for his or her own winning, the media applauses it without posing any difficult questions. And so on. At least, in this free country of ours, we have various opinions, various parallel societies, all living side-by-side."

For a second, Saskia wants to ask why the underground, like these countries that Mr. Sind are referring to, is trying to control information, when all and everybody have a mobile phone and with it an abundance of information readily available at the snap of their fingers. But just before she goes ahead and asks, she remembers that it is no different from above ground or the countries Mr. Sind was referring to in this welcome speech. Thus, in the world above, people can also access all information, and yet, people tend to search only information that reinforces what they already think and believe to be true. Saskia shakes her head as she thinks that she is no longer able to distinguish between true and false. She wonders that maybe the parallel underground is in fact no more parallel than the world above. She is confused.

Saskia says, "It sounds to me as if you believe United States is faring much better than these other countries. I very much doubt that. People here, despite having access to free information, also live in echo chambers. Anyway, it is always easy for those with privileges and power to talk about the rights and freedoms of others. In this fine country of ours, mass poverty is spreading like a contagious disease. Poor people have no *other* rights than to speak their minds, but no one listens! Anyway, how can you form a critical opinion if you were never taught to read, little less think critically? How can you make your opinion count if you live marginalized at the fringe of society? This is not fair!"

Mr. Sind replies, "Well, life isn't fair." As if *she* doesn't know that.

Mr. Sind is sitting observing her as if he reads her mind. Saskia is getting more and more uncomfortable, shifting around in her chair, until she gets up to say, "Anyway, it was very kind of you to drop by and bid me welcome. I really appreciate that!" Mr. Sind doesn't reply. He just looks at her. After a moment's silence, he gets up and leaves.

Saskia's mind is racing. "Shit! Did I spill too much information? Share too many of my crazy ideas to him? Will he tell Kate and the others? Will I get thrown out of the underground for my radical views?" While lying in bed, Saskia stares at the high-gloss, off-white ceiling of her alcove. She is starring up out of habit. While in her room at sub-level 2, seeing people's footsteps above her bed, transcended her into a deep and comforting sleep in which she felt connected with the outside world. Now, she feels far removed from everything. Far away from her children. She starts crying. She misses Ava and Max. She knows that they will be missing her. They will be wondering where she has gone to.

She never got a chance to explain to them that she advanced to sub-level 3. Now, Annona is left with the task of explaining it to them. They will not be told that she has no choice in the matter. That she refused to advance without them. That she would rather have stayed at sub-level 2 together with them than advance to this nondescript existence at sub-level 3. It is not until she decides she will go straight back to sub-level 2 the following day and wait for Ava and Max until they get back from their assignments that she is able to let go and fall asleep.

The next morning, Saskia makes an early start to return to sub-level 2. It takes her two hours or more to go to sub-level 2, because she gets lost on her way, multiple times. On several occasions, she stumbles across a door revealing the uninhabited underground. In those instances, she is confronted with the heavy smell of decaying metal, human excrements, and rats. At one point, she opens a door into a massive warehouse housing a vegetation factory. It is an infinite storage room with plants growing on some kind of tissue suspended from the ceiling and tied to the floor. Between the suspended tissues covered in fresh natural vegetation, there are LED lights that flood the plants with a blueish and reddish light. A mist is sprayed into the air from the ceiling. Initially, Saskia gets worried, when she is mistakenly sprayed by the mist, but then she reckons that if the plants don't die from the mist, she will also not die.

The whole operation is as clinical as the brightly lit long corridors and private cells of sub-level 3. Saskia walks between the tissues covered in vegetation. It feels like walking in a trimmed jungle bathed in fluorescent light. There are tomatoes, peas, strawberries, potatoes, spinach, cucumbers, apples, bananas, and so on. Luckily, the plants release their natural scent, reminding Saskia of the natural world amidst this highly controlled artificial environment. There are no humans to be found anywhere. Everything is automated. Like in the world beyond, there is little to no need for manual labor anymore. Labor has been replaced by robotics and artificial intelligence; a development that led to millions of homeless people. They lost their poorly paid jobs to the robots. Unable to pay their rent and mortgages, they lost their homes. The rest is a tale of yesterday's glory.

Sometime in the late afternoon, Saskia arrives at sub-level 2. She is quite exhausted by the strain of trying to find her way and the long trip through the underground. During her travel, she contemplated various times what would happen if she got lost and never came back. She thinks, no one, apart from her children would care. It is her own responsibility to find her way back to her children. It is her own responsibility to survive for her children.

Saskia goes straight to Ava and Max's rooms and knocks. She pulls the handles, before anyone can answer. The doors are locked. She gets a chair and makes herself comfortable in front of their rooms, waiting. After about an hour, Annona appears. She is excited and wants to hear what life is like at sub-level 3. "I don't know. It is very strange. I am not even sure, what to say. It is very organized. Very tidy. Almost synthetic," Saskia says and anxiously asks Annona, "When are Ava and Max coming back? Do you know? Where are they?"

Annona seems wary of telling her. Then she answers, "We are preparing a large raid that will soon happen. All the different combat units are working together on this raid. That is why there are no people here! They are all away on training." Saskia hasn't noticed that the plant floor is empty until Annona points it out.

"Right… a large raid. Sounds daunting," Saskia mumbles till she affirmatively asks, "When are they back?" Annona answers while turning around to leave, "This evening. Maybe late…"

That evening, they cry and hug as they are reunited. Max says, "We didn't know what had happened to you! Where did you go!"

Saskia looks surprised. "But you can always ask Annona. She knows what is going on."

Ava says, "We did! She said, she also didn't know where you had gone to."

Saskia's gut feeling that the underground is trying to keep families, parents, and children apart, disconnected, separated, and alone is confirmed. "Look! You must always, *always*, know that I would never willingly leave you. You are my children. I will never leave you and always be there for you. Don't believe what people around here say. Something sinister is going on."

Max looks at her. "I tell you what that is… We are preparing this big raid. Massive. We are hundreds, maybe thousands, of fighters down here. You won't believe it!"

That night, they all sleep in one bed. All together. Saskia holds her children tight. The next morning, she feels as if she hardly closed an eye. Her body is arching from straining her muscles in the tight grip all night. After breakfast, she says, "Let's go on a train ride! Get away for the day." Her children explain that they are expected at training. At seven, it starts. "No, no, no. We are going away. We have little time together before I will have to return to sub-level 3. And you have little time before the raid!" Saskia decides that they should just sneak out, without telling anyone. She hopes nobody will find out that they are missing until it is too late. After all, there is such commotion, chaos, and people everywhere from different combat units assembling on the plant floor and getting ready for training and the big raid.

Ava and Max are as excited to go on this train ride, as they were after Saskia successfully stole the diamond from Dr. Glenmore, and they went to Ocean Station on holiday. Her children are wide eyed looking around and out of the windows. The train ascends the underground somewhere on Upper Manhattan. They are steadily moving across the city on an elevated flyover. They cross the Bronx Bridge into West Bronx. Transcending Marble Hill, they look out of the window. It is a beautiful sunny but cold day. The sky is bright blue. The trees line up along the streets. As they snail along the elevated flyover, they inadvertently intrude into people's homes, peering straight into their private lives.

It feels as if they are riding one of those model trains in a miniature landscape. Yet, reality hits hard when they take a closer look at what goes on around them. The streets are packed with tents and makeshift shelters. Hordes of homeless people drift aimlessly around in the streets. In fact, the streets seem to only belong to the homeless people. They assemble around small open fires along the sidewalk warming their permanently cold bodies. Some homeless people have barricaded roads to traffic to take over the sparse communal space the city provides for living. People live in a massive refugee camp sprawling along the streets of New York. Street by street, neighborhood by neighborhood, the infinite refugee camp will eventually consume the entire city. The refugee camp stretches for as long as the eye can see.

At one point, the train stops, and Ava points out of the window, while exclaiming, "Look! Look! Mama!" They look straight into a dark and dinky living room. From the ceiling, the body of a man is dangling. "Don't look, kids. Look away!" Saskia exclaims, when it dawns on her what they are looking at. "It is probably suicide," she says. Later, while entering 238th Street station, they unwillingly witness the assault of a woman, who is beaten and raped by three men. "What is the world coming to," Saskia says while continuing, "I don't think, we should get off the train. The world seems dauntingly dangerous. Suddenly, the hell hole seems like a peaceful sanctuary compared to this world." When the train reaches the end of the line, at Van Cortlandt Park—242nd Street, they stay on the train waiting for it to make its return trip back across the Harlem River and into Manhattan proper. Saskia can't wait to get back.

When Saskia, Ava and Max return to sub-level 2, they hardly speak a word to each other. What should have been a wonderful field trip out into the city turned into a jarring awakening to the harsh realities of the outside world. The world seems crumbling around them. *With or without the big raid, the city is collapsing,* Saskia thinks. They find themselves unexpectedly drawn to this strange abyss, the hell hole, that now constitutes the only reality they know. Paradoxically, it seems more familiar and less daunting than the world outside. Saskia, overwhelmed by the uncertainty of their situation, pulls her children close. She kisses her children. She hugs them holding them firmly in her grip. She doesn't know, when and if she will see them again. She silently prays that they will remain safe in her absence. The whole thing is too terrible to bear.

Once back at sub-level 3, Saskia goes about her daily tasks sleepwalking. She is demotivated and detached from the world above and below, and its abstract notion of the cause. Yet, within a couple of days, she learns more about the grand design of the underground settlement, when Mr. Sind shares insights that change her forever.

Mr. Sind explains to Saskia that, the following day, they have a reunion in the large hall in the rail grave. "What is the reunion about?" Saskia is curious to understand what the people at sub-level 3 spend their time on, apart from meticulously following rules and regulations along systems and structures that hardly seem to make any sense. It is like the rules and regulations have been put in place to keep the members of sub-level 3 busy and complaisant. Rules and regulations lead to system and structures that lead to new rules and regulations and new systems and structures, and so it continues ad infinitum to no apparent end, other than keep people busy with absolutely nothing, while sub-level 1 and 2 settlers, robotics and artificial intelligence do the real work.

Mr. Sind sits down. "Well, hear me out and listen carefully... We are planning the rebellion that will start with a big bang or a big raid, which marks the starting shot of the civil war. We expect the establishment will retaliate, in full force. They will send the police and probably also the military. We have amassed our own artillery and trained our combat units to go into a lengthy and tough battle." Mr. Sind looks at Saskia to make sure she understands the severity of the situation.

Mr. Sind continues, "When I say 'we,' I am actually not just referring to our settlement, but similar hidden settlements across many, many other mid-sized to large cities in the United States. For instance, even though, I have not myself been in touch with the settlement in Los Angeles, I know, massive homelessness is pushing the hidden settlement there to the brink of imploding. The distress, hopelessness, and homelessness are so pervasive that the leaders struggle containing their communities for much longer. We want to time these attacks across all U.S. cities to take place simultaneously. Therefore, it is no good if Los Angeles erupts prematurely and as a stand-alone event. One big attack in one city can be stopped by the authorities, but hundreds or thousands of big attacks across *all* U.S. cities simultaneously cannot be stopped by anyone. We will ride an avalanche of revenge across the country." Saskia is quiet and in shock.

Mr. Sind continues, "To prevent one city from going off prematurely, such as Los Angeles, we need to speed up the date of our attack for all attacks to implode and explode at the same time. When Los Angeles and Baltimore are on the verge of breaking into a full-fledged war, we, in New York, must speed up our process."

Saskia is sitting shaking her head. After a while, she comes to her senses and says, "I had *no* idea I was part of such an effort. No idea! I am not even sure I *want* to be part of it. It doesn't sound like a good idea, at all! We are sitting on a ticking time bomb. Once it erupts, who knows what will happen!" Saskia thinks of her children.

Mr. Sind nods while looking down at the floor. "Listen, nobody thinks this is a good idea, anymore, maybe apart from a few loose cannons, that is. We created a monster that we can no longer control. But I guess, the same can be said of society, above ground... a monster that no one can control. It is not as if *anyone* really planned it... Oh well, maybe some of the wealthy backers planned it. You know, people like Skyman and his associates."

Saskia looks up. "Who are Skyman's associates? Kate also spoke about them. Yet, I have never seen them nor heard their names."

Mr. Sind continues to look at the floor. He looks contemplative as he says, "Skyman is not his real name. None of them use their real names. We see them at sub-level 3. The ones we work with closest with at sub-level 3 are called Storm, Raven, and Nightshade. And then of course Skyman, who is probably our closest ally. He funds us. That is his main role. I am not sure, the funds are all his own, or if he also gets donations from other people, his associates. I think, he probably gets donations from his associates. That is millions of dollars poured into our settlement and 'the cause' for the past decade. Skyman managed that. That is why people are so in awe with him down here!"

Saskia is still in shock when she asks, "Who are the others, you mentioned? What do they do?"

Mr. Sind treads carefully as he says, "I know that Nightshade has a high position in the New York district attorney's office. I think, she is the Manhattan District Attorney. Raven, also a woman, has a high position in the police. I am not sure what her position is though. Storm is a vice president of the real estate division in the New York State Department of Financial Services. Called NYDFS. Do you know of that?"

Saskia nods no. Mr. Sind continues, "It enforces the laws on the financial industry, including banks, insurance companies, mortgage providers, *etcetera*. Skyman is also in the financial business, *and* he owns a cyberwar company. He is in the private sector, while Storm, Raven, and Nightshade are all in the public sector."

Saskia asks, "Why do these people support a rebellion? It just doesn't make any sense!"

Mr. Sind pauses again, before answering, "I think, all these individuals, mainly from the public sector, have deep knowledge of the inside workings of society, and they are profoundly disappointed with what they see every day, day in, and day out. Somehow, they have become disillusioned with the lay of the land. Maybe through their work. Supporting the rebellion and the cause is by most viewed as a last resort. But also, as the only viable way out of all this mess. I have mainly engaged with Storm, and I know he became totally embroiled and frustrated by the DOMA program that was supposed to offer accessible mortgages and simplify homeownership for the poorer segments of the population. The program pretty much failed, like all other government initiatives designed to help the poor. When Storm was approached by Nightshade, the Manhattan District Attorney, to support the cause, he was ripe and swept up by the moment, I guess. However, as you know, you can always enter the underground, but never leave. That also applies to our backers. I think, Storm has since had his doubts, but he cannot leave the cause. That would be too dangerous." Saskia still can't believe what she is hearing.

Under normal circumstances, if such ever exist, Mr. Sind would not have spilled all this information to Saskia, but the closer they get to the big raid, the more audacious people in the underground become. It is as if, now that the world is going to hell anyway, we may as well give into whatever pleasure and urge we have. This also explains why Annona did not prevent Saskia and her kids from sneaking out and going on a day excursion in the middle of training for the big raid.

Mr. Sind gets up to leave. "I have a meeting now in preparation of the reunion with some of the leadership of the other cities tomorrow. We have some last-minute details to sort out."

Saskia says, "Of course. Of course. Thank you for explaining all this to me."

The following day, the atmosphere at breakfast in the large hall in the rail grave is filled with anticipation and anxiousness. People are either very chatty or sitting alone, quiet, and secluded. We all react differently. That afternoon, the sub-level 3 leaders of the New York, Baltimore, Pittsburgh, and Philadelphia settlements meet for the first and the last time before releasing the mobs on their cities.

The city settlements of New York, Baltimore, Pittsburgh, Philadelphia, and elsewhere across U.S. cities function as autonomous entities, like self-sustaining cells in a terror network. At sub-level 3, each city settlement has established operational units with dedicated recruitment, financing, lobbying, military operations, and social media presence. These units operate independently, only connecting and interacting if and when necessary. Each unit, sub-level, and settlement is organized like a self-contained terror cell with a distinct mission and the ability to act independently of other units, sub-levels, and settlements.

At sub-level 2, each combat unit is a self-contained terror cell. Each terror cell at city level, settlement, sub-level, and unit is trained to operate independently and together to cause maximum destruction with minimal effort. Information is strictly on a need-to-know basis. Information takes the form of actionable orders that push this massive locomotive forward at great velocity. Once, it is set into motion, nothing and no one can stop it. It is a network of networks so intricate and intertwined, it is impossible to detangle, even for its members and leaders. This is also what precipitated this unhinged monster's relentless march onward and upward.

The big raid is not like the large-scale military operations that the government frequently deploys worldwide, such as Afghanistan, Iraq, Syria, Libya, Somalia, and Yemen. Instead, the hidden settlements sizzle under the surface of cities, like an army of poisonous spiders infiltrating even the tiniest crevices of every street and structure, or a swarm of infectious grasshoppers materializing out of nowhere, swarming in massive numbers through the city's open doors and windows. The hidden settlements need no central command. Years of training means that each cell knows exactly what to do once the starting shot sounds.

The hidden settlements need no large-scale media stunt to win the heads and hearts of the population, like governments need to justify their clandestine military pilgrimages, because the hidden settlements *are* the population. They embroil and embody the great majority of the population that has finally stepped off the endless, meaningless hamster hell wheel of a human existence at the bottom of a bottomless society.

That afternoon, everybody flocks to the large hall in the rail grave. There is no special decoration, no special foods and drinks, no special nothing. The settlement remains a dialed down, peeled to its core operation of bare minimums. The New York leadership consisting of about twenty people in total is standing at the far end of the hall. They are waiting for the leaders of the Baltimore, Pittsburgh, and Philadelphia settlements. When the doors open, the hall quiets, and about five to ten leaders from each of the collaborative cities' settlements walk through the door.

The leaders each have their own color; Baltimore is dressed in a black uniform; Pittsburgh has a brownish gray; and Philadelphia has a rusty colored orange. The leaders enter exuding an air of quiet confidence and humble dignity. They nod their heads hesitantly smiling to the crowds. Everybody knows what is at stake here. Everybody is grateful and in gratitude of everybody else's support and sacrifice. "Together we can do this! Alone we will die under the weight of injustice of society!" Kate yells out before stepping aside to hand over the word to Skyman.

Skyman bids welcome. He speaks of 'the cause' in a controlled yet greatly enthusiastic manner. "Enough is enough. It is time to take things into our own hands. To course correct decades, even centuries, of injustice done to us by the very few at the very top of society. The richest people in society sit on trillions of dollars. The top ten percent of the wealthiest Americans sit on seventy percent of the country's wealth. Their wealth is growing by the hour without them lifting a finger. The bottom fifty percent of the population only sit on two percent of all the country's wealth. The poorest part of the population lives in poverty comparable only to the poorest countries in the world. This makes America the country in the Western World with the biggest social inequality. The most massive poverty. Since the nineteen fifties, when the American Dream died, the rich have become richer, while everybody else have become poorer and poorer." Skyman builds himself up into a rage. "I count myself amongst the wealthiest of Americans. Yet, I recognize that this society cannot persist. If we don't change, and change fast, we will *all* end up in the hell hole! The change is not about initiating another program for social housing, making accessible mortgages for the poorest of the population, creating jobs for the unskilled, launching better public education, *etcetera*. We tried that. Many times, over and over again. And we failed. Real change cannot come until the old institutions, political and non-political, public and private, that form the foundation of this unjust society are torn down, once and for all. Only by tearing down these old dinosaurs, breaking their inept rules and regulations, dependencies and interdependences, can we build a new and brighter future for the people of this nation."

A youngish woman, who Saskia has seen before on a couple of occasions, gets up and immediately takes over from Skyman, who sits down. "New York has the highest concentration of extreme wealth in America. Yet here we are! We live with debilitating injustice, poverty, homelessness, famine, desperation, and *no future*. We will no longer just accept our destinies without a fight!" The people in the room roar and raise their right fist ready to fight.

After several more fire speeches, each leader from the Baltimore, Pittsburgh, and Philadelphia settlements takes turns to talk about the injustice and poverty of their city and how many fighters they have assembled and how ready for combat they are. It is all very exciting and encouraging, until you think about it. Then it just seems hopeless. But last resorts are always hopeless. That is why they are last resorts.

After the speeches, people start moving around the hall. Mr. Sind, who is originally from Philadelphia is happy to see his fellow city folks. Kate visited the Baltimore settlement a year back and enjoys rekindling her friendship with its city leaders. Saskia sees Skyman making his way across the hall. He is coming toward her. She wants to flee, but as they have both acknowledged each other's presence, fleeing is pointless. It will just make things even more awkward between them. Saskia decides to stay put, so that Skyman must edge his way through the crowds and across the hall. "Congratulations!" is the first thing he says to her, while approaching her with open arms.

Saskia acts as if she hardly grasps his presence, as she says, "Thank you!" out into the air in front of her. There are two places where former lovers can talk privately. One place is where they are all alone. Another place is where they are in a room filled to the brink with people and noise, as the commotion and chatter muffle their intimate conversation.

Skyman launches into what seems like a carefully scripted speech. "Saskia, listen. I know now that what we had was special. I hugely enjoyed your company. Hell! I would love to still spend time with you. Lots of time! It was never my intention to let our relationship ebb out. I guess, our worlds just drifted apart. But it doesn't have to be like that. We can make a conscious decision to see each other. To be together. Maybe not officially... I guess, what I am trying to say is that I want us to continue seeing each other!"

While Skyman is talking, Saskia is thinking and asking herself, if what they had was actually a relationship prompting her to ask, "Do you think we had a relationship?" Saskia raises her glance looking at him straight in the eyes. "I mean, we never discussed it. I am not sure I would call whatever we had 'a relationship.'"

Skyman is taken aback. Then he says, "Look, I don't care what we call it. All I am saying, or rather asking, is if we can be together again? I miss you. We had such a laugh." Saskia is flattered until he says, "We had such a laugh." *Is that all it was? A laugh? Some fun amidst all the gloom and doom of the hell hole.* On the other hand, Saskia is thinking. *If the world is coming to an end, what is the harm of having a bit of fun.*

This is how they reinitiate their affair. From her position at sub-level 3, Saskia is free to visit Skyman without having to explain her whereabouts and ask for permission to leave. Each time they see each other, they dine, chat, and make love. Every morning after they have had sex, she is presented with the "regret" pill. Every time, she is presented with the "regret" pill, she regrets their empty dead-end relationship. Not because she would ever consider getting pregnant, but because the "regret" pill reminds her of how fleeing and superficial their relationship is. They are committed to each other when they are together. Never beyond.

Saskia doesn't recall at what point in their relationship, Skyman starts leaving money on the desk in the bedroom before he leaves for work early in the morning. She is sad and disappointed that he thinks he can buy her. Buy her sex. In fact, Skyman is not buying her nor her sex. He is trying to give her the means by which she can become an independent person, who is able to make her own choices. It is still pitiful. In the end, Saskia decides not to take the money that just sits there, on the desk, quietly accumulating, serving as a testament to their dead-end relationship. Since most things between them are left unspoken, their relationship becomes more and more trapped in misunderstandings and mistrust.

At sub-level 3, her days revolve around attending endless meetings. She receives detailed briefings from the sub-level 2 combat units, including their objectives and the damage they seek to achieve during the big raid. Saskia thinks that, if nothing else, her being at sub-level 3 means that she gets an overview over the battle plan and ground.

The battle plan consists of mainly two different straits of action. One, is to create as much fear and chaos as possible by releasing thousands of homeless people on the streets of New York all at once. Most New Yorkers do not realize the magnitude of homelessness existing in their city. The authorities will be preoccupied with trying to retain this chaotic situation. The other strait of action consists of smashing things, blowing up, and setting fire to buildings, bridges, and other infrastructure. Together these two straits of action will wreak havoc. Ava is in the unit that will instigate chaos. She will lead a group of homeless people at street level. She has orders to steer clear of the authorities, to run around and behind them. Max is in a combat unit that will go head-to-head into fighting with the authorities. Saskia is consumed by thinking how she can rescue Ava and Max from the warzone. They will flee, far away from this and that world.

Every time Saskia is in a meeting, all she can think about are the implications on her children, and how she can rescue them from the imminent danger and possible death by escaping and running away. At one meeting, Skyman and Saskia meet again. The atmosphere between them is awkward, as they just spent the night together. Now, they are sitting opposite each other, at a meeting with lots of other people. Saskia doesn't typically attend the same meetings as Skyman, but due to their recent assignment to the same workgroup overseeing the underground's electricity supply, they now find themselves in the same meeting and room.

"We need to figure out how to disable the city's electricity during the upcoming raid!"

Kate explains to which Mr. Sind says, "But if we turn off all the city's electricity, we, too, lose our electricity in the underground, which will be debilitating for *our* war efforts."

Kate looks at Mr. Sind, while saying, "We need to determine if it is possible to keep an emergency generator for the underground electricity running while shutting off the rest of the electricity for the entire city. Otherwise, we will just have to lose our electricity, which may not matter, if we all have to surface anyway. We need to consider our options and carefully plan."

Kate turns her attention to Saskia and says, "We know the location of Con Edison's main operating room. The main switch for the Manhattan's power is housed there."

Saskia gets nervous, as all eyes rest on her. "But we cannot just walk into the main operating room of Con Edison. It will be heavily secured and guarded."

"Humm..." Kate is thinking aloud. "How did you get into the high security basement of the Langmore? We can find out who works there, and you can befriend them? You are good at that! It helped you both at Dr. Glenmore and the Langmore Hospital!" Kate says to Saskia.

At this point, Skyman intervenes. He proposes using Saskia as a honey trap. "We can find out who operates the main switch. It should be possible to access that information. And then you can work your way into the heart of the operation through this person." Saskia is totally shocked to hear Skyman's proposal. She is also hurt and angry. She thinks she will never ever again be with him. He is ambushing and abusing her.

To make things worse, Kate exclaims, "But she is not pretty enough to be used as a honey trap! Is she?" Skyman looks at Kate surprised.

There are cracks along the streets of Madison and Lexington Avenues that are spreading to Fifth Avenue and the streets running diagonal between these avenues. The city is slowly being overtaken by the underground forces carving their way up to the surface. The city will sink into the underground. Skyscrapers will tumble and become piles of gravel. As the underground surfaces, what is below ground will emerge above ground, while streets, bridges, and buildings will tumble into the hell hole.

Chapter Seven

Brady gets up every morning at six. She has done so all her life. In fact, she cannot remember when and why she started getting up every morning at six. Even at weekends, her consciousness calls her in her dreams around five-thirty. Sometimes, she hears it calling her name, as her consciousness knocks on the door of her subconsciousness. "Claudia, Claudia. Wake up!" The consciousness calls her by first name, as Brady and her consciousness are well acquainted. Other times, her consciousness wanders into her dreams, disrupting them, and causing her to wake up. Both incidents are extremely annoying, but they are only annoying till Brady is fully awake; after which, she somehow forgets about her intruding and bothersome consciousness.

This morning, her consciousness has approached her in the least subtle manner. It is almost yelling her name making her wake up with a jolt. Once, Brady comes to her senses, she sits up calmly on her sofa bed looking around her office. The problem with living in your office, or working in your home, is that you never really get any time off. At least for overachievers, such as Brady, that is the case. Even though, nobody requested her services since she opened her private eye operation about two months ago, she gets up at six every morning, goes for a run, and starts investigating.

In her mind, she is solving cases printed in the media. When there are not sufficient cases in the media to be solved, she reverts to the Langmore Hospital. The problem with reverting to the Langmore case is that her otherwise cool, detached, and objective approach to case investigation is accompanied by bittersweet and resentful hatred at the injustice of the way she was treated. She hates the police. She hates society. Turning from enthusiastic friend to foe is not unusual when people are justly or unjustly punished, proportionally or disproportionally. In fact, this is where most of societies' most adamant adversaries come here. They have felt upon themselves the dark flipside of society. They are the undergrowth snarling its way up through the creeds and cracks of society.

 Brady grabs a black coffee before going for a short run. At seven, she is behind her desk in her office-cum-bedroom that has hidden the bedroom away for the day. This morning, Brady's mind is circling around the Langmore case, again. During her investigations, she kept numerous files on the case at home that she never handed back, when she was tossed out of the force. These case files are sitting neatly organized in the large bookcase covering the entire wall opposite the kitchen. This morning, again, she is going through the files of material and boxes of evidence.

 Around nine o'clock, a hard knock on the door sounds. Brady gets a shock. For a moment, she thinks the knock will break the thin glass window in the door. Before she knows it, a tall and corpulent man is standing in the doorway. He is well dressed to the extent that it reveals his vanity and decadence. A dark blue suit, a cold-pressed shirt with thin blue stripes, a tie, and brightly blue colored silk socks tucked into silk soft tanned colored suede loafers. "Sorry, I didn't mean to startle you!" he says in a loud voice that matches his corpulent corpus. He has the confidence that comes from being born, bred, and brainwashed into wealth and privilege. There is nothing about him that confess of any work done, ever, other than discussing with his team of wealth managers how best to grow his substantial family wealth, if one can call that work.

"No," Brady says, while getting up to fetch a chair. "You didn't startle me... Well, maybe. But that is just because I was deep in my own thoughts." He stops and nods.

Brady puts the chair down. "Please."

He sits down, and it immediately becomes clear that he is weighed down by something heavy. "Where do I start..."

Brady smiles politely. "Start by introducing yourself, please." Brady has seen photos of Mr. Marlowe on numerous occasions, but, at this point, she does not dare to think that it is actually Mr. Marlowe sitting right in front of her.

He nods again. "I am Christopher Marlowe. Just call me Chris."

Mr. Marlowe can see that Brady is astonished. *Could he be THE Mr. Marlowe? What does he want from me?*

Brady thinks to herself, as Mr. Marlowe says, "Look! I know, you know, who I am. And I know, who you are. So, let's get straight to the point. I was told that you received the original material or evidence that enabled Midtown Precinct South to open and pursue the case against the Langmore Hospital and Dr. Hinnemann—"

Brady interrupts, which is a bad habit of hers. She doesn't mean to be rude. She just gets overexcited. There are even times, when she quite deliberately interrupts, because she knows, she needs to make an important question that she needs further ahead in the conversation. "Sorry for interrupting," Brady says, even though, she isn't. "But how come you know this? How do *you* know that I received this evidence? Who told you?"

Mr. Marlowe looks at her. "Never mind that! Do you want to hear why I am here?" He is obviously very annoyed with being interrupted; something that never happens to him, as people automatically treat Mr. Marlowe with great care and respect, even, when they don't know who he is.

"Yes, yes, go on," Brady insists.

Mr. Marlowe continues, "Anyway, I know someone sent you this material anonymously. Secretly. I need to know who! You understand? I need to know *who* wants to get at the Langmore Hospital and Dr. Hinnemann? And for what *reason*?"

Brady cannot believe her ears. While Brady was still in the force, Mr. Marlowe was one of the chief suspects. Not only does he have strong financial links to the Langmore Hospital and Dr. Hinnemann, but he also publicly advocates for the good work and exoneration the Langmore Hospital, Dr. Hinnemann, and everybody else prosecuted in the case. He and his crowd funding buddies even finances the legal expenses of all the people prosecuted. "I am not sure, *you* know, who *I* am... I am the investigator who started the whole case at the hospital. I led the whole investigation. Until they tossed me out on ass and elbows for no apparent reason!" Saskia doesn't understand why Mr. Marlowe wants to engage the very person who unraveled the whole case against the Langmore Hospital and Dr. Hinnemann to find who is behind the original denouncement. *Why is it even important to know who gathered the evidence and sent it to me?* she thinks. In that moment, she gets an eerie feeling that Mr. Marlowe could be involved in getting her fired. She doesn't quite understand where this feeling comes from, but, sure enough, it is there.

Mr. Marlowe is particularly vengeful, in part, his spoiled upbringing meant he always got everything he ever wanted. Therefore, whenever he encounters resistance, he becomes extremely revengeful. He tells those close to him, who have dared to confront him on the matter, that to him it is just business. He tells them, and himself, that he just wants justice and only means business. He says there is nothing personal to these spiteful attacks that he spends the majority of his life planning and executing. In fact, they are extremely personal. These attacks mask the spoiled child that insists on getting his way, at all costs. Things must conform to whatever he believes. His world is clearly drawn in black or white. Now, Brady gets the uneasy feeling that Mr. Marlowe has ulterior motives for engaging her to find the secret source of the evidence. Fair enough, it is smart to ask her, who received the evidence, to find the source, who sent the evidence, but if he was indeed the one, who got her fired from the force, then he may be gathering more damming evidence against her, for some unknown reason. Brady is confused. "Is he out to get me? Or does he indeed want to find the secret source of the evidence against the Langmore Hospital? Or both?" Her mind is racing.

They sit and stare at each other trying to read the mind of the other. Then Mr. Marlowe says, "*I* know who *you* are. That is why I am here! I am here because you received the evidence. I am presuming that whoever sent that file wants to hurt the hospital. Right? Otherwise, why go through the trouble of gathering evidence and sending evidence to you. But why you? You see... Why you? Do you know who sent it?"

Brady shakes her head. "Of course, I don't know. If we knew that, we would have dragged that person into the station and made him or her talk."

There is a moment of silence between them, again. Then Mr. Marlowe continues, "Do you want the job? Or not?"

Brady replies before she can even think, "Of course! I continue to do my own investigations into the case. In this way, I can get paid while investigating." Brady smiles. Mr. Marlowe does not return her smile. He gets up to leave. "Hold on!" Brady says. "I need to know why you want to know this?"

Mr. Marlowe gets annoyed, again, as he turns around to ask, "Why?"

Brady replies, "I need as much information as possible to do this investigation. I mean, are there any people out there you can think of who want to damage the Langmore Hospital and Dr. Hinnemann? Or even you? I know, you financed the hospital since way back. And today, you and others finance the legal expenses of Dr. Hinnemann and his accomplices. I also know your wife had an organ transplant at the Langmore. I hope she is better..."

Mr. Marlowe walks back to Brady's desk. He stops behind the chair; he was sitting in leaning his hands on the back of the chair. "Okay. It is no secret that I financed the establishment of the hospital about twenty years ago. Since then, I have worked very closely with the hospital and, in particular, with Dr. Hinnemann, who has also been there since the beginning. Today, I consider Dr. Hinnemann a friend really."

Brady asks, "Did you not notice anything sinister going on? Did you not question, where the organs came from?"

Mr. Marlowe replies, "Why would I? Anyway, I didn't run the hospital. I just invested and promoted it at any given opportunity to make sure my investment thrived. I didn't deal with the particulars. The problem is that I have gotten a lot of wealthy investors involved in this endeavor, and they are all ripshit at me for what happened. They want to withdraw their investments, but how can that happen!

And we all want to know, who caused all this shit. Hold whoever did this accountable."

Brady looks interested. "Humm... Okay, I get it. But is it not a good thing that criminal activities are revealed? I suppose you and your fellow investors do not knowingly want to support criminal activities, such as human trafficking and the stealing of organs?"

Mr. Marlowe is annoyed again. "I am not asking you to pass judgement. All I am asking you is to find who is out to get us. Do you think you can do that? Or should I take my business elsewhere?"

After Mr. Marlowe leaves, Brady beats herself up for always being so open mouthed and confrontational. *At least, she got the job,* she thinks to herself, as she goes through her files of material and evidence sent by the anonymous source, again. She looks at the photos. There is nothing that reveals their origin. Brady is completely lost with where to start.

After starring at the material and evidence for a couple of hours, Brady gets up to go to her drawing broad that was one of her pricier purchases for her new office. She starts writing. "Who would want to hurt Dr. Hinnemann or Mr. Marlowe? Who are Mr. Marlowe's fellow investors? What activities are they engaged in? Are they involved in human trafficking?" She needs to understand, who are the potential enemies of Mr. Marlowe and his associates to understand who would want to damage them. For that, she needs to understand what line of business they are in. She starts her own, mainly online, investigation of Mr. Marlowe and his associates. Within about half an hour, she stumbles across an article about Mr. Marlowe written four years ago by a friend of hers. Her friend, Noah, works at the New York Daily News, a crime tabloid newspaper. They arrange to meet at a bar opposite the Langmore Hospital at six that evening.

It turns out, Noah has his own reasons for meeting with Brady at such short notice. Noah is all too eager to share what he knows about Mr. Marlowe and his connection to the Langmore Hospital in exchange of information on the criminal investigation into the Langmore Hospital and Dr. Hinnemann. Noah explains that Mr. Marlowe's family's wealth stems from the medical drugs industry. "They made their fortune in antidepressants. In the early eighties, they sold their company to one of the large U.S. manufacturers of medical drugs. Great business! That is how they made their fortune. Since then, Mr. Marlowe and his family have invested in the medical industry, mainly buying stocks in flagship pharmaceuticals. The Marlowe family runs their own wealth management office that employees about sixty people. It is a large operation. The family and the wealth management office have been on the radar of the authorities on various occasions, including for insider dealing and money laundering. Mr. Christopher Marlowe is the patriarch of the family. He is the chairman of the board of the family foundation that holds all the family's wealth. Essentially, he has a say in all major investment decisions."

"Right," Brady says contemplative. "That means, he would definitely have been involved in purchasing the

Langmore Hospital, when it was old run-down hospital. He would also know about the substantial investment needed for bringing it up to date and into one of the best-known private hospitals for organ transplants in the U.S. He would have been hands-on with those decisions, right?"

Noah nods. "You bet!"

"To what extent do you think that Mr. Marlowe is involved in the hospital's daily running and its covert operations? I mean, do you think, he is aware what was going on with the migrants? Do you think, he was involved in the trafficking of migrants?"

Brady looks at Noah, intensely, who says with doubt in his voice, "Well, I was going to ask you the very same questions?" They both stare at the large mirror on the other side of the bar.

Then Brady says, "My sense is that Mr. Marlowe is involved. For two reasons. First, you mentioned that the family wealth management office has come under scrutiny from the authorities regarding potential money laundering. Previously, while I was still in the force, we observed a strong link between money laundering and human trafficking in this case. I mean, it looks like they take crime monies from drugs, maybe legal medical drugs sold illegally, to pay for the trafficking of illegal migrants. Then, these monies are washed when patients get their operations at the hospital. The hospital and their investors receive the full revenue of the medical operations but do not list any of the costs, because the procurement of organs is illegal. Thus, drug money is used to cover all expenses, including furnishing the operating theaters in the basement, paying overtime and hush money for the staff, and funding the clandestine operations. They list the organs as donated, sometimes postmortem, while clients pay legit money for legit operations. Secondly, why is Mr. Marlowe so interested in discovering the identity of those behind the denouncement of the hospital in the first place? That seems suspicious. If he was just investing in an above-board business that turned awry, he would naturally want to alienate himself from the enterprise, not dig deeper into learning who is behind the denouncement, would he? It is as if he is trying to identify which one of his enemies is having it out for him, so that he can silence that person before the authorities catch up with him."

Noah nods while still looking at the mirror on the wall behind the bar counter. Brady says with disappointment in her voice, "Anyway, whether or not Mr. Marlowe is involved with the human trafficking, clandestine organ transplants, and God knows what doesn't change the fact that I accepted the job of finding out who is behind the denouncement of the Langmore Hospital and Dr. Hinnemann. In desperation of getting *some* business, earning a living, I accepted a job from the very people that I would have been prosecuting had I still been in the force. What a pretty mess!"

Noah asks, "Okay. So, you were investigating this case, while you were still in the police? That explains why he came to you."

Brady turns to look at Noah. "Yes. I also received the anonymous package with all the material and evidence that kick started the whole investigation at the police. I swear, management seemed to be against this case unraveling from the very beginning. I swear. The whole thing was prearranged. That is why I was tossed out. So, the two knuckleheads, Sullivan and Davis, could take over the investigation. Either Sullivan and Davis are stupid, which I doubt, or they are corrupt. And management is probably also corrupt." Noah can see how painful it is for Brady to talk about her exit from the force. He decides not to say anything. He just nods in understanding.

At this point, Noah straightens his back and slowly turns to Brady. "Okay… This is what we need to do. I'll share all my evidence, which might be a bit dated by now, but it still provides some significant insights. In return, you let me in on your investigation. By sharing our evidence and combining our knowledge, we'll get to the bottom of this, together."

Brady looks at Noah. "Hold on! I need to find the anonymous source who sent the evidence. I'm not here to build a case against Mr. Marlowe, the Langmore Hospital, and Dr. Hinnemann. Besides, orders from the top dictate that Mr. Marlowe and his accomplices will walk. Mark my words, they will walk free. Dr. Hinnemann is being thrown under the bus as a scapegoat to give the appearance that someone is being held accountable. He's not innocent, but he is just one piece in this puzzle. The real masterminds behind the trafficking and money laundering will walk away, leaving Mr. Marlowe and his high-net-worth investors in the clear."

Noah is shocked, as he exclaims, "Wow! So, you think that the top of the police, the mayor, and other high level city officials know that Mr. Marlowe and his investors are involved in criminal activities, and still, they would rather turn a blind eye than bring them to justice. Why? Because these people finance the mayor's political campaigns and politics?"

Brady replies, "Look, I don't know what to think anymore. But no, I don't believe that the chief and the mayor are aware of Mr. Marlowe's criminal activities and then intentionally let him walk. They simply don't want to rock the boat. The city relies heavily on financial support from Mr. Marlowe and his investors. Through their financial support, they hold significant influence over the city's affairs. Following the money trail connected to the Langmore and Dr. Hinnemann will eventually lead us to Mr. Marlowe and the rest of the top echelon of society. Their financial support inevitably reaches high-ranking officials, including the chief and the mayor. Money and politics intertwine. They protect each other. Therefore, the people in charge and with influence, such as the chief and the mayor, would rather not *know* than be confronted with the uncomfortable truth that they have been dealing with criminals."

As the evening unfolds, Brady and Noah get more and more drunk. They reminisce about old days. They originally met some eight years ago when Brady had just started in the police force. She was a newly appointed assistant criminal investigator. As this was her first job in the force, she was told to seal off the area of a homicide scene, which normally falls to street petrol. The homicide scene resulted from drug and arms gangs warring in the streets of New York and mowing each other down in broad daylight. In those days, Noah was a freelance crime reporter, cruising the streets at night.

Both Brady and Noah spent several hours waiting for the chief investigator to arrive at the crime scene. During those hours, they became friends by exchanging horror stories about New York's all-pervasive crime. Brady was hopeful that their acquaintance would lead to romance. Luckily, Noah reciprocated her feelings and asked her out, and they started a relationship that was doomed to fail from the get-go. They both lived for New York crime. Crime was all they were excited about and consumed by. It was their only shared passion. Yet, Brady was not allowed to discuss her work with outsiders, and specifically, she was not allowed to leak information to this hungry up-and-coming freelance journalist, Noah. As time passed, crime became the elephant in the room. They both knew of the arrest of a high-profile arms dealer, but Brady refused to answer any of Noah's prying questions. On several occasions, she had divulged confidential information to Noah, who eagerly gobbled the information and spat it out again on the pages of the New York Daily News the following day. After a heated argument late that evening about loyalty and betrayal, they finally decided to go their separate ways.

Now they are together in the bar, intoxicated by their drunkenness and the familiar presence of an old lover. Brady looks at Noah, who is tall and tanned, likely acquired by spending most of his days waiting in the streets or in the van of his photographer with the window open. He has a good head of hair, albeit notoriously messy. Noah looks like a journalist. It is strange how we must look like our profession to gain credibility.

Suddenly, the door to the bar opens, and the late-day shift from the Langmore Hospital enters. They speak loudly about the arrest of Dr. Hinnemann that occurred earlier that day. Brady and Noah snap out of their intoxication and turn to watch the newcomers move across the bar. Miguel is one of the newcomers. He wants his beer now. He is too tired and thirsty to ask anyone else what they want. Impatiently, he weaves down to the barman. While waiting for his beer, Miguel calms down. He turns around to look at his colleagues and smiles. Then he turns, shaking his head, as he mutters to himself, "What a mess!"

Brady is standing right next to him. She concurs, "Yes, what a mess."

Miguel turns to Brady. "You know what happened today?"

"Yes. I heard about it. I also used to work with the Langmore Hospital."

He replies, "You left the hospital before the shit hit the fan! Good for you."

Brady asks, "Well, will all this have any implications for you? I mean, it was just a small group of people who were involved in these atrocities. The vast majority of people working in the hospital will be left to go about their work and lives as before."

Miguel looks at Brady as if she has just fallen out of a tree. "Are you shitting me? Don't you see... If Dr. Hinnemann is convicted, and hideous crimes at the hospital are revealed, including smuggling of migrants and stealing their organs, then we will be shut down. *Everybody* will lose their jobs. Do you think that crimes of this magnitude can be revealed without the hospital and *all* its employees suffering?" Miguel is annoyed. He picks up his beer and walks away.

Brady has lived her life somewhat sheltered from the realities of the cruelty of doing business, such as at the privately owned and run Langmore Hospital. This sheltered existence away from the harsh realities of business, human survival, and greed has allowed her to keep her neat and somewhat naïve ideology intact. She secretly despises people who profit excessively. In the Western World, business is where Darwinian principals, in their purest form, rule. It is not each individual who is to blame for the greed and selfish fighting to get ahead of the game at the expense of those less fortunate. It is our society that, sometime in the early Industrial Revolution, around the mid to late eighteenth century, decided that all resources should be valued according to their mechanized manufacturing and industrial production value. As a result, in the Western World, everybody, apart from those in public office who receive their salaries regardless of production output, must succumb to Darwin's principles of survival of the fittest. Brady sits with her nose high in the sky, thinking that wealthy businessmen and women are greedy, corrupt, and delinquent—something she knows nothing about, as she has not had *her* livelihood depend on the battle of survival of the fittest, until now, that is.

Brady gets up and wobbles over to Miguel. She wants to apologize for not recognizing the terrible predicament that all the employees of the Langmore Hospital are in. "Sorry. I understand that it is a bittersweet situation to be in. I mean, nobody approves of illegal migrants being forced to sell their organs to wealthy New Yorkers, but I totally understand the broader ramifications of the recent revelations. I am sorry, you are all propelled into total disarray. Uncertainty. I also recently unjustly lost my job. It is terrible," Brady says, shaking her head and looking down.

Fortunately, Miguel is forthcoming. "Don't worry. We are all super sensitive at the moment. People ask themselves how this could have happened right under our noses and on our shifts without anyone noticing it?"

A woman standing next to Miguel says, "Our lives have been turned upside down. We are standing back holding a bag of shit. All the good people already left the Langmore. The doctors and nurses easily found new jobs elsewhere, but we, the unskilled, don't know what is going to happen to us."

Miguel nods in agreement and says, "Anyway, our days were numbered even before Dr. Hinnemann pulled this trick on us. I drive a cart in the basement. Management had already laid off over half of the drivers and porters who were all replaced by robots. We are dispensable. The robots are the only ones indispensable."

After a while, Noah walks over to them and introduces himself. The woman, standing next to Miguel, asks if he works at the Langmore or is otherwise connected to the hospital. Noah says he is a crime reporter for the New York Daily News. The woman smiles as she says, "So, you came here to snoop?" Noah explains, in his defense, he didn't know the bar was a meeting place for Langmore employees.

Brady asks, "Do you know how it all blew up? How did it all come out into the open? Was it carelessness?"

Miguel and the woman look at each other, then Miguel says, "Nobody knows for sure, but I stumbled across a woman who seemed suspicious. The first time I met her, she was wandering around in the basement, lost. She said, she was new in the hospital. Then it turned out that she had already lost her employee ID. In retrospect, it seems strange to start a new job and lose your ID immediately after. Now, thinking back; maybe she didn't work at the hospital at all. Unknowingly, I helped her get a new ID by taking her to a friend of mine at facility management. Maybe I helped her get a fake ID."

Brady immediately sobers and asks in suspense, "Who was she?"

Miguel inspects Brady apprehensively. "I don't know. There was another highly suspicious incident with this woman. She was in the basement when the alarm sounded. When I look back, I wonder what she was doing in the basement at that time. She came out of the section in the basement that is sealed off from most personnel. Only Dr. Hinnemann and a few other people have clearance to enter that section. When the alarm sounded, guards were right behind her chasing her down the corridor. I gave her a lift and got her out of a very hotspot. It turns out the section was where they held the illegal migrants and conducted the covert operations. I didn't know that. And now, I don't know, if I did a good deed, or if I am to blame for all of us losing our jobs. Maybe both." Brady can hardly believe her ears and luck. Most things in life cannot be planned. They happen by total coincidence. It is this lack of control, this total randomness by which most things in life occur, that largely defines the destiny of most people.

"Shit! So, you helped the woman, who uncovered the whole thing?" Brady inquires.

Miguel contemplates. "It is difficult to tell, but I think so. I think, she must have been in the basement snooping around."

Noah asks, "Who is she? What does she look like?"

All eyes are on Miguel. "She is about thirty something. Maybe early thirties… Short hair. Slim and medium height."

Noah resigns. "That describes everybody and nobody. Do you have her name?"

Miguel smiles, as he says, "Elisabeth Taylor." They all laugh.

Brady is thinking. She feels that the description could match the woman she encountered a couple of times. Once at the Glenmore's, and the second time, outside the hospital on the day of the raid. It was that second time that Brady felt was more than just a coincidence, but she had pushed her gut feeling out of her mind at the time, because she was too busy handling the chaotic situation. Now, she regrets not reacting on her gut feeling at the time.

Noah agrees to walk Brady home. Now, none of them are thinking of having sex. Instead, they have sobered up and are excited about the bombshell discovery. "I have seen the woman, Elisabeth Taylor, before. I investigated a suicide in Upper New York, Fifth Avenue. A posh couple. Elisabeth Taylor, which was not the name she used back then, was working there as a cleaner. That is how I recognized her, when I saw her standing outside the Langmore watching the raid. You see, for her to be at the scene of crime at two different incidents and match the description of Miguel cannot be a coincidence! I also got a distinct feeling that she was somehow involved in the raid of the Langmore Hospital, but I decided not to pursue that feeling."

Noah reflects, "That was a pity, but you couldn't know that back then. How do we find her? Do you know where to look?"

Brady answers, "Well, she gave me her address when I questioned her at the Glenmore's. I guess, it was a phony address. She was not there, when I checked it out later in the Glenmore investigation. Still, it is the only lead we have right now. We should look up the place tomorrow. Maybe there are clues."

The following day, Brady and Noah walk to the apartment in the old brownstone on West 117th Street. The place has been swept clean with a toothbrush. There is nothing. Just a sparsely furnished, run-down apartment that was vacated quite a while ago. Dust has settled on the floors. They leave the apartment disappointed.

On the way down the stairs, they bump into a young man. They ask if he knows where the woman, who used to live on the fourth floor, lives now. He looks them up and down and says, "Who's asking?"

Neither Brady nor Noah knows what to say. "Well... We think, she has some important information for us."

The man says, "I don't know a lot. But I am willing to share the little I know, if you make it worth my while." They pay the man off.

He tells them that there were several people in the apartment. "People come and leave that apartment. Often, for long periods of time, it is empty and then suddenly inhabited by entirely new people, who stick to themselves, till they too evaporate. This goes on and on. I think, it is some kind of criminal organization. Maybe a safehouse for some people on the run. It is hard to tell, but it is no ordinary place."

Brady is annoyed. "That is little help. Did you see a woman? Early to mid-thirties? White. Short hair. Medium height and quite slim."

The young man is thinking. Then he says, "Yes! I saw her. She left in the mornings and came back early evenings. Most days. I think, she had a real job."

Noah says, "Where can we find her?"

The young man starts to turn around. "How the hell do I know!"

Just before he enters his apartment door, he turns. "By the way, these men, who cleaned the place. They dropped something on their way out. They were carrying these large black dumpster bags into a van parked downstairs. But on their way out, they dropped something. I picked it up and yelled at them, but they didn't react; and then they left. So I put it on the shelf by the door, in case they come back." The young man reaches to grab a brown envelope.

Brady is desperately trying to mask her eagerness, as she slowly reaches to take the envelope from him. The man retracts it. "Hold on! You can't just have it! I am beginning to think, this wrapper means quite a lot to you two snooping journalists or whatever you are. You must pay a finder's fee!"

Noah calmly asks, "How much?"

"Should we say a hundred?"

Noah digs deep into his pockets and retrieves a bundle of notes and coins. He counts them under the watchful eyes of Brady and the young man. "Eighty-nine and something. Does that work?" The young man waves his hand. He gives them the envelope and turns to leave. Then he is gone.

Once back on the street, Noah opens the wrapper carefully like excavating a rare prehistoric artifact. Brady says impatiently, "Come on! What are you waiting for!" Inside there is a map of some kind of underground. "What on earth is that?" Brady exclaims revealing disappointment in her voice.

There is also a delicate drawing of a crown sitting in a glass cage. Careful lines are drawn for the infrared sensors protecting the crown. Noah takes out the maps and drawings. "What the hell is this! Anyway, let's go to the corner deli, sit down, and take a proper look at these strange papers."

The deli is a dinky affair. A relic predating the recent gentrification of the neighborhood. It smells of old wet carpets and wood. The wallpaper has a kind of Art Deco motive with palm leaves. No doubt this place was once the pride and glory of the neighborhood. Today, it testifies to a time long gone. A couple of old men and an even older woman sit at the counter making small talk with themselves. "Two coffees!" Noah yells as he and Brady rush into the deli in a frantic state. The two men and woman turn to look at them. They haven't seen such force of energy for decades.

In this inconspicuous place, Brady and Noah can take their time to trawl through their find. "Okay... a map of the underground. You agree? It is probably the New York underground, because there are references to some familiar underground trainlines." Noah points to the references. Brady is looking at the drawing of Nefertiti's crown. "And a beautiful drawing of what reads as Nefertiti's crown. Do you think it is worth something?"

Noah turns the paper. "No. It is a reproduction. Like a photocopy, but the glass case and infrared lines have been added... There is a map here of the entire underground, including below the Langmore Hospital!" Brady doesn't respond. She is online to search "Nefertiti's crown," and she finds out that it was recently displayed at the Met.

"Wow!" she exclaims. "There is a commentary from a visitor about a strange incident at the Met about the same time as the whole Langmore Hospital case blew up. This incident looks like a theft of the crown from right under the nose of the museum's security and in broad daylight."

Noah is looking over Brady's shoulder to see what it reads. "Okay, so we have here an underground map of both the Met and the Langmore Hospital, and a detailed drawing of Nefertiti's crown with lines to indicate where the security sensors are. Then we have theft of Nefertiti's crown, and the unraveling of the Langmore Hospital's clandestine organ transplants."

Brady leans back. "These two incidents are tied together by this woman. But how?"

As they walk down the street and turn to say goodbye after an eventful day, Noah reasons, "If we can get security footage from the Met of the theft of Nefertiti's crown, we know, what this woman looks like. We can collect a visual of her. If I get that, you can go back to some of your old colleagues at the police and get them to run this visual through the face recognition software to try to locate her whereabouts."

Brady ponders, *Look, I left the force on no good terms. Very difficult... And I decided never to talk to any of my old colleagues ever again. I just wanted out and never to turn back again. But I really want to get to the bottom of this. It is too intriguing. I mean, what is the connect between the Langmore and Nefertiti's crown, and who is this woman? Why is she doing this?"*

Brady looks down. *Okay, I will get in touch with Lizzy. She is a decent person, and we were friends—of sorts.*

*

Mr. Marlowe comes to hear what Brady has discovered. Brady explains, "Well, I am pretty sure, it is a woman in her early to mid-thirties, slim and short hair, who infiltrated the Langmore. She got into the basement, where the covert operations took place. I think, it is safe to say that *she* gathered the evidence on the operations in the basement, and that she or someone else subsequently sent this evidence to me." Mr. Marlowe nods reflectively. He is pleased with what Brady discovered so far.

Mr. Marlowe asks, "Who is she? And what are her motives?"

Brady shakes her head. "I don't know. When I interrogated the personnel at the Langmore, while I was still in the force, one of the guards told me that he let a woman into the sealed off area of the basement. She also fits the description that the cart driver, Miguel, gave of a woman he dealt with on several occasions. For instance, he helped her get a new ID, probably a fake ID, and he helped her escape the guards, when the alarm sounded in the basement. When he helped her escape, he didn't understand why the guards were chasing her. He also doesn't know who she is."

Mr. Marlowe gets upset. "He shouldn't have helped her! It is bloody anarchy at the hospital. He should have handed her over to the guards!"

Brady nods and continues, "Yes. But he didn't. Anyway, I met this woman at the Glenmore's when Mrs.

Glenmore committed suicide. Do you know the Glenmore's?"

Mr. Marlowe looks surprised. "I know Dr. Glenmore. Everybody knows him. But I don't see the connection between Dr. Glenmore and the Langmore Hospital. Or between Dr. Glenmore and Dr. Hinnemann. I doubt, they knew each other."

Brady looks at Mr. Marlowe. "The connection is probably you. You know Dr. Glenmore and Dr. Hinnemann, and you invested heavily in the Langmore Hospital."

Mr. Marlowe looks astonished. "So, someone is out to get me! I knew it!"

Brady tilts her head. "It is too early to tell. But let's just say, someone is out to get you… Who could it be?"

Mr. Marlowe replies, "Look! Anyone in my position has many enemies. That goes with the territory. But I can't think of anyone who would hurt Dr. Glenmore, who is just an acquaintance, Dr. Hinnemann, and the Langmore Hospital just to get at me. There are far more effective, and less round-about, ways to get at me."

Brady says acknowledging, "I'm not saying someone wants to get at you. But maybe you are part of a group, a kind of collective. Maybe it's some kind of gang war. Does that make sense?" Mr. Marlowe gets annoyed by Brady's association to gang wars. He does not perceive himself as a low-life criminal engaged in gang wars. His crimes are far more sophisticated.

*

Noah comes later that afternoon. "I have done some digging. One of the guards at the Met is apparently the uncle of one of the journalists at my paper. This guard does nightshifts. He has shared information with the New York Daily News on a couple of occasions through his nephew, who is the journalists at my paper. The information was mainly about the Met Gala and what goes on behind the scenes. So, celebrity stuff that we ended up selling to some tabloid paper. We paid him for the information. I got his nephew to get in touch him, and we arranged that he run through the footage of the theft, while alone on duty in the video surveillance room. I followed the video of the theft via facetime. Not ideal. But then I got him to send me a file of some decent photos and a smaller video cut of her." Noah shakes his head. "I am telling you! This woman is a pro! She calmly switches the real crown for the fake after having gotten the guards out of the room. I could hardly believe my eyes! My colleague at the newspaper wanted to break the story, but he agreed not to because his uncle will probably lose his job if the story runs. But strange that the story has not been covered by the media already…"

Brady lights up. "I can take this footage to Lizzy!" She arranges to meet Lizzy in a bar after hours the subsequent day. The bar is near enough to Midtown Precinct South to make it convenient for Lizzy to meet and far enough from Midtown Precinct South for Brady not to encounter any of her old colleagues. Lizzy rushes up to Brady as soon as she sees her. "Oh my God. What happened? You just disappeared one day. I couldn't get in touch with you. After a while, I went back to your old apartment, but you were gone!"

Brady doesn't know what to say. She musters the courage to talk. "Well, I was kicked out on ass and elbows. You know... Sullivan. He was out to get me from day one, as you rightly suspected. I should have listened to you. But I am not sure that would have changed anything."

Lizzy exclaims, "You know! To make matters worse, it is as you suspected, the whole Langmore case is quietly going away. Dr. Hinnemann, Mr. Marlowe, his accomplices, and everybody else hide behind a veil of legislative bullshit. I am beginning to think that the law is made for those who want to use it viciously to their own end, to enrich themselves or get revenge or whatever. The law is not made to protect ordinary people."

Brady nods. "Well, I used to think that I could actually make a difference by joining the force. I used to think that people doing wrong could be held accountable. Now, I just think that the law is used by people to settle scores and get ahead." Lizzy looks down.

"I am so happy you reached out to me. I really missed you. And I was worried for you. Where did you go?" Brady is too ashamed to tell Lizzy that she is in fact now working for Mr. Marlowe and his lot. "I set up my own private eye. That is why I also wanted to see you. I need your help to identify a woman, who stole Nefertiti's crown at the Met."

"I haven't heard of that. How strange... Well, did the Met give you the assignment to find the thief?" Brady nods in confirmation. "So, it is all underboard? Okay, I may be able to help you. What do you need?" Brady explains how she needs to find the woman by running her visuals through the face recognition software. "I will try the stations and bus terminals first," she says and gets up to leave.

*

Noah has done some snooping of his own. After spending weeks getting caught up in Brady's web of investigation, he returns to the Langmore investigation and tries to assess the connection between the main protagonists of the hospital and Dr. Glenmore to see how the woman, Brady is looking for, could have been present at both scenes of crime. It turns out that Mr. Marlowe and all the other investors of the Langmore Hospital, *and* Dr. Glenmore are all part of "old money." They have inherited their wealth and spread out their investments across properties, stocks, and shares. The only strong common denominator linking them is "old money," and that they all know each other, invest together, and marry into each other's families. Some of the investments are totally intertwined. For instance, several investors in the Langmore Hospital have their own flagship investment projects that Mr. Marlowe reciprocally invested in. "Do you see? You invest in the Langmore, and I reciprocate by investing in your project. For example, Mr. Harrington owns a company that builds and renovates hospitals. The Langmore Hospital contracted his company to refurbish the basement. In return, Mr. Harrington invested in some business venture of Mr. Marlowe's, which is a start-up company working on a new antidepressant drug. In this way, it becomes totally impossible to disentangle the web of take-and-give investments. They even swap investments by exchanging stocks and shares. I doubt the tax authorities can figure out what goes on. Some of the women are also swapped, so to speak. They married several men in this top echelon of old New York wealth. They divorce and remarry, divorce and remarry, and so on. In that way, they all become related, through some bizarre kinship, where you, as a man, can father a child that is raised by another man, whom you do business with. As a young man or woman, you may inherit two men, your paternal father and your stepdad through your mother's new marriage, and then you marry into a third family of old money. It is a tightknit web of wealth that sits on over seventy percent of all New York wealth, while only representing three percent of the city's population. It is actually rather claustrophobic. But also, very discerning. Very discerning."

Brady looks at Noah and says, "Humm… That is a very *loose* connection, but I guess, at least, it is a connection. Who would want to damage these old families enough to take matters into their own hands? I mean, we all know that there are massive injustices in society. Some people are born into great wealth, while others are born into great poverty. What do they call it? Lottery of the womb? Still, for someone to actually do something about this, risk their freedom and life, is altogether a different matter!"

Noah reflects, "I think maybe there is a group of people out there, like a vigilante group, that is shaking up things and breaking the foundation of the establishment. The police, courts, and public authorities are useless. If anything, they protect the super-rich by protecting the status quo, rather than ensuring justice for all. So, this citizen patrol or community security group on steroids is taking matters into their own hands."

Brady adds, "Well, they have kind of gone awry. It is hardly your regular neighborhood watch group."

Noah smiles. "Look, we have so many homeless people. So many people just wandering aimlessly around in the streets looking to make a living. They have nothing. No education. No money. No future. What little is left of the middle class has left the city. We are stuck here with the super-poor and the super-rich."

Brady is thinking. "So now the super-poor and the super-rich are going into war with each other?"

Noah replies, "I don't know. Maybe poor people have just reached the breaking point."

Brady says while in deep contemplation, "I just don't see where this woman fits into everything. It just doesn't make sense! If your theory is correct, then she seems to be singlehandedly taking on New York's "old money" establishment. But why? And surely, she is not able to dismantle both the Glenmore's household and more importantly the Langmore Hospital on her own! In addition to stealing Nefertiti's crown from the Met. She must be working with more people. Maybe that's where your theory on the vigilance group on steroids consisting of the homeless people fits in?"

It is frustrating that, unlike reality, fiction must make sense. If fiction doesn't make sense, it seems unbelievable and incredible. Contrary, if reality makes sense, it too seems unbelievable and incredible. This is because, we recognize, that we cannot control life, but we can control the narrative of fiction.

Brady says, "Before I left the force, we had an enormous increase in crime. It is up by fifty percent during the last ten years. It is a ticking time bomb. Did you hear about all the raids on Madison Avenue? The luxury stores moved to the upper floors of the buildings. They are no longer at street level. It is simply too dangerous. Even drug stores and supermarkets are raided. People are hungry. A recent report from Famine shows that the poorest thirty percent of Americans die twenty years earlier than the wealthiest ten percent of Americans, due to malnutrition. These numbers compare to some of the poorest countries in the world! The establishment says that poor people make poor lifestyle choices, but many people have next to no choices. The authorities want to improve public education so that the poorest people are *educated* into making better lifestyle choices, including schooled for future-proof jobs."

Noah tilts his head, as he says, "Still jobs are disappearing. Jobs are becoming more and more scarce due to automated technology, artificial intelligence, robotics, and so on, all of which are highly reliable and work relentlessly round-the-clock. No jobs are future-proof. No job—no money. No money—no food. Even the establishment should be able to understand that!"

What has the world come to. The American Dream has turned into a Waking Nightmare, where if you are *not* amongst the wealthiest ten percent of Americans, you are basically doomed. The middle-class, suffering declining living standards since the nineteen-sixties, barely make ends meet, while the poorest thirty percent of Americans live a waking nightmare. "If anything, it has only just gotten worse," Noah looks at Brady, while he continues, "The disparities between those who have and those who do *not* have are great and growing. Maybe groups in society are mobilizing for social justice? The authorities have been talking about improving public health, education, and jobs for decades, centuries, all the while it has only just gotten worse and worse."

"So, how do we find this vigilance group on steroids?" Brady asks.

Noah raises his shoulders. "I don't know... Maybe we should look around in the streets. Ask some homeless people. They are everywhere."

Chapter Eight

Everything moves at double speed. They need to be prepared for the big attack that is only weeks away. Kate's newly appointed executive assistant, Robin, comes to Saskia's room with news on Saskia's upcoming assignment of cutting off the electricity supply of New York City. The city black-out and stand-still must be timed with the big attack on the city. Cutting off the electricity is a most effective weapon, as electricity is the thin line that separates chaos and order. In this city, where despair is sizzling under the surface, a black-out will send the city over the edge. Electricity symbolizes the institutional authority of the old establishment. Once, it is lost, the raging and rampant mobs will take to the streets and take over the city.

Robin explains, "I have your ID card with the highest clearance to the Con Edison." As Robin walks toward her, he reaches out his right hand with the card. Saskia reluctantly takes it. Robin continues, "We have identified the person, the Switch Master, or Chief Power Switch Operator, in charge of the main electricity switch at Con Edison. His name is Mr. James, Jonathan James." Robin shows Saskia a photo of Jonathan James on his phone.

Robin is a young man in his twenties. He is well spoken, has good schooling and a bachelor's degree from

NYU Wagner School of Public Service for which he received a scholarship. He comes from a modest background. His parents live in New Jersey and commute every day into Manhattan for work. Robin's father works in the city's Roads and Parks Department as a middle manager overseeing the maintenance of street trees. He is at a loss as to why the city can't finance the planting of more trees. He tirelessly explains city management that car tires randomly catching fire due to extreme heat or roads turning into rivers during heavy downpours can be helped with the greening of the city. "Afterall, the fires and floods also carry substantial costs. Many more costs than planting trees!" he insists. However, the city, and the country at large, are accustomed to reacting and responding with short-term thinking and strategies. It's an entirely different matter to proactively invest in the long-term future of the city and country, looking beyond the elected four-year period in office of the mayor, the police commissioner and other high-ranking officials who are at the mercy of the mayor. None of the people in power, anywhere, think beyond their own elected period in office, which prevents any change from happening. At worst, any improvements made during one term is reversed during the next. And so on and on it goes.

 Robin's mother is a nurse at the Bellevue Hospital Center. Robin's parents possess some of the few jobs left in the city that require the physical presence of human beings. Most of the remaining middle-class workers are either working out of their suburban homes, or they have entirely lost their jobs. After decades of long commutes and hard work, both Robin's parents are looking forward to living off their public pensions.

Some people say Robin is related to Raven, one of the main high-level supporters of the underground. Raven was recently promoted from Department Chief of the Special Operations Bureau to First Deputy Commissioner in New York's police force. It is frightening to think that the person who will measure and manage the response to the underground's big attack is part of the underground itself. Both as a Department Chief and First Deputy Commissioner, Raven is primarily responsible for emergency responses, tactical operations, counterterrorism, SWAT teams, and other high-risk situations. Saskia gets chills running down her spine thinking of this, as she asks herself, if Raven will altogether prevent an adequate response to the underground's strike, when the day comes. The underground has penetrated and permeated the city right under the watchful eyes of its guardians.

Saskia gets up early the next morning to go Con Edison's headquarters at 4 Irving Place, on the corner of East 14th Street and 3rd Avenue. There is a strangely violent wind raging that morning. Like an evil omen trying to warn the city's inhabitants of what is in waiting. But nobody listens. They are too busy going about their daily errands to connect with themselves and the world beyond.

Saskia was told that the Distribution Control Center (DCC) and possibly the main switch, both are located at Con Edison's headquarters at 4 Irving Place. The underground has created a fictitious position for her as a monitoring technician. Con Edison's HR system confirms this, as does her new ID card. During her preparation in the underground, Saskia receives a quick crash course on how to operate the monitors and analyze data from various electrical systems and equipment within the DCC. Yet, the course is more crash than course, and she feels more confused than confident about taking on her fictitious position as monitoring technician.

"Why can't I get a job as an administrative assistant or communications operator? I think, I can actually do those jobs! Which is more than I can say about this job!" Saskia pleads with Robin.

"We already thought of that. You will be called out very fast in those positions, as you are clueless on who's who, and where everybody and everything is. You see, Con Edison is unlikely to hire an outsider for the DCC. As a monitoring technician, you can bluff. You can act as if you know what is going on the screens. As long as everything is fine, you don't need to do anything but monitor. I think, you can hold up the façade for a couple of days. Don't you?"

Saskia doesn't answer. Her mind stopped mid-sentence at "you can bluff."

They went through the deliberations of finding the fictitious job that enables Saskia to go undercover until the day of the big attack, after which no one cares what happens to her. "One last thing…" Robin says before he walks out of the door. "We have removed the monitoring technician, whose job you are replacing. Otherwise, they don't need you, do they?"

While Saskia walks along the windy streets of New York that almost serve as air tunnels for the wind to pick up pace, she is trying to prepare herself for her new job. She thinks she must seem knowledgeable, yet humble, as she has a relatively junior position. She has studied Mr. James's factsheet. He is in his early fifties, married and has two grown up children who have both left home in pursuit of their college education. "He doesn't seem like the kind of man who would have an office affair with a woman in a junior position." Saskia expresses frustration with her mission and doubts her ability to carry it out as planned and instructed by the leaders. "If he doesn't want to get intimate with me and spill the beans, what do I do?"

Robin looks at her disinterested. "Then I am sure you will find another way. We need to switch off the electricity of the city in time for big attack. You have three days! Three days, that's it! Your mission is critical to 'the cause'!"

As she walks along the windy streets, she feels alone and lonely. She also doesn't understand how she ended up in this highly compromising position. How did she go from being a homeless mother of two to being embroiled in highly criminal activities conspiring to topple the political and economic leadership of New York through civil war? It dawns on her that she will spend the rest of her life in prison if she is caught.

In this way, our destiny is precisely what greets us when we try to avoid our destiny. For instance, when we take the shortcut through the alleyway to get home faster and meet our rapist or murderer, we meet our destiny. No matter the alternative and round-about routes you may take, destiny always catches up with you. It always wins.

Saskia, Kate, Annona, Robin, Lucky, Trish, Trash, Troll, Preacher, Raven, Storm, Nightshade, Skyman, and everybody else entangled in the underground are guilty by default. It doesn't matter if the homeless people found their way into the underground looking for shelter and food and then unknowingly and unwillingly got sucked into the intricate criminal web of the underground. Once, you have emptied all other options, pulled the handle of that door and take your first steps down the stairway leading to the underground, you become guilty of a whole suite of criminal offences, by default. This is the last resort. This is the only option still standing when all other options have been exhausted. Had she known at the time that she would end up playing a central role in a big attack designed to topple the city's old establishment, she would not have gone down those stairs. But she didn't know, and she didn't have any other options. Nobody knows what each one of us are capable of, when we are out of options. When we grow up with violence, drugs and destruction as the only reality known to us. When we live with injustice and corruption and have nowhere to turn to for help.

What are the forces that define the kind of society we live in? Who decides what is right and wrong? And what grants them the power to define right and wrong in society? How can anyone justify a society that pushes so many people to the brink of desperation? How can anyone justify the justice in the extreme human suffering that so many people are born into? Or the extreme luxury that other few people are born into? We use words such as "democracy," "justice," and "the law" to explain why our society makes sense, when in fact there is no sense making of the meaningless human suffering and injustice suffered by millions of people. Does democracy succeed when democratic societies fail? What good is freedom if society is unjust, people are wronged, and live pitiful existences depleted of choices? Is freedom not precisely the ability to make choices, freely? For those at the bottom of society, there are no choices.

Change does happen in society. Nevertheless, instead of change being a linear progression from bad to good, from little to plenty and so on, change sways from one end of the spectrum to another, with currents of influence washing over society like ebbs and tides. Never landing, never sustaining the passage of time. Always shifting. These tendencies might address some past mistakes, yet they rarely address the persistent issues of poverty, famine, injustice and violence that continue to afflict the majority of those living in supposedly free democracies.

Saskia walks through the main entrance of Con Edison, which is almost hidden by the scaffolding wrapped around the building. In New York City, continuous construction is an ever-present sight, transforming buildings, streets and infrastructure over and over again. Once inside, Saskia catches the attention of a guard approaching her. "Can I help you, ma'am?"

Saskia quickly responds, "I am starting work at the DCC today, but I don't know how where to go." She shows him her fake ID. The guard takes a moment to call Mr. James's secretary and inform her about Saskia's arrival. Their conversation lasts forever. Saskia is getting nervous. Only if she is lucky, the underground has informed Mr. James's secretary, known as Blondie, of her turning up for work at the DCC today. Eventually, the guard informs Saskia that Blondie will be there in a moment.

Blondie arrives looking confused. She is a slim, elderly woman with thin, frizzy white hair, and a radiant, rosy glow on her face that reflects her positive attitude and good-natured spirit. Positive people appear to age at a slower pace than the rest of us, as if their abundance of positivity can decelerate the relentless march of mortality. It is precisely because Blondie is such a good-natured person, who doesn't take herself too seriously that she doesn't mind her nickname Blondie. "I am sorry, if I seem out of sorts, but nobody told me you would be starting at DCC today. I guess, we must fill your post immediately. It is a critical job overseeing the networks." Saskia smiles. Blondie continues, "Well, they never tell us anything. But I don't understand how this could slip. Who did you talk to at HR?" Saskia sighs with relief, as she knows the name of the person, she must refer to. It is someone supporting "the cause."

"I talked to Jennifer Martinez."

Blondie says, "Oh, I don't know her. I will call HR, just to make sure. You are not in trouble or anything. We just need to be careful, because DCC is at the heart of the operation."

Saskia nods and says, "I know. Better safe than sorry."

Saskia sits down in the small boot with massive screens at 180 degrees. A wave of exhaustion washes over her at the sight of the screens. DCC is dark allowing the monitors to light up like stars on the night sky. Sound is muffled in the room, seemingly for no apparent reason. *I guess, if you really understand what you are looking at, it makes it more interesting*, she thinks to herself.

"We have lunch at twelve-thirty in our kitchen, where you also find the coffee maker," Blondie says pointing toward a door leading to the kitchen. She continues, "Mr. James is not in yet. He attends a meeting in town. But as soon as he gets in, I will present you." She walks away, and Saskia exhales a deep sigh of relief.

So far, so good. For the next two hours, Saskia is starring at what seems like a series of small blinking dots along a labyrinth of lines. She is trying to identify different constellations of stars on her night sky, Orion, Cassiopeia, Crux, Leo and so on. Sometimes a dot starts moving slowly along the line, breaking up a constellation. At first, Saskia gets nervous when this happened, but after two hours of starring at the stars in the dark universe of DCC, she is positively numb. Her brain has experienced a short-circuit.

"That was fast!" Mr. James walks over toward Saskia. Blondie nervously tailing him. She still looks somewhat confused. Saskia jumps up, waking from her slumber. "Well, welcome," he says. "You have difficult shoes to fill. Mr. Pavis, your predecessor, did an imminent job. He prevented several major incidents. The system is so complex and in severe need of serious restoration. It breaks down randomly due to overloading. Not to talk of reoccurring flooding. Or road workers zapping the cables. Well, you know!" Saskia takes an instant liking to Mr. James, but it is clear as daylight that Mr. James and she are never going to become intimate. She finds him utterly unattractive, *and* he is too decent a man to cheat on his wife.

Later at lunch, Saskia asks, "What happened to Mr. Pavis, my predecessor?" Two of her colleagues abruptly get up to leave the lunch table. They don't want to be privy to this conversation.

Mr. James answers that Mr. Pavis had an accident and lost his life. "Just married with his high school sweetheart, and he had his whole life ahead of him."

"What type of accident?" Saskia bravely asks.

"He was killed in a robbery at a gas station near his home. It is so meaningless. Such a loss." Somberness kills their conversation, and shortly afterward, Saskia is back starring at the stars.

This time living in the world above ground amongst the earthlings, Saskia lives alone in a rented room in a corner building located in Hell's Kitchen, adjacent to the Garment District. Her room has a small kitchenette at one end of the room. A door leads to a small toilet. She fixes a shower hose to the tap of the sink and takes a shower almost on top of the toilet, for lack of space. Alternatively, there are shared toilets in the hallway, where two toilettes have been removed and replaced by a plastic shower cabin. The accumulated dirt and scale make it almost unbearable to shower there. Saskia spends her first day at the new place cleaning and ends up showering in her toilet praying not to cause water damage in the building. That would draw unnecessary attention to her.

*

On her first Sunday off, she visits Tony Dapolito Recreation Center in Greenwich Village. Here, she sees Troll and Preacher getting out of the pool, as she gets in. She nods politely to them. They look at each other perplexed. They don't recognize her. In this setting, stripped of their racks, they look almost normal. She wonders, if they have stopped standing in the streets of New York screaming from the top of their lungs.

Saskia is racing back and forth in the pool. She is a very capable swimmer, which was highly unusual, because where she grew up, most kids never learned to swim. Suddenly, when touching the pool coping to make a turnaround, someone grabs hold of her hand, hard. Robin, who has become her new handler, replacing Annona, is towering above her, fully dressed. The lifeguard is yelling to him to leave the pool area. "I am being chased away, but I need to talk to you!" Robin says hurried. "Meet me at the deli on the opposite corner in fifteen minutes!"

Her short hair is still wet, as she enters the deli.

"Having a nice time?" Robin asks ironically. "Please take your time with your mission…"

Saskia replies, "This is my day off. My one day a week off. *And* I have no shower in the establishment you rented for me. By the way!"

After a day or two at DCC, it dawns on Saskia that despite Kate's assurance about knowing the main switch's location, Saskia only knows DCC's whereabouts and that Mr. James heads the technical core of the operation. "Did you tell Kate and the other leaders that, in fact, we do not know where the main switch is? That this operation may take longer than expected because I need to locate the main switch?" Saskia is almost trying to catch her breath in anticipation of the long and relentless run laying ahead of her.

"Kate knows. I don't know if the other leaders know. We are all very busy planning and putting into motion the big attack. There is no time for talking through nitty-gritty details," Robin says somewhat annoyed.

"I would hardly call it a nitty-gritty detail!" Saskia says resigning.

Robin explains, "You need to find the main switch, fast!" It is clear, by now, that Mr. James is not going to fall into her honey trap, or any other trap for that sake. Back at sub-level 3, Kate restates her initial concern that Saskia is simply not pretty enough to work as a honey trap.

Robin continues, "The big attack can happen any day now. We are ready! But we cannot proceed before we know, for sure, that there will be a total black-out when we strike. That is the whole plan. Our plan hinges on you shutting off the electricity. Do you understand?" Robin looks at her intensively in the eyes. Saskia may have overlooked the importance of her mission.

She feels somewhat remorseful, but still manages to reply with simulated authority in her voice. "There is *no* main switch at DCC, if such a switch even existed! Tomorrow, I will try to look at my screens with fresh eyes to see if there, anywhere, is an accumulation of lines, which could represent a cable hub. But please remember, I can only see the networks of Brooklyn on my screens."

On her way back to her hobble, she passes Troll and Preacher, who have put back on their old dirty racks. "Do you know what is about to happen?" Preacher yells and continues, "The city is about to tumble to its grave. Everybody will die!"

Troll chips in, "Yay, yay. Doomsday has come! Doomsday has come!" As always, Troll and Preacher speak the truth. As always, nobody listens.

On her screens, there are six such cable hubs, just in Brooklyn. But Con Edison also supplies Manhattan, the Bronx, Queens, and parts of Westchester County; those networks are on her colleagues' screens. Maybe one of the other boroughs holds the main switch. She probes at lunch in a rather insistent manner, prompting Mike, who oversees the networks of Manhattan, to reply, "There is *one* main switch in my network, but that only turns on and off the electricity in Manhattan. There is no main switch for all the boroughs supplied by ConEd. I think, such a switch is a myth!"

*

About a week after Brady and Lizzy met, a text message ticks in on Brady's phone. *Meet me the same bar as last time at six!* The message is from Lizzy. Brady calls Noah to tell him that Lizzy wants to meet. Brady is so grateful for Lizzy's help. She feels slightly guilty that she told Lizzy a lie about her motives. She told Lizzy that she is tasked with finding the thief, who stole Nefertiti's crown from the Met, when in fact she is helping the "bad guys" now and drafting the unknowing Lizzy to help her.

She knows that Lizzy will get into great trouble and lose her job if anyone finds out that she is helping her. "Look, I found several matches of your mystery woman around Grand Central Station and this strange door in Lexington Avenue that she comes in and out of. I have no idea where the door leads, other than the underground of the station and maybe it's electricity supply. But this woman doesn't work there, I think."

Brady looks at the photos of the woman entering and exiting the Westside door of Grand Central Station. On some of the pictures the woman looks carefully over her shoulder as to check if anyone sees her. On two photos, she is seen with Ava and Max. "Her children, hum?"

"Maybe. Probably."

After chatting about the Langmore case, Sullivan, Davis, and Benson, Brady talks a bit about the woman on the photos. "I tell you why I am suspicious. Firstly, this woman worked in Glenmore's household, when Mrs. Glenmore committed suicide, which Dr. Glenmore vehemently denied happened. To be honest, I agree with him. Who goes to a dinner party, and then to bed. Then gets up in the middle of the night and jumps out of the window. Another case that we will never get to the bottom of. Anyway, this woman..."

Brady violently points at the photos. "This woman was there, and she was at the raid of the Langmore Hospital, outside. We caught each other's eyes, but I was too busy to take proper notice. And now! She turns out to have stolen Nefertiti's crown without anyone alerting the police!"

"Wow! She is like a master thief or something!" Lizzy doesn't comprehend that Brady is working on more than just the Met investigation. She thinks it is a coincidence that it is the same woman.

Before they part, Lizzy restates, "If you want to find her, you must watch the Grand Central Westside door at Lexington Avenue. She keeps on popping up there."

The subsequent morning, Brady sets up her surveillance station from a highchair in the window frame of the café on the opposite side of Lexington Avenue.

*

In the early afternoon, Saskia decides to go back into the underground and personally deliver the news of the Manhattan main switch to Kate and Robin. As Saskia approaches the door on Lexington Avenue, Brady gets off her highchair in the window frame of the café on the opposite side of Lexington Avenue. She stands and watches carefully as Saskia looks over her shoulder, knocks three times twice and the door opens. She vanishes.

Brady is so excited about her observation that she forgets to take out her phone and capture the moment. She calls Noah, who commands, "Stay there! When she comes out, you follow her."

Saskia's journey through the underground takes more than three hours. She runs through the argument again and again in her head in preparation of her talk with Kate and Robin. Saskia reasons that shutting off the electricity of Manhattan alone should be enough for the successful completion of the attack plan.

"Okay," Kate says, somewhat surprised at seeing Saskia back at sub-level 3. "Can you turn off the main switch of Manhattan, then? I think that is enough. Most certainly!" Kate leans back into her chair. "You did it again, Saskia. You are fucking amazing. I will report to the leaders that we stick to the schedule. You need to shut off the electricity tomorrow at precisely three in the morning in the city that needs light 24/7. You know, we have numerous studies that show that when cities experience blackouts, it is only a matter of time before they fall prey to dark side, the crooks that come out of the woodworks."

Saskia is bewildered. "But I am not working nightshift tomorrow!"

Kate gets up, as she says, "You will make it work. I don't care, if you blow your cover in the process, as long as you switch off the electricity tomorrow at three in the morning and keep it switched off!"

Just before Kate turns around to leave, she asks, "Do you need something from us?"

Saskia is thinking on her toes. "Yes! I need some special forces to come and rescue me."

Kate smiles. "To be honest that is *not* a priority."

Saskia insists, "Only if you take over control of DCC, can we make sure that the electricity stays off. I cannot singlehandedly fight off everybody, guards, police and who knows. They will do anything in their power to put the power back on. I need reinforcement, if we are to succeed in keeping the electricity shut off."

Robin walks Saskia to the door leading to the maze of the underground. He stops in front of the door and says, "I will make sure there is reinforcement for you. This is too important a piece in the mission for it to slip." Before bidding her the last farewell, Robin says, "Saskia! The reinforcement you solicit will come disguised as NYPD Special Forces, who will turn sides during the attack and start protecting us! That is the work of Raven and others."

Saskia is running. She barely makes it to sub-level 2 before the doors shut for the night. As she runs along the swallow passage at the edge of the plant floor, she passes Annona, who, upon recognizing her, swiftly looks the other way. Saskia knocks hard on the door of Ava, who opens it and hushes her. "You are waking everybody!"

Saskia whispers while catching her breath, "You and Max must gather your stuff and come with me. Now!" Ava has become a grown woman during the time in the underground. This is not just prompted by the passage of time, but also by the responsibilities resting on her shoulders.

Ava waves frantically for Saskia to enter her room. "What are you talking about? No one is allowed to leave their posts. The attack will happen tomorrow!"

Saskia leans forward toward Ava wanting to embrace her, as she says, "I know. That is why I have come to get you. I have a rented room in the city, where we can all stay."

Ava takes a couple of steps backward and looks at her. "The city is no safer than the underground. Everything above ground will be pulverized by the attack. Also, your rental room."

Saskia shakes her head. "You don't understand. We need to stick together. It doesn't matter where we are when the attack happens. As long as we are together. Anyway, if everything above ground is pulverized, then the underground will collapse at the weight of crushing buildings, roads and bridges. The city will fall into the hell hole."

Her children are the only ones, Saskia can hold on to keep her from going under. Her sole mission is that the three of them remain united amidst the rapidly approaching chaos and carnage. Ava is apprehensive, but still, she follows Saskia into Max's room. After a short while, they are standing with a backpack each, ready to ascend the underground. As they walk toward the exit at the far end of the plant floor, they pass Annona again. At first, she stops to observe them. Then she turns around and acts as if she didn't see them. She is letting them off the hook. Indifference and unlawfulness foreshadowing the pending civil war have started to fester everywhere, also in the underground.

On their way back to the hovel on the corner of the 8th Avenue and West 37th Street, Saskia notices a woman on the other side of the street, who is intensely observing her. First, she looks back at the woman, but then she ignores her, as she starts talking to her children. In the meantime, the woman on the other side of the street continues to stare at her. Saskia thinks she may have seen her before but since living in the underground, Saskia has met so many new people that she has given up trying to remember who's who. Saskia feels as if the woman follows them, but she knocks it out of her head.

Ava and Max are in awe with the entrance hall. "Whoa!" Ava says looking up at the stucco carvings in the ceiling.

"I am sorry to say that it is only the entrance of this building that is this impressive." Saskia does not want them to have too high expectations. "My room, our room, is really just a room. It is dark and run down. But I have cleaned it and stocked it with good food." Both her children's faces light up at the prospect of getting a homemade meal from their mother. Regardless, how poorly mothers cook, children always recall their mothers' homemade meals with fondness.

Saskia opens the door to her rental and lets Ava and Max enter before her. She remains outside for a short while to turn around to see if she is followed by the woman from the street. She has the eerie feeling that someone is observing them. True enough, at the end of the corridor,

Brady is standing. She makes no effort to hide herself or the fact that she has been following them. In that split second, Saskia considers, if she should walk down the corridor and ask Brady who is she and what she wants. But Ava and Max are calling her to get in.

Once in the room, Max pulls the top madras onto the floor. "I can sleep here!" Max says. Saskia smiles. She is too tired to cook, but forces herself to succumb to her children's begging. *After all, who knows when they will next time be able to cook and enjoy homemade food?* she thinks, while cringing at the thought this might become their last supper. They might lose each other altogether once the strike hits. Before shutting her eyes, Saskia thinks of who the woman, who followed them, could be. She feels she has seen the woman before, but she cannot recall where. Before she knows it, Saskia, too, is in deep sleep.

The next day, Brady knocks on Saskia's door. She has brought fresh breakfast bread with her. "I am sorry to disturb you," Brady says apologetic, when realizing she has woken Saskia up. "You probably noticed that I followed you yesterday." Saskia is totally taken aback. She has strict orders not to interact with any earthlings, but she can hardly run. There is nowhere to run to. "I startled you!" Brady continues, "Look! I will get straight to the point. We met at the Glenmore's and then again outside the Langmore Hospital. Do you remember? I was the principal investigator of the Langmore Hospital." Brady looks at Saskia inspecting her to see her reaction.

"I know, who you are now!" Saskia exclaims as she suddenly recalls that she sent all the evidence gathered on the Langmore Hospital to the woman standing opposite her. "You are with the police?" Saskia asks, while almost breaking into a panic sweat at the thought of having been called out by the police.

Brady sees Saskia is getting nervous and hurries to say, "I am no longer with the police. I was tossed out on ass and elbows for some insane accusation of wrongdoing that I didn't do! Well, I did it to bring the swindler to justice. But I am not proud of it..." Now, Saskia calms down.

"Right, right... Well, please come in."

Max sits up on the madras on the floor rubs his eyes, while Ava moans something incomprehensible. Saskia makes a sign to hush Brady, and they proceed to the other end of the room, where the kitchenette is, to brew some coffee. Brady and Saskia do some small talk about the dire living conditions in the building commenting on the single mothers living there with young children. Saskia asks, "What are you doing now? I mean, you left the police..."

"I set up a private eye office, in the Garment District. Not far from here."

"So, you are still chasing the bad guys?"

Brady doesn't know what to answer. She can't say that she is now doing the bidding of the bad guys. "It's complicated. I worked in an insurance frauds department for years. Then I left to join the police because I felt I could make a real difference. Bring the bad guys to justice. But law enforcement and the law don't always deliver justice. Actually, I don't know what they do, but it isn't justice. The police and broader law enforcement are just righteous, elevated in their fucking righteousness." Brady pauses. Saskia can see that Brady gets emotional.

Brady continues, "Everybody wants to think they are doing the right thing. Everybody wants to think they can separate right from wrong and that *they* are sitting on the moral high ground. In fact, there is no right or wrong. In fact, it is the very people who think they are sitting on the moral high ground, those very people walk around with blinkers. They are more interest in persuading others of their own righteousness than exploring all the facets of life. They want to force feed their righteous views to everybody else, rather than explore and understand the world." Brady is still emotional. Her disillusion with the ways of the world is profound. Without many words, the two women find that they have more in common than most people.

With no further ado, Brady asks, "You are the one who sent me the evidence on the Langmore Hospital, right?" Saskia is in shock. She doesn't know, what to say. Brady continues, "You wanted me to catch Dr. Hinnemann and his accomplishes, right?" Saskia still doesn't answer. Her eyes are trying to find a safe place to fixate on. They sit there, both, in their own thoughts, almost catatonic, starring into the air.

Brady volunteers, "I was fired before I could get to the bottom of the case. I was fired to prevent me from getting to the bottom of the case and bringing these crooks to justice!" Saskia looks up at her horrified at the realization that the Langmore investigation was shut down by the police, without justice. Brady continues, "These people, wealthy old money people, have infiltrated the police, high up, and somehow, they dug up dirt on me, from way back, when I worked with insurance fraud. You see, back then, this wealthy guy, also old money, burned down a large housing complex, when the financial crisis hit in 2008. You remember, the Fannie Mae and Freddie Mac and their risky *government-sponsored* securities." Brady feels release as she volunteers her story that she never shared with anyone else before. In fact, she doesn't understand why all this information is pouring out of her now. Maybe she feels, Saskia also operates in the gray zone of real justice.

"Anyway, I bent the rules slightly to make sure this guy was unable to claim his humongous insurance and eventually he did get some kind of fine. The fine, of course, didn't measure up to his crime of insurance fraud, but still... I made a powerful enemy in that moment, who seems to be working with other power people in the city. In the end, when the crooked policemen, Sullivan and Davis, wanted rid of me, they somehow liaised with these powerful people. Or maybe the powerful people liaise with Sullivan and Davis to shut down the Langmore investigation by having me fired from the force? You see, Sullivan and Davis are very ambitious, and they also wanted rid of me so that they can advance off the back of my case, our case! Anyway, who knows... By some freak accident sudden the old money enemy from my past and Sullivan and Davis share the objective to get rid of me from the investigation and the force. Maybe they have always been working together helping each other to get ahead of the game." Brady is still in shock when recalling the chaotic course of events that turned her life upside down.

Brady continues, "Well, I wanted to follow the money trail, in the Langmore case. I wanted to look at the broader picture. Investigate who was behind the human trafficking of illegal migrants. I wanted to find out if there was money laundering taking place. You know. I wanted to reveal *everything*. Bring it all into light. But I was stopped by this concoction of criminals working together across both crime and law enforcement." Brady is biting her lower lip indicating she has unresolved issues bottled up inside of her.

Suddenly, Saskia exclaims, almost as if talking to herself, "It is unbelievable! Just unbelievable! I should have known."

Brady feels bad that Saskia went through the risk and hardship of gathering evidence to see little, in any, justice done, and the real villains walk free. Brady tries to console Saskia by saying, "You know what the irony of all this is? I continued working on the Langmore case after I was forced out of NYPD, and I traced the financing of the Langmore Hospital to Mr. Marlowe and his associates. You may have heard of him. He did a big interview in the New York Times about the good deeds of the hospital, when in fact he is heavily invested in the hospital and just looking out for himself, his investments and associates. Literally, Mr. Marlowe and his associates financed the whole hospital."

Saskia shakes her head. She doesn't read newspapers. The only stories she hears are the ones swirling around in the underground. Brady continues, "Anyway, the irony is that one day, out of the blue, Mr. Marlowe looks me up at my office to investigate who are behind the unraveling of Langmore and Dr. Hinnemann!"

Saskia stares at her. "I guess that is me!"

Brady nods her head in an affirmative manner. "Yes, I guess it is. I kind of knew it was you, but I had no idea where to find you. And then yesterday you walked back through that door on Lexington Avenue, and I was able to follow you and your kids from there!"

Abruptly, Saskia gets up, as she realizes she doesn't have time for talking with Brady about this case that she thought she had already dealt with. Right now, she has a war to wage. She realizes that if Brady rats her out to Mr. Marlowe and his people, she will be in deep trouble. She might, even, be prevented from going through with her mission, and then the whole underground will come after her. If she doesn't turn off the electricity, the mobs of New York will hunt her down to the end of the world. Anyone and everybody will look for her. Nowhere will be safe if she doesn't turn off the electricity and thereby completes her last mission for the racketed world going to hell. She must hold off Brady, Mr. Marlowe and his people until *after* the big attack, after which nothing matters anymore. She must not be late for work.

"What do you think of the whole thing?" Saskia probes Brady, while trying to remain calm. Saskia continues, "I mean. Don't you think that the people behind these atrocities should be convicted? They are trafficking illegal migrants and robbing them of their organs. I suspect that some of the migrants might even have been killed in the process."

Brady looks at her. "Of course, I think, they should be brought to justice, but that is no longer my job. Is it? I am no longer with the police. Instead, I have been solicited by the criminals, who I was pursuing, to find the source of the denouncement, and that's you! Sitting right in front of me!"

Saskia says, "Okay. Calm down! I am not the villain here. These people want to kill me."

Brady says in a dry tone of voice, "Probably."

Saskia says, "This is insane. The whole world is in upheaval, and we are sitting here discussing some payback of a crazy rich guy."

Brady asks, "What do you mean 'upheaval'?"

Saskia is contemplating if she should let Brady in on her mission. Making Brady complicit, might prevent Brady from throwing Saskia to the lions. Saskia is caught between a rock and a hard place, when she reluctantly starts explaining, "Yes, upheaval... I am working with some *other* powerful people, who are planning to topple the political and economic leadership of the city."

Brady leans back. "Okay that explains..."

Saskia tilts her head. "That explains what?"

Brady continues, somewhat off guard, "The only thing linking you to both the crime scenes of the Glenmore's and the Langmore Hospital is that both episodes involve high net value individuals, who are deeply entangled in the "old money" establishment of New York. You worked as a cleaner at the Glenmore household and then you pop up again outside in front of the Langmore Hospital the day we do the big raid of the hospital. The last revelation that confirmed my suspicion was when I met some people working at the Langmore, who talked about you being at the Langmore in the basement on a run, when the alarm sounded. I still don't know where Nefertiti's crown fits into all this."

Saskia gets defensive. "I didn't know that they were doing these horrible crimes at the Langmore Hospital. I stumbled across those crimes, and then I wanted to get to the bottom of the case, because I felt terrible for those migrants."

Brady says, "Very honorable. I don't doubt your noble intentions, but the whole thing blew up in my face. Even the illegal migrants seemed to support Dr. Hinnemann and the Langmore Hospital. Suddenly, everybody seemed to be against me and my colleague Lizzy."

Saskia says, "That is not my fault. I mean, I was trying to do the right thing. I hope you don't deliver me to these people. Who are they? No. Don't tell me. There is no time for this." Brady looks confused.

Saskia includes Brady in the imminent war plans to hopefully prevent Brady from handing her over to Mr. Marlowe and his people who are looking to revenge themselves on her. "As I said, I *also* work for some powerful people. These people want to topple the establishment, which includes this Mr. Marlowe, by the sound of things," Saskia says and stops. She already said this, but she hardly dares to venture beyond. Still, she convinces herself that the immediate task of shutting off the electricity must be completed, tonight.

After tonight, once in war, who knows where they will be. Giving the full story will help her convince Brady to let her go. After all, Saskia is just a hand puppet. Nevertheless, the whole rebellion hinges on her completing this important assignment. "There are hundreds, maybe thousands, of homeless people in this city. Well, they *were* homeless. Then they got sucked into the underground."

Saskia pauses and continues, "We are planning a civil war that will start right now with a big attack that echoes across other big cities in the Unites States. You see, you cannot hand me over to Mr. Marlowe and his lot, because if we want some justice in the world, we need to topple the establishment."

Brady looks contemplative. "It sounds to me like you are replacing one establishment with another, this underground. I am not sure it makes a whole lot of difference." Even though, Brady talks like she is disillusioned, Saskia and she share their pursuit for bringing the people who have wracked havoc to their lives and society to justice. In fact, Saskia's rant has sparked hope for a better future in Brady.

Saskia tries to reason. "Wealth is accumulated in very few hands. People are starving to death. Poverty is spreading like a contagious pandemic working its way up to the middle class. Anyway, whether you support this rebellion, I *need* to go to work this afternoon. There is no time to waste."

With that, she gets up, turning to see if Brady tries to stop her. Brady doesn't. Daringly, Saskia asks, "Can you look out for my children, please, while I am gone? I will be back tomorrow morning." Desperation flows from her eyes as she pleads with Brady for help. They agreed to meet the following day at noon by the Bow Bridge in Central Park.

It is one-thirty p.m. by the time Saskia walks over to Ava and Max, who are now sitting on the bed, to give them a hug. She kisses them. "You heard everything. This mission is important. I need to get it right. And then we run. The three of us. Run! Get the hell out of this city that will fall to the ground." Saskia sheds a tear, while she hugs them, hard. Suddenly, she fears, she may never see them again. "I love you. I love you. We must survive. We must stay together. I'll meet you tomorrow at noon by the Bow Bridge in Central Park."

Walking along the streets, Saskia tries to focus on the pressing task at hand. But she is easily distracted. She looks around the streets at the people going about their daily errands, grabbing lunch, picking up children from school, meeting loved ones, going home, *etcetera*.

The majority of individuals aspire to align their lives harmoniously with what is considered "normal." They cluster around the widely accepted values and objectives, seeking a shared sense of stability. Paradoxically, as more people gravitate toward this concept of normality, it often transforms into apathetic conformity and even intolerance.

Over time, conformity tightens its grip, resembling a restrictive straitjacket for those who exist beyond its boundaries. This predicament can drive those who are excluded from conformity's grasp to a point of desperation, leading them to embark on a civil war as a last-ditch effort to secure a life that is both dignified and meaningful.

In New York, the majority finds themselves marginalized from "normality," unable to access fundamental life resources such as employment, education, and healthcare. As these homeless individuals roam the streets and fall into the abyss of the underground, they become complicit in pursuing civil unrest and war as their final recourse to attain the essential and purposeful lives they seek. Both normality and conformity convey an image of an aspirational existence, yet paradoxically breed intolerance toward anyone standing outside these boundaries.

As Saskia walks through the entrance to Con Edison, her blood is pumping, and her heart is beating fast. She is nervous. The black-out is not scheduled for several hours, so she needs to calm herself, and place her faith in the underground, herself, Kate, Robin, Raven and all the others instrumental in the big attack. She has a long night shift ahead of her. Recognizing that Saskia is tired, Mr. James proposes that she takes a quick nap before most of the personnel checks out that evening leaving her and Mike to oversee all the networks. She can't sleep. She is laying in the bunkbed starring at the ceiling. She hopes her mission is completed without any loss of lives at the DCC.

Still completely sleep deprived, she is sitting starring at the twinkling stars on her monitors, when her phone vibrates at two forty-five. She gets up with a shock. This is it! It's now! She starts wandering around DCC, stopping at the monitors furthest away, when she yells loudly to Mike, "Come over here! Something looks off! Can you check it out, please?"

Mike, also in a slumber, gets up frantically and makes his way over to her. "It looks normal to me..." he says curious while continuing, "What did you see?"

Saskia doesn't know what to say but stutters, "I—I don't know. Something blinking and then suddenly it disappeared altogether. Like it was shut off." They both stare at the monitor when Saskia points. "Around here, I think."

Mike leans closer to the screen to inspect it, while confirming, "Right, yes. I see."

Saskia starts walking further and further away till she leaps toward Mike's monitors with the Manhattan network. She grabs the controller, places the cursor over the central Manhattan electricity hub on the screen and enters the delete code she was given by Robin to shut off the electricity at the heart of the city's network. Mike turns around and runs toward her yelling, "What are you doing? Have you lost her mind!" He pushes her aside. She falls over his large chair. Mike looks back and forth between Saskia on the floor and his screen that is blinking red and sounding an alarm. "What the fuck!" he yells. The electricity is off. Saskia gets up and runs toward the main door. She presses a red bottom next to the door to keep the door shut. Now, no one can get in or out.

At this point, it becomes clear to Mike that Saskia is consciously sabotaging the electricity supply of the city. After desperately trying to unsuccessfully enter different counter codes to get the electricity back on, Mike moves toward the door. She doesn't know how he intends to apprehend her. He is much larger than her, both taller and wider, but he is not fit, like she is. They start what looks like a dance. Mike moves slowly toward Saskia. She edges her way along the tables with the screens, while she pushes the large gamer chairs out into the middle of room, where Mike is standing. He gets annoyed with dancing with her, as he starts to groan and thrust himself at her. Saskia makes a fast step aside. Mike falls to the floor. He gets up again, now red in his head with fury.

They continue the dance for what seems an eternity. Until, suddenly, light in the glass dome above them is turned on. Controlling one of the essential lifelines of the city, Con Edison has an emergency generator that turns on the lights only in the building. This makes Mike stop up and yell toward the dome above. "Hallo! Hallo! Is there anyone up there? Help us! We are stuck here. I am stuck here with a crazy person who shut off the electricity in Manhattan!" Con Edison guards and employees gather above them in the large dome. They can see them but not hear them. The dome is made of bulletproof glass offering maximum protection of the DCC, the heart of the operation and city. In another attempt to protect the DCC from outside attacks, once you push the red bottom next to the door, DCC is completely sealed off to the outside. No one can get in, or out. She can see people banging heavily on the glass and screaming loudly, but no sound gets through the thick glass. All the while, Mike is jumping up and down pointing at Saskia yelling, "It was her! It was her who shut off the electricity!" No one can hear him.

Suddenly, Mike turns to Saskia, grabs her around the neck and squeezes hard. She feels herself losing consciousness as the guards desperately pull out their guns and start shooting at the glass, but the glass doesn't budge, not even an inch. Only a select few at Con Edison have access to the DCC once it's been shut down in emergency. Even fewer can overrule the shutdown and restore electricity once the delete code is entered. Therefore, when the police arrive about fifteen minutes after three in the morning, they too are shut out of DCC. The dome above becomes crowded with guards, police officers, and employees all trying to catch a glimpse of the action below. But there is nothing to see. Only Mike, still hammering away on his computer, and Saskia lying unconscious on the floor.

After about half an hour, Mr. James rushes into the DCC wearing his pajamas under a raincoat. He runs over to Saskia, screaming for someone to call 911. She regains consciousness but remains lying on the floor. The guards restrain Mike as he frantically tries to break free yelling, "It wasn't me! It wasn't me!"

Later, Saskia wakes up in an unfamiliar hospital with a syringe in her right hand. Blood has stained the clean white sheets. Waking up, it dawns on her what she has done. She is sad and desperately scared. The hospital is immersed in chaos. The only reason she made it to the hospital is that her strike was one of the first in the big attack. It occurred before the city had fallen to the underground. Now, the hospital is filled to the rim with people weeping, mourning and missing limbs. Each scream penetrates her body and fills her soul of sorrow. Saskia is lying in bed becoming more and more conscious of the magnitude of events that occurred while she was locked up in DCC and the hospital. She knows she must rejoice her children. She arranged with Brady that they would all meet on the Bow Bridge in Central Park at noon the day after the big attack. She doesn't know, how many days have passed since she was hospitalized. But she does know that there is no time to lose.

A curtain separates her bed from the other beds lined up in the ER. A police officer stands guard on the other side of the curtain at the end of her bed. She doesn't know what to make of it. Is the office there to protect or arrest her? Regardless, she needs to get out of the hospital and back to Ava and Max. A nurse enters to checks on her, asking if she's all right. As Saskia tries to respond, she realizes her throat hurts. The nurse is gone before Saskia can mutter a word.

As soon as the nurse leaves, Saskia gently pulls the syringe out of her right hand. The pain of seeing the needle exiting her skin hurts more than the actual physical pain. She quietly gets out of bed and sneaks down on the floor opening the door in the nightstand. Behind the door, on a shelf, her clothes are neatly folded and placed. She sits on the floor putting on her clothes without making a sound. Anyway, the tumult and noise around her muffles everything. Luckily, just as the nurse returns to check up on her, she is called away by a police investigator, who enters ER asking how Saskia is doing. While they are talking, Saskia sneaks behind the curtain to the patient next to her and continues until, about five beds away, a patient yells, "Who are you?" With that Saskia runs out into the middle of ER and toward the door, down the corridor and stairway, and out of the hospital. A policeman and the investigator are right behind her. She is running. Running for her life. Somewhere along the way, she loses the policeman and the investigator. She stops to catch her breath. She reaches her pockets searching for her phone. It is gone. *Shit!* she thinks.

She is running toward Central Park, but she is totally disoriented as the cityscape is completely transformed. As dawn breaks, the darkness of the night lifts revealing the annihilation of the city. With a new day, Saskia knows that she must have missed the day of their agreed meeting. The air is thick with cement dust, choking her throat and lungs. Cars have collided. Buildings have collapsed. People mummified in cement dust wander around like statues crying and screaming angrily at the world. Orphaned children walk around weeping. Other children sit silently suffering in total shock. There are no landmarks left to show her the way to Central Park, Bow Bridge and her children. She is fumbling in the dark.

After several hours, when she reaches the edge of Central Park, her body is aching. She enters the park, which was, seemingly, one of several centers of fighting during the big attack. The park is littered with dead bodies. She stumbles across battered bodies calling out of help. Fixated on getting the Bow Bridge, Brady ignores everything around her. The bridge has fallen like everything else around her. Her children and Brady are nowhere to be found. They probably waited at Bow Bridge, as they agree. Maybe they waited for a day or two and then decided to leave the city. With the realization that she has arrived too late, she collapses. Sleep startles her. When she wakes up, in the early evening, she recognizes, she will not find her children in the city. Saskia gets up and starts walking into the fallen city.

Chapter Nine

The city is pulverized. As a new day dusks, the thick layer of cement engulfing the city reveals the sun as a distant hint of light. Saskia holds both hands out in front of her, fumbling her way through the dense cement air. She is unable to breathe, choking, and suffocating. Yet, she keeps moving forward, toward her children. No one is following her anymore. She is moving into the city and toward the apocalypse, moving toward death. The further into the city she moves, the more death and destruction she encounters.

After a short while, decimated with exhaustion, Saskia slows her pace. A little later, she drags her feet after her. Later yet, she is crawling. At first, she doesn't notice the dead bodies dotting the gray landscape in bright red. At first, she doesn't hear the cries and screams of agony from bodies trapped under buildings. At one point, she stumbles over a leg sticking out from under a building block. Upon contact with her, the leg immediately starts to wriggle in a cry for help. She looks at the leg horrified. She knows that, somewhere, a real person is attached to the leg. Yet, she cannot feel any human empathy. She only feels horror and disgust. She hurries away and onward.

Toward the evening, Saskia realizes she is starving. But there is no food anywhere to be found. She sits down on a building block. Stopping up in the middle of the frenzied search for her children, it dawns on her that she will never find her children in the city. If they survived this total annihilation, they will be elsewhere.

Saskia feels tired, exhausted, as a deep and deceitful sleep creeps up on her. In that moment, she realizes that if she gives in to the sleep, she will never wake again. Rather, she will slowly and painlessly suffocate in her sleep, passing on to a brighter and better world beyond this one that humanity has completely destroyed. Weeping, Saskia lifts her heavy body off the building block. She contemplates for a short second which way to go but decides that it doesn't matter. The best way, the only way, is forward.

After some hours, Saskia arrives at the edge of a river. Somewhere in the far distance, she sees what looks like the George Washington Bridge collapsed into the Hudson River. Building blocks have fallen into the river. Above the massive building blocks, shadows of mummified people are moving, trying to cross to the other side of the Hudson River. Saskia knows that once she crosses the river and turns her back to the city, she has effectively given up all hope of finding her children in the rubbles. She prays that her children are amongst the survivors who left the city.

Saskia decides she, too, must get to the other side. Behind her, as the night breaks, Manhattan descends into total blackness. In front of her, along the coast of Brooklyn, a string of lights appeared as shimmering stars of hope. Behind her, massive buildings are still collapsing at an ear-deafening noise. By now, she is both deaf and numb. She no longer hears the noise of the collapsing city. The city is not safe. In a few days, Manhattan will be all but completely destroyed.

Before she knows it, she joins the hundreds of walking dead scattered across the building blocks in the river. No one talks. Everyone is climbing, crawling, and clinging onto the jagged cement blocks, trying to make it to the other side that remains intact. Some people on the other side of the Hudson River are holding torches throwing rays of light across the river. Other people are in rowing boats with lanterns, rocking back and forth. There are too few boats and too many walking dead.

At one point, Saskia collapses in a puddle of pebble stones indented between two massive building blocks. Unwillingly, she resigns to a deep sleep that is stronger and more insistent than she is. Her eyelids feel heavy. *I flee this world for a moment to gain strength to continue at a later time*, she thinks. Just before closing her eyes, she observes herself at a distance. Her consciousness is hovering above her lifeless body tossed randomly over a cement slack. She sees herself closing her eyes. If they remain closed, her soul will ascend from its earthly vessel. All that will be left to testify to her life on earth is this empty vessel; a slab of rotten meat that lies stretched across a block of stone. She closes her eyes unable to fight death any longer.

Someone is clapping her cheeks, hard. She gasps for air while opening her eyes. For a split second, Saskia thinks that maybe it was all just a terrible nightmare. Maybe it never happened. Reality seems too unreal for any of this to have happened. Someone is pouring freshwater into her mouth and over her face. She gasps for air and life. It dawns on her that she is alive in this nightmare of a life. Someone hauled her back from the dead. She is back in living hell. She fumbles and grabs hold of a man's arm while staring disoriented into his eyes. "She is alive! She is alive!" the man yells. Other people climb over the building blocks, hurrying at snail's pace. They lift her onto a stretcher, tying some clothes to keep her body fixed on the stretcher as they meticulously move across the jagged surface. She is too exhausted to fear that they could fall or drop her over one of the hard pointed corners of a building block.

Once on the other side, an elderly woman gives her a cup of freshwater and some bread. She drinks and eats in desperation and in silence. She looks up at the woman and utters her first words since in the DCC. "Thank you." The woman smiles and lifts Saskia to her feet. Slowly, they move along a cobbled street dating back to the 1890s. The old street and its brick buildings are a stark reminder of how transient human lives are. The buildings, like the tress in the forest, stand the test of time, while human beings are just testing time.

Saskia is welcomed into a wooden terraced house. The house is painted in a rusty red color with black window frames and a black main door. It is a small house. All the houses along the street are identical, but they all adorn different colors. There is something artificial about the street. It is as if the building entrepreneur wanted to reassemble the beach town of his childhood but did so with cheap and makeshift materials, in the middle of bustling Jersey City. The neighborhood is lower middle class, but prices have risen moderately due to the flight of the middle classes from New York City into the surrounding hinterland. Nevertheless, the neighborhood also testifies to the increasing distress and poverty of the population at large, as it succumbed to increasing gang violence, almost daily random shootings, drugs, and homelessness.

Today, in the face of an epic disaster, people have come together to help each other by opening their homes to total strangers offering them shelter and food. Saskia lies down on the single bed in the room of an adolescent girl. The room has My Little Pony wallpaper that has been almost entirely covered by posters of different idols, none of whom Saskia recognizes. She falls into a deep sleep, dreaming that she is rejoined and rejoiced by Ava and Max. While still asleep, tears of relief and happiness run down her cheeks. When she wakes up from her dream in the early morning hours, those very same tears are now of sadness and sorrow.

Saskia gets up. For the first time since leaving the hospital, she feels her body. She feels every bone in her body aching. She is battered and bruised. She moves slowly into the heart of the house, the kitchen, where several people of all ages are sitting and chatting in low voices. They have been up all night, and are, now, surrounded around a warm breakfast. When Saskia enters the kitchen, a man gets up and fetches some water and food for her. He places it on the table, pulls a chair out and opens his right hand to bid her welcome to the table. Saskia sits down and eats in silence.

Everybody is looking at her. Whenever she looks up and catches someone's eyes, that person smiles with pity back at her. The woman of the house, who brought her home with her, enters the kitchen and says, "You can stay here for as long as I wish. Just stay here until you are well and know where to go." Saskia is deeply grateful for her not posing any prying questions. All she wants is to be left alone. Alone to suffer and grieve.

After a couple of days, Saskia becomes eager to search for her children. She is restless. "I have to leave now and go look for my daughter and son," she explains at breakfast, when only the woman and daughter are present. The rest of the family and many other people from the street, neighborhood, city, and region have crossed over into Manhattan to scavenge for people still alive.

The woman explains, "There is a large missing person center near the PATH that NamUs and the local police set up. There is a data center there, where you can go online to see if your children have tried to get in touch with you. You can also talk to workers from Amber Alert, who specialize in finding lost children. You can put a search out for your children through Amber Alert."

The young teenage girl, whose room Saskia is camping in, gets up and says, "I will take you there! We can leave whenever you are ready."

About half an hour later, Saskia and the teenage girl cautiously leave the safety of the rusty red wooden house, carefully navigating through the fog of dust until the outline of a massive tent emerges before them. The closer they get to the tent, the more people are congregating in the streets. There are four entries into the tent, all heavily guarded by armed soldiers. After two hours of standing in line, Saskia stands face-to-face with a young soldier. "What's your name?"

Saskia suddenly thinks that she might be wanted by the authorities. On the other hand, if she does not give her real name, she will never find her children. Nervously she gives her real name. "Saskia Winslow." The soldier notes the name on a piece of paper and lets her enter the tent.

Inside the tent, there are thousands of people wandering around. Hundreds of computers are lined up on top of tiny low tables that look like school desks. There is an expansive area with metal bunk beds next to an eating area. Everywhere there are staffers in bright colored vests and jackets with the large letters reading Amber Alert, Red Cross, ShelterBox, Mercy, and so on. There is a multitude of organizations, volunteers, and regular citizens running to the aid of the survivors. Saskia gets a rush of gratitude until she recalls and asks herself, where were all these organizations and people when we needed them to help us out of poverty, famine, desperation, and the hell hole! Where were they when she and her children were sitting in Grand Central Station and had nowhere to go, no food and no future?

Saskia is anxious to find a free computer. Eventually, she accesses her email account, but there is no mail from Ava and Max. The only message is from her mother in

Kentucky, titled *Are you alive?* Quickly, Saskia responds to her mother, asking if there's any word from Ava and Max. Saskia stares at the screen, as if willing her children or mother to contact her at that very moment.

A man in a light blue "All Hands and Hearts" sweatshirt approaches her. "Can I help you?" he asks gently. Saskia remains lost in her thoughts, stirring at the computer screen. He places a comforting hand on her shoulder, causing her to startle. "I am looking for my children. Ava and Max..." she says, still fixated on the screen.

The man offers, "Come with me to the Amber Alert center. You can register your children as missing there, and they will try to match them using their data registration, street cameras, and facial recognition software. It is all very sophisticated, and we *will* find your children."

Saskia follows the man, and after another two hours, she finds herself sitting with an Amber Alert man at a desk with a large computer. They input all the necessary details, including online photos of both children, which the software scans and searches across all data and cameras in the U.S. The man in the yellow jacket sighs. "I am sorry, but there is no match." He quickly adds, "It doesn't necessarily mean anything. It's still too early to tell. They could still be out there somewhere. All street cameras in Manhattan were turned off shortly before the attack, which has affected other parts of New York state. But there's still hope for your children."

Saskia stares intensely at the screen searching for any overlooked detail. Then she asks, "What do I do now? Wait? And for how long?"

The man gives her an understanding look, even though he doesn't understand. Then he says, "Look, the streets are full of military vehicles that all have cameras. There are also drones with cameras everywhere. Data keeps on coming in. New people are discovered every hour, every minute. You will have to check again tomorrow."

Saskia looks at him bewildered. "So, I leave the tent and start all over tomorrow? Waiting in line for hours to check if new data has come that tells me if they are alive, and where they were last seen?"

The man nods affirmatively and says, "I know it sounds frustrating, but what else can you do?" Saskia gets up with a deep sigh and walks away.

A determined young woman from ShelterBox, her short hair bleached, strides purposefully up to Saskia. "I overheard your conversation with Ben, from Amber Alert. You'll find yourself going in circles if you keep returning here every day. It is endless. It doesn't lead anywhere," the young woman explains.

Saskia is grateful for her honesty. "So, what do I do then? Should I just wander the streets and search my children there?" she asks.

The woman responds, "An elderly man mentioned to me yesterday a military data center operated by DISA, somewhere on a secret location in Maryland. They've got real-time data on all citizens, gathered from various cameras, including private security cameras in stores, parking lots, computers. They process and correlate all those images in real time. That would be your best shot. The military has the most up-to-date surveillance system, and it is nationwide."

Saskia looks at her puzzled, questioning, "But where exactly is that place?" As the woman starts to move away, she says, "The man mentioned Hagerstown. You should give that a try! I would do that if I were in your shoes."

Saskia doesn't bother to go back to the rusty red wooden house to get her few remaining things and bid farewell to the family that nursed and nurtured her back to life. She decides that finding Ava and Max takes precedence over everything else. She heads straight for Hagerstown.

She walks down random streets looking for a van or car that she can steal. Most vehicles are gone. Saskia presumes that they are used for the rescue mission, or maybe someone else stole them before she could get to it. It is quite obvious that Saskia is looking for a car to steal as she swiftly proceeds down the street. At one point, she gets into a station car, without bothering to close its door, she starts to fiddle with the emission to see if she can get it started. The car makes a roaring noise sparking hope till it dies. "The cars have broken down from all the cement dust that has gotten into the engine," a man volunteers. He is standing next to her station car looking at Saskia through the open car door. "Where are you going?" he continues.

Saskia gets out of the dead car and stops in front of him. His name is Leroy. He is wearing a dark wide ribbed velvet trousers and a knitted sweater with holes. There are cement particles covering his hair and sweater. Saskia thinks he is probably around sixty years old, but maybe the gray veil of dust makes him look older than he is. His demeanor is youthful.

"I am going to look for my children. We got separated during this insane attack. Well, I was taken to hospital at the inception of the attack and when I got out, they were gone." Saskia's throat is closing. She pauses. "So, you need a car? Where are you going?"

"Direction Maryland..." Leroy looks her up and down and then piercing her eyes, he proposes, "We can travel together. I am going the same direction." Saskia nods. They start pulling handles of cars together, until Leroy suddenly starts a white van that he is maneuvering out onto the narrow street. "Jump in!"

They don't get very far, when Leroy exclaims, "Hold on! I know her!" He stops the van abruptly and yells out of the window, "Ana! What are you doing here? You want a lift?" Ana, a young Hispanic woman in her early twenties, turns around and waves while jumping up and down. The van has stopped next to Ana. Saskia opens the door and Ana jumps in.

"What a great coincidence that I found you here? You are also going to the datacenter?"

Leroy looks nervous. Without answering, he says, "This is Saskia. I just met her in the street trying to steal a car, and we decided to carpool, as she is also heading to Maryland. I just met her."

"Ohh..." Ana nods knowingly.

Leroy and Ana, like herself, have lost themselves, their loved ones and belongings. There is an intense smell of sweat and dirt in the van. The trip almost takes a whole day. Leaving the city, the landscape transforms into an expansive lush green forest with valleys donning deep blue rivers and lakes. Saskia is grateful to move far away from the warzone in New York. Secretly, it pains her to have contributed to the war. It is still unclear if the underground or the overlords of New York won the war. Maybe no one won or lost, as is customary in this date and age, where wars are fought to no end other than growing the wealth of the private individuals, contractors, and companies.

The landscape is changing, opening up and revealing the wide horizon, as they enter rural farming land heading into Maryland. Saskia looks out of the window contemplating if she should share her end destination with Leroy and Ana. After all, she doesn't know for sure that the national military data center exists, where it is and how to get in. It seems that Leroy and Ana share her end destination, since Ana revealingly mentioned a "data center," when she onboarded their van. *Maybe joining forces with these seemingly like-minded revolutionaries will help me find what I am looking for.* Saskia thinks to herself. *They look like people of the underground. Then again,* she reflects, *everybody leaving New York City looks haggard and battle worn.* Regardless of where you come from, everybody leaving the city looks helpless and homeless.

The closer they get to Baltimore, the denser the air becomes. Daylight dims, as if swallowed by the surrounding dust. Leroy, Ana, and Saskia gasp and cry as they recognize that Baltimore, too, has succumbed to what is now referred to as the rebel forces in the media. From afar, Baltimore looks like a massive dust ball extending far beyond the perimeters of the city. Just like New York City before it, Baltimore, too, has been reduced to particles and debris.

They stop at Bel Air, thirty miles from Baltimore. Leroy, Ana and Saskia get out of the van, bewildered. Around them, several people are crying inconsolably, as they had pinned their hopes on joining relatives in Baltimore who could offer them shelter.

Saskia asks Leroy and Ana, "How do I get to Frederick?" They look at her astonished.

Leroy replies with a question, "Why are you going there?"

Saskia lies, "I am looking for a relative who lives there."

Leroy and Ana look at each other. Suddenly, a middle-aged woman, standing next to them, says, "I am also going in that direction. Maybe I can come with you?"

Leroy looks at Ana and says, "There is room for one more in the van." Realizing that they are all traveling to Frederick, they decided to travel together for mutual security. The new passenger is called Aria Vega. She is in her early sixties. She is short and voluptuous. Saskia cannot figure out if she is native American or Latin American with indigenous roots. She decides it doesn't matter.

Amidst an air of secrecy, Saskia detects a sense of familiarity about her fellow travelers, suspecting, once again, their involvement with the underground. Her curiosity makes her ponder, why her fellow travelers are also journeying toward Frederick, the same destination as her own. Could it be that they share a common objective: to find the data center near Hagerstown? Yet, Saskia remains guarded, refraining from divulging her own origins and final destination.

In any event, the underground seems light years away. Like a different lifetime. Saskia contemplates that much like New York, the underground's presence might now be fragmented, perhaps even evaporated, receding into the shadows from where it emerged. Vanished. Crawled back into the hole it came from. Saskia and the three passengers sit in silence, their gaze exchanges unspoken words. It is as if they share a secret pact, each person preserving their own concealed truth.

Three days after Leroy, Ana, and Saskia set on their journey, they enter Frederick, which seems spared mass destruction. Even though, it, too, is racked, plundered, and deserted. They stand and look at each other waiting for the first person to make a move. Then Saskia cautiously asks, "It seems that we may all be going to Hagerstown?" She looks around to see, if someone acknowledges what she is talking about, or if they should just continue the blinking contest.

Ana audaciously says, "I am going to the military's national data center. But it is not in Hagerstown. It is at some unknown secret location in the Tussey Mountains."

Aria Vega, Leroy, and Saskia lower their shoulders with ease, as they nod and mumble, "Me, too..."

Saskia is confused, as she asks, "Why are you going there? I mean, I know why *I* am going there, to look for my two children, who I lost in the big attack in New York."

At this point, Leroy explains that the data center is a key strategic stronghold in the war against the old establishment. "We suspect that the military center does not only scan places and people but also gathers information, such as counter terror intelligence, as they call it, when they spy on us and other groups moving at the fringe of society. They intercept our communication, keep track of certain high-level people's whereabouts, *etcetera*. If we want to win and sustain victory, we must get to this information and make sure that *they* do not have access to it."

All of them look intensively at Leroy as if he is divulging top-secret information. In fact, he *is* disclosing secret information, but they all possess this information, and they are all, for different reasons, journeying to the data center.

The top-secret data center in the Tussey Mountains is part of the United States' Defense Information Systems Agency (DISA). There is one other data center in the U.S. called the Utah Data Center, also known as the Intelligence Community Comprehensive National Cybersecurity Initiative Data Center. That center is operated by the National Security Agency (NSA). Unlike the DISA data center, the secret location of which is somewhere in the Tussey Mountains, the location of the NSA data center, in Utah, is common knowledge.

Saskia is hoping to find her children with the help of the top-secret DISA data center, as recommended to her by the young woman from ShelterBox. Leroy is a data specialist, who was told by the leaders of the underground to go to the data center immediately after the big attack. Ana is the daughter of one of the leaders. She is searching for her father, and she overheard a conversation where her father and other leaders agreed to convene at the center immediately after the big attack. Aria Vega is herself a leader, who was instructed to go to the center after the big attack.

Half an hour into their journey from Frederick to Hagerstown, the van breaks down. Leroy is barely able to roll it to the side of the street before it refuses to move an inch more. They are in an area that has yet to decide if it is urban or rural. Further down a dusty road, there is an auto repair workshop. Leroy crawls out of the van. It is clear that his body is aching. As he starts making his way down the dusty road, Ana runs up next to him. Aria Vega and Saskia don't say a word. They watch.

After a while, Leroy and Ana return in a tow truck, with a smile, and a man behind the wheel. The truck is bright electric blue. Its owner is equally inauspicious, loud, and bright. He says his name is Ranger. He says, he knows where the data center is, but Saskia doubts it's true. She suspects he just tells them whatever they want to hear to get the assignment and money that Leroy offered him upon their safe arrival.

Beyond the suburban areas, the landscape transitions to countryside with rolling hills, open fields, farms, and rural roads. Saskia sits next to Aria Vega in the backseat of Ranger's truck. "Are we sure the DISA data center has been taken over by our people? I mean, if we go there, and it is still run by the military, what do we do?"

Aria Vega nods.

"I have been thinking the same thing. Rumor has it that the rebels are *in* the data center. That they have taken over control with the center. Getting stronghold of the DISA data center was a top priority during our early planning efforts, because as long as the authorities track and trace us, we are lame ducks. From the very offset of the revolution, we knew that we needed to disable all government-controlled spyware used to monitor and control so-called hostile groups in society."

Saskia says reflective, "So the idea is to disable the systems? Or is the idea to take over control of the systems and use them to serve our cause?"

Aria Vega answers, "The former. But there are also voices, strong voices, in our community who want to preserve and use the spyware for our own purposes, for our own cause. Personally, I think, we must destroy the systems. As long as these systems exist, we risk them falling into the wrong hands and getting used to control us or, even worse, fight us. The whole rebellion and our cause are also about resisting the monitoring and control of *all* citizens. How can we ever become free if the monitoring and controlling persist?"

Aria Vega is getting upset as she proceeds to answer her own question. "If we continue to monitor and control groups of society, we are just as bad as they are. All we do then is to shift targeted discrimination from one group to another. Secretly monitoring and controlling citizens are far greater threats than any other violation of privacy. Such a threat erodes trust in society, and it crushes any healthy criticism for fear of retribution. It gives us a false sense of security. If we continue to monitor and control citizens, we will see the same expansive self-censorship as we have now, just based on a different ideology: our ideology and our cause. The cause does *not* justify the means! The cause and the means must be the same. They must both be evidence of the same ideology."

Saskia nods. "Yay… I guess, it's like saying that the end goal is the only important thing, when in fact, it's the *process* of getting to the goal that is at least as important as the goal itself. At the end of the day, the end goal for all of us is identical: we are all going to die. That's the end goal for every human being! So, what we are left with is infusing our lives with a purposeful meaning. It's the process called life that's important. Not the end goal called death that has been predetermined for all of us. If we monitor and control people, we may get them to behave as we want, but life becomes stifled and stagnant, devoid of joy, experiences, and innovation."

The systems and structures are the means by which these financially, legally, and politically influential people of the old establishment shield the status quo and safeguard society. Monitoring and controlling populations, however important, with the use of the data center in the Tussey Mountains is but one means by which the old establishment maintains their grip on the prevailing structure of society.

Again, we find ourselves at a critical juncture: the underground and their cross-city peers want to tear down the antiquated and inequitable financial, legal, and political systems and structures permeating society. These systems, on one hand, exacerbate inherent social injustices and, on the other, safeguard the privileges, influence, and affluence of the elite echelons. To destroy these unjust systems and structures, the underground and its allies must infiltrate and dismantle the established order, along with its financial, legal, and political frameworks that uphold this unfair society.

Now the question remains: to what extent should the underground and its accomplices deploy, to their own advantage, the very same methods, tools, and institutions that were used to safeguard the old establishment? Or are these methods, tools, and institutions de facto degenerative? Thus, can systems and structures ever fulfil a good and meaningful purpose? Or do they have a propensity to land in the hands of power grabbing individuals? Is there a tipping point at which systems and structures cease to serve the populace in a meaningful manner? Is there a tipping point at which systems and structures preserve existing injustices locking society into a state of stagnation?

Is there any justification for people in power, such as governmental authorities, to monitor and control their citizens? Or does a free society mean the freedom from surveillance, exaggerated use of power and coercion, and (self-)censorship. Supporters of the status quo and the old establishment argue that antiquated and inequitable financial, legal, and political systems and structures undergo reform from within. Conversely, the underground and its allies have waited too long for too little to happen. They believe that the only way to achieve genuine transformation and betterment for those at the bottom of society, where most of the population has congregated, is to start at a clean slate. However, Saskia asks herself, if they are really starting at a clean slate, when the leadership of the underground and its allies have taken over the data center in the Tussey Mountains and now monitor and control citizens in much the same way as the old establishment did. *Though motivations might differ, if the methods, tools, and institutions remain unaltered, it is merely a matter of time before we fall back into old habits*, Saskia thinks. This apprehension shadows her thoughts.

They pass Hagerstown and follow the signs to Hancock. That evening, they camp in a cave in the Tussey Mountains. All the five of them, Aria Vega, Leroy, Ana, Saskia and the Ranger, are so exhausted, they fall into a deep sleep immediately upon laying down on the rock-hard surface of the cave floor. In fact, they are so exhausted they oversleep until eight a.m. the next morning. "Wake up! Wake up!" Ana exclaims running around franticly. They get up and start wandering around in the cave, still drunk of sleep, to collect their stuff and get ready for the onward journey.

"Today is the day, we will be rekindled with our family and friends," Ana says in an upbeat tone of voice. Leroy says, "Well, we still don't know, for sure, *where* in this vast expanse of forests, rolling hills, and valleys the data center is."

The Ranger says, "We've been traversing this land for days, crisscrossing its expanse. The most probable location now lies on the opposite side of that valley!" Ana smiles at the Ranger. Saskia doesn't smile. She winces at the thought of Ava and Max, who are somewhere out there in the world. Her heart is literally aching with hurt.

She hopes Brady stayed with Ava and Max. Saskia believes that if Brady showed them mercy and took them under her wing, they are safe somewhere out there, waiting to be found.

They only have a bit of freshwater and scant provisions left for the journey. They stand at the cave's entrance, observing as the Ranger assesses and readies the aging tow truck for the onward expedition. "We only have just enough gasoline for one day's travel. Sorry guys!" Saskia's frustration with the Ranger is becoming evident. Throughout the entirety of the journey, she feels the Ranger is lackadaisical and carefree, bordering on immaturity, in understanding the severity and importance of their journey. He also seems clueless as to what is going on in the big cities across the country, many of which have been destroyed to obviation, seemingly without him noticing or caring much about it. Now, the Ranger saunters around the truck that looks as if it could collapse any moment.

Five minutes later, they are forcing their way up into the Tussey Mountains on a narrow and steep trail that they must climb before they ascend the mountain where the DISA data center is supposedly located. Suddenly, they hear an enormous crack from the sky. They all look up. The sky is clear, and the sun is spitting clear white fire. The Ranger says, "I don't know what that was, but it may have been a noise from the data center. We are getting close."

The crack returns. They all look up. "It is definitely coming from the sky," Leroy says.

"Well... it can also be a noise from the ground echoed up and out by the mountains," the Ranger says all knowingly, when he in fact does not know what he is talking about.

They are making their way up the mountains, when the third crack is accompanied with a massive thunder hitting the ground right next to them. "That was definitely a thunder!" Ana says. Before anyone can answer, they are caught in a torrential downpour. There is no time to put up the hood of the truck. All attempts to shield themselves from the downpour are pointless.

After a few seconds, the raindrops transmute into large balls of solid ice. They instinctively flinch evading the forceful hits from the hundreds of ice projectiles relentlessly hitting them. It becomes unmistakably clear that the truck cannot navigate this weather. The canopy of water drowns out all attempts to communicate between them. Nevertheless, they can see the Ranger's agitated and panicked screaming. Giving up at making any sense, the

Ranger hurls himself out of the truck. Swift as thought, each one of them abandons the truck like deserting a sinking ship. The moment Saskia's feet touch the ground, she senses shifting earth beneath her. The deluge has caused a landslide that is moving like a massive river down the mountain side. Nowhere is safe. In the blink of an eye, the truck is out of sight. Saskia will soon follow suit unless she finds a steady footing. Fueled by desperation and fear, Saskia and the others crawl up the mountain. They scramble for what seems an eternity till the downpour resides and the landslide slows.

After another couple of minutes, the scorching sun reemerges instantly evaporating the water drying everything around them. They have reached the top of the mountain, where they collapse with exhaustion onto a level expanse of concrete.

Chapter Ten

After days of crisscrossing the Tussey Mountains, and by total serendipity, they arrive at a concealed site nestled between two ascending cliffs within the canyon range. Unbeknownst to them, a massive cement bunker, covered in ivy, lies beneath them—the DISA's enigmatic data center. "How do we get in?" Saskia inquires, once she gains enough strength to utter a word. No one responds but Leroy, who gestures in uncertainty. Suddenly, this strange creature appears out of nowhere.

It exclaims, "Saskia! God am I happy to see you! Where have you been?" Saskia tries to sit up, but she is too weak.

The creature looks entirely unfamiliar. It is human, but wearing a mask with oriental features, including Asian eyes, high protruding cheekbones and a nose with minimal projection. The mask shows a cheerful person with long white pigtails swaying calmly in the breeze. "Saskia!" the woman behind the mask insists.

"Do I know you?" Saskia mumbles.

"It's Kate! You know! From the underground. Sub-level 3!"

Saskia looks at the masked woman astonished. "Kate! Why are you wearing a mask?"

Kate tips her head. "I forgot, I was wearing a mask. I had an accident. During the big attack, I burned my face. It is a miracle, I survived."

Kate still looks blissful, or rather her mask looks blissful, despite delivering the terrifying news. Saskia is trying to collect herself. Behind Kate two guards appear. Kate orders them to help bring the almost lifeless bodies into the compound. More guards come to their aid, as they are, all five, carried on stretchers into the data center. Once inside, the guards place the stretchers on pokes in a dark and cool room, while medical staff hooks them up on IV lines for fluids and medications to be directly delivered into their bloodstreams. There must have been sleeping medicine in the IV fluids.

Saskia wakes up feeling she has been brought back to life from death. Kate reappears. This time, she is wearing the mask of what looks like an elderly wise Chinese man whose face is pale yellow with Asian slanted eyes. The mask is angry with a frown and deep nasolabial folds extending from the sides of the nose to the corners of the mouth. On top of the mask, is a high bone or horn, almost like a unicorn. Behind the horn, long white hair flows. Saskia says, "It is very confusing with those masks, Kate. I mean, I don't know if you are in a good or bad mood."

Kate turns her head to look at her as she says, "You know me, Saskia! I am *always* in a good mood." Even though, Saskia wants to, she does not ask why Kate put on the mask of an elderly Chinese man, who looks angry. She is lost for words. She is perplexed asking herself if the masks show Kate's true identity or if they mask her true identity from others. Several things race through Saskia's head. Firstly, Saskia is surprised to meet Kate in the middle of the Tussey Mountains. Secondly, she is remains uncertain if she is indeed talking to Kate or an impostor. Anyone could be hiding behind that mask!

Saskia descends the stretcher slowly. Her body is aching. Kate says, "Slow now. Slow now..." A nurse approaches. She removes the IV line. Saskia looks around the room. She is the first one of her traveling companions to get out of bed.

She looks around the room and soon realizes that Aria Vega is not there. "Where is Aria? Where is Aria Vega?"

Saskia asks bewildered, "Did she not make it? The landslide. Did she not make it?"

Leroy, Ana, and the Ranger are moving. Kate steps over next to Saskia. "Aria Vega is one of the biggest leaders in the rebellion. She is being looked after in a different section."

In that moment, a well-rested and recovered Aria Vega enters. Kate, still wearing her old Chinese man mask, turns around to face the entrance, while her long white hair catch a breeze. Aria Vega steps forward and says, "I am Aria Vega!"

Saskia is astonished. "I am happy to see you are all well!"

Soon after, they all six—Kate, Aria Vega, Leroy, Ana, the Ranger, and Saskia—make their way down a tunnel, where some artists are painting what appears like a large mural on the barren cement walls. Just as they pass by, one of the artists turns to Kate and waves to a particular portrait of Kate wearing a cat mask with three eyes and four ears. Each eye is its own bright color: blue, yellow and green. Saskia thinks it is peculiar to portray a masked Kate. The portrait doesn't reveal the real person, but the masked persona. *How can it be portrait, when the person portrayed is masked.*

Once at the end of the corridor, Kate pushes open a large iron door, revealing an expanse that seems infinite. Darkness shrouds the space, obscuring its outer dimensions. The pungent odor of synthetic carpets is ghastly. Three colossal screens illuminate the room. The first screen rapidly scans the surface of the earth at high velocity pausing each time it encounters something suspicious looking. The subsequent screen zooms into an array of individual cameras, scanning with frenzied speed to identify specific faces using facial recognition systems. The third screen displays the movements and gatherings of people. In cases of heightened human activity, the system magnifies the view to scrutinize and share instantaneous data on the observed activity.

"This is monitoring and controlling at a whole new level!" exclaims Kate while putting her arms up into the air and spinning around in the middle of the floor. Behind them, there is an amphitheater with hundreds of desks with large computer screens.

"Are all these people, manning the computers, ours?" Saskia asks in astonishment.

"Well…" Kate starts. "Most of them are our people, but some of them are 'legacy workers,' who worked here before we took control with the data center. They were given a choice... If you can call it a choice to be killed or collaborate."

Saskia realizes that there are guards patrolling the aisles. Saskia walks slowly over to Aria Vega. "Do you think we will destroy the systems?" Aria Vega turns to Saskia and looks her in the eyes and nods no. They both have an eerie feeling that something profoundly wrong is happening.

After Saskia has reflected a bit on the magnitude of monitoring done by the old establishment and its government and that will now persist with the so-called new freedom seeking rebels, she moves over next to Kate. "I have come all this way to look for Ava and Max," she dares to say. "I am hoping that these systems, especially the one doing facial recognition, will help me find them."

Kate makes a deep sigh of exhaustion. "Of course," she says and turns to Saskia. "Of course, you are looking for your children. We tried to separate families in the underground. Families are toxic. Don't you know that!"

Saskia says, "Some families are toxic, but my children are just children. They are good and kind children, and I need to find them. I love them, and I miss them. Please help me!" Saskia wants to drop on her knees, but resists.

Kate examines her with in inspective look. "We actually use these systems on a regular basis to locate lost people. I will help you. But then you must continue to fight the battle for freedom and equality. You give me your soul, and I give you your children. That's the deal! Do you take it?" Saskia knows that if she extends her right hand, shakes Kate's hand, and seals the deal, she is committed to serving the rebellion and its cause for the rest of her life. Still, she has no choice. She must find Ava and Max. She shakes Kate's hand.

"Now then!" Kate exclaims clapping her hands with excitement. "We need to convene for dinner. I will take you there." Like the corridors that have artists working away to decorate them, the former sterile canteen has been transformed into a colorful display of narrative tales unfolding on each wall. In the dining hall, as it is called now, the tales of victory in each New York, Baltimore, Los Angeles and Houston unfold. One city tale adorning each one wall of the subterranean mega room.

Kate says, "Obviously, Aria Vega will sit at the high table. You guys can sit somewhere else." With no further ado, Aria Vega is whisked away by Kate. Saskia sees many familiar faces in the dining hall. Suddenly, she feels a hand on her shoulder. She turns around to see Annona. Saskia gasps with surprise. They embrace.

"You survived!" Saskia almost yells. No one around them takes much notice. The scene is quite common these days.

Annona and Saskia sit down in a quiet place far removed from the bustling crowds. "Do you know if my children, Ava and Max, survived? Do you know where they are?" Saskia's urgency can't be contained.

"I truly don't know," Annona replies with a touch of sadness in her voice. "Once the major attack began, chaos engulfed everything. People scattered in all directions, vanishing into thin air. Many might not have survived. I'm sorry, Saskia."

Saskia's determination remains unwavering. "I can sense it in my mother heart—they're alive. They're out there, waiting for me to find them."

They share a silent meal, as Saskia contemplates the origin of their comparatively modest meal. Despite their victory, an air of uneasy anticipation looms. Victory seems almost tenuous, destined to crumble at any moment. There are many recognizable faces from the underground, but there are even more new faces, some of whom have switched allegiances under duress. The possibility that they might band together and mount a counter-rebellion crosses Saskia's mind. She doubts that whatever replaced the old establishment is much better and noble in its cause. The only certainty they have now is total uncertainty.

"How have you been faring?" Saskia asks forcing herself to seem interested in Annona's life journey when she is, in fact, only interested in her own and the survival of her children.

Annona turns to her, somewhat surprised by Saskia's interest in her well-being. "What can I say… I would be lying to you if I said, I have been well." She forces a smile on to her face. "In some ways, I think, my blessing is that I am all alone in this world. It seems to both level out my joy and certainly also my pain. Since most people, these days, feel pain in abundance of having lost loved ones, I seem to have a relatively easier ride than most people. Does that make sense?"

Saskia nods. "Tell me about everybody else! What happened to Lucky, Trish, and Trash. What happened to Becky? And what about Skyman and Mr. Sind?" In that instant, she is reminded that she hasn't shed a thought to Skyman since the big attack. All her waking hours have been singular focused on finding Ava and Max.

Annona turns to her with a choked smile. "Skyman is doing well. I am sure. He is residing, or should I say hiding, in his large country house in Amagansett, East Hampton. He is still one of the leaders. If anything, he has become an even bigger man!"

Saskia looks out in front of her. "We knew *that* would happen. Sometimes I think we were all helpful fools doing the bidding of a small handful of power craving, blood thirsty individuals, such as Skyman. We helped him and a few others like him ascend to power by demolishing everything that stood in their way. We handed them the world on a clean slate that they are now free to mold it in their own image. Who says, they are better than the ones before them? Who says that they will create a better and more equal world for us? We have just been running a fool's errand!"

Annona doesn't say anything. Then she straightens her back and says, "Look! You can say this to me. You know, you can trust me. But do never, ever, say this to anyone else. They will kill you. I promise you. They will kill you!"

They sit and stare into the air. The people crowding the room calmed down once food was served. Saskia gets the sense that people are genuinely hungry. She resonates that it is not a good sign that they don't have enough food to properly feed everybody. Hungry people become easily agitated. Saskia and Annona already finished their meal.

"What about Mr. Sind?" Saskia says to change the subject and atmosphere between them.

"Mr. Sind? Did you know him well?" Annona inquires and continues before Saskia can reply. "Mr. Sind was a complex person. He was obviously intelligent. But I think, he had a destructive streak, almost like a death wish. He came from great wealth and joined the rebellion to spite his family, I think. He survived the big attack and had the world at his feet but became a drunk and a drug addict. Can you believe it? After having survived the big attack and coming out on top, he tried to commit suicide by hanging himself!"

Saskia is still looking ahead, when she says, "Hmm... Yes. In some ways, I *can* believe that. He was a total survivor. He was smart, as you say. But joining the underground to spite others seems like a waste of talent. Self-destruction is a cry for help, so they say. Maybe he wanted his family to come and rescue him from the underground. Self-destruction is also entirely self-absorbed. It is all about putting yourself and your suffering at the center of your own and other's lives. Look at me! Look at me! Instead of finding a meaningful purpose in life. Self-destruction is all about taking rather than giving."

Annona doesn't say anything. Saskia concludes, "Anyway, it is a pity that he died. A real pity. I liked him."

Annona turns to her and says, "He didn't die! He *attempted* to hang himself, but like most people trying to kill themselves, he survived the attempt. Instead of dying, he got some kind of irreversible brain damage. He is now living with his brother, I think, in a permanent vegetative state on a life aid machine."

Saskia feels that her life in the underground was a time pocket. A time and place apart from this time and place. She feels that the people she met in the underground should have stayed in the underground. That is where they belonged. That is where they thrived. When she looks back at her relatively short life, it feels as if she lived many different lives.

The next day, Kate and Aria Vega come to look Saskia up. Aria Vega likes her, she senses, while she always felt that Kate has a façade behind which she is hiding. It seems a suitable irony that Kate is the chosen one for living with wearing a mask. Maybe she is happier wearing a mask, Saskia reasons. Aria Vega says, "We have come to help you find your children!" With that, they all proceed to the infinite room with the surveillance and spyware monitoring systems. They walk over to one of the desks at the lowest tier of the amphitheater, where they stop and Aria Vega says, "You know Leroy! He will help us locate your children." Saskia is bursting with anticipation.

Leroy asks, "Do you have a photo of them?" Saskia doesn't. "Well... Is there an old class photo in a school yearbook? Such photos are online. Or something else? Are they on social media?" Leroy says and continues, "We need a photo of both kids to run them through the facial recognition software." Aria Vega and Kate decide to leave Leroy and Saskia to work in peace.

After a couple of hours, they locate a photo of each Ava and Max that is suitable for the search. Leroy cleans the photos and runs them through the age progression software. When Saskia sees the final images of her children, she weeps. Leroy puts a hand around her shoulder. "Don't despair. You are here to find them. You have come this far. You'll find them. Let's run their photos through the middle screen that has all the individual cameras and the facial recognition software. It may take several hours. Maybe days. You don't need to wait around here…" Saskia doesn't want to leave. Her eyes remain fixated on the gigantic middle screen as it rapidly cycles through thousands of cameras within minutes. Once in a while, a camera stops and the screen is enlarged. Saskia's heart stops! The contours of one of the children's faces fill the screen, prompting an attempt to find a match. So far, no match has been found.

After six hours, both Leroy and Saskia are dozing off behind Leroy's big computer screen. Saskia reaches out and shakes Leroy to wake him when she realizes that the big center screen is lightening up with a repeated message written in large red letters. "Match found!" She gets up and starts jumping up and down.

"Okay! That must be Ava. She is… Wait!" he says, while taking the image to the third gigantic screen that hovers above cityscapes and landscapes trying to identify and scrutinize irregularities. "She is in the Catskill Mountains, not far from New York!"

Saskia is jumping up and down with joy. "I will go get my stuff and set out toward the East Coast and New York immediately!" she says.

Leroy says worried, "No, no... This needs to be planned. What if they are traveling and by the time you get to the Catskill Mountains, they have moved on? And what about Max? Don't we need to find him too?"

Saskia sits down. "You are right. We need to find him also. I was just assuming that he would be together with Ava." They narrow their search for Max to a one-mile radius of Ava and find him. With that Saskia insists on leaving as soon as possible.

Kate and Annona approach Saskia's bunk bed. "Are you leaving us?" Kate inquires, adding, "You made a commitment to keep working for us. You can't just leave at your own accord."

Saskia makes a weary sigh. "What now? Can't you just let me go and trust that I will return here with both Ava and Max?"

Kate exchanges a glance with Annona before looking back at Saskia. "Nope! Unfortunately, not. We need you to take an encrypted code reader to Skyman. He's capable of cracking it open and extracting any messages it contains."

Saskia's mind races, pondering the request. Among all the potential tasks she could be assigned, this is the one she's least eager to undertake. "My priority is to find my children; then I go with *them* to Amagansett on Long Island. Catskill Mountains are along the way to Amagansett. That is the way to do this." Kate reluctantly relents. It is unclear to Saskia, if Kate's resistance stems from a personal disliking of her or if it's simply Kate's nature. Kate is wearing the happy mask with the pigtails today.

Again, Annona is tasked with preparing Saskia for her assignment. Saskia is handed an antiquated mobile phone that looks like a relic from another era. "Only the old phones function offline on the old telco network. All newer models use the internet and therefore, they are very easily hacked. You can *only* call me and Leroy from this phone. Leroy keeps up to date of the whereabouts of your children."

Annona takes a large intricately carved wooden case out of a large bag she has been dragging along the floor. "This assignment is important. Skyman must get this encrypted code reader!" she says, as she opens the case and takes out a strange looking compass of sorts. It is of gold colored metal. In its center, there is a screen with decoded deciphered information rolling across in a steady stream. "That thing is far bigger than I anticipated, and it looks really heavy! You are dragging it along the floor!"

The next morning Saskia is teamed up with the Ranger. She regrets not having told Annona that the Ranger is totally useless, bordering stupid. She is annoyed, not least with herself. She hands him the straps to the massive bag with the encrypted code reader. "Take this!" Annona jumps up. "Watch out! It is really important. It must not break!" The total ignorance of the Ranger means that he is excited about going on the trip.

"You know we are heading into a warzone?" Saskia insensitively points out as they take off in the truck.

Leaving the Tussey Mountains, they arrive back at Hagerstown, where they stock up on provision and fuel. Having told the Ranger upfront that she doesn't want to talk to him, the Ranger is excited to be back in his hometown, Hagerstown, where he meets and greets many people on the streets. Saskia is getting impatient and hurries him. At some point, Saskia asks herself, if she is simply annoyed with the Ranger for being constantly upbeat and cheerful amidst civil war, total upheaval, and chaos.

After staying overnight in a hostel, they continue onward across Maryland, where the weather forecast warns of strong storms. About five days into their journey, they see Baltimore emerge in the distant horizon. "Last time, I was here, Baltimore was one big dust ball. You couldn't see a thing!" Saskia says out aloud. Now, the city's few still standing skyscrapers are towering over a mountain of debris. There are blinks in between the buildings and debris testifying to intense human activity. Saskia ponders over who is rebuilding the city: the rebel forces or the old establishment.

Saskia is in daily dialogue with Leroy, who confirms that Ava and Max are still in the Catskill Mountains. As they draw closer to their journey's first destination, in the distant mist, the Catskill Mountains unveil themselves as a breathtaking quilt of verdant greens, sunlit yellows and rich auburn hues of foliage. Once in the mountains, we are engulfed by the intense scent of pine and wildflowers. At this world wonder worries seem to fade into insignificance. The immensity of nature diminishes the significance of humans and their relentless search for wealth, influence, and acknowledgement. In any event, human presence on mother earth is but a blink second. Yet, we ascribe such enormous importance to ourselves.

The Ranger and Saskia stop at a small settlement that oozes of peace and serenity. Saskia is filled with appreciation at the thought of her children having been nestled far away from the brutal war in this natural sanctuary. While the Ranger is checking the truck and sorting their stuff, Saskia walks determined toward the settlement that is about 1500 feet away further down the valley. After a short walk, she stops at a natural cliff overhang where she can see the entire settlement below in the valley.

Suddenly, Saskia sees Brady. She jumps up and down waving, while calling out Brady's name. Saskia is grateful that Brady stayed with Ava and Max. Brady doesn't see her. Behind Brady, Max appears. He is walking up to Brady. Saskia struggles holding back her tears of sheer happiness. No one can see nor hear her from her current post, so she decides to run down into the valley and the settlement. She runs as fast as she can. Like a deer, she jumps effortlessly over branches and stones at great velocity. At the bottom of the valley, she looks around for Max. "He was just here!" she thinks aloud while looking around franticly.

"Mother?" a frail voice behind her inquires. "Mommy?"

Saskia turns about to see Ava standing right in front of her. They both fall into each other's arms, hugging and sobbing. "I thought, I would never see you again. I missed you so much!" Ava sobs.

"I never stopped looking for you. I would have looked for you for the rest of my life!" Saskia reassures her. Saskia says, once they have wiped away their tears, "I just saw Max and Brady from the cliff up there." Saskia turns to point at the cliff. The Ranger is standing up there now. He is not looking at them, but rather out over the breathtaking mountainous landscape. "He is my driver," Saskia says and turns to Ava, who asks, "You have a driver?"

"Don't be fooled. I am nobody, but I must deliver this strange machine to Skyman at his second home on Long Island. The machine is important. Or rather getting the machine to Skyman is important... I am still a nobody!"

Crossing a wide lawn in a fresh vibrant green color, they walk toward a large rusty colored red barn with a black roof. Bright yellow buttercups sporadically dot the lawn. "Max went to the barn, our food hall, for supper. We eat dinner at six every evening," Ava says with a smile. "How did you find us? We are supposed to be totally hidden away from the world here nested between the large mountains and tug far into the infinite forest," Ava inquires.

Saskia replies, "That is a long story. But I am still stuck in the underground, or rebel forces as they are now called. I have to run this errand for them and in return they helped me find you. A quid pro quo. But it never ends, does it? There really is no way out of the underground."

Ava asks, "You have to go back to the underground?"

Saskia reflects, "I don't think so, but I have to deliver the machine to Skyman. Otherwise, they will come look for us to get the machine, and punish me. Also, I know there is no point in running away and hiding from them. They have the means to find anyone, they are looking for."

As they are entering the barn, Ava turns to say, "We are happy here." Saskia nods reflectively.

Once inside, Max runs toward her, knocking over several chairs. "Mother, Mother!" he screams. Again, they weep.

She kisses his head and runs her fingers through his hair, that is wet with her tears. "I cannot believe we are together again. This is all I have been able to think about since I lost you in New York. For three months, I have been spending all my waking hours working my way back to you." Saskia is still sobbing.

Max asks, "But how did you find us? We are supposed to be totally hidden from everybody out here!"

Saskia says, "You are not hidden. I mean, if no one is looking for you, you might be hidden out here, but I was looking for you."

Brady comes over and gives her a warm hug, while she whispers into her ear, "They missed you." Both Saskia and Brady are on the same team now: team survival. Nothing else matters now.

They sit down at one of the long tables with their bowl of soup. Saskia explains how she traveled to Frederick, then Hagerstown and into the Tussey Mountains to find the DISA data center in some unknown location in the mountains. She tells of her new friends, Aria Vega, who is one of the foremost leaders of the rebel forces, and Leroy, an IT specialist, and Ana, who was looking for her father. Saskia talks about her reencounter with Kate, who is wearing masks, strange masks that freaks her out! And Annona, who hasn't changed a bit. Lots of familiar faces that she can't put a name to. And people that she did not see, Lucky, Trish, Trash and Becky. "What about Hammer?" Max asks.

"No, I also didn't see him either."

"You never met Skyman and Mr. Sind?" she asks.

"No, we didn't."

"Well, you will soon meet Skyman..." she says. Both Ava and Max are looking into their soup.

Then Ava asks, "Do we *have* to come? I mean, we have peace here. There are no dangers. No war!"

Saskia replies, "Let me think about this. I will stay here for some days. The travel is safe. We will go in the truck and around the big cities, where the fighting persists." After a while Saskia adds, "The thing is, nowhere is safe. Fighting can come here too. And then when I return to look for you, you will be gone! Again—"

Brady intervenes, "But I will look after them. And we can find a way to stay in touch."

"Let me think about it."

Over dinner, they all explain what happened during the big attack. How Saskia was found, near dead, on some building blocks fallen into Hudson River. A kind family nursed her back to life. How she went to the massive tent, a refugee camp, where Amber Alert, Red Cross,

ShelterBox, Mercy, and all the aid organizations were. How a young woman from ShelterBox pointed her in the direction of Hagerstown, and so on. "What a crazy story!" Max says.

"Except it is not a story. It is real life. A battle for survival. I really don't want to leave this place. There is peace here, and people are kind. Nobody talks about the rebellion here. Nobody cares what side of the war you are on. Here we are all just equal," Ava says.

"On that note!" Brady exclaims. "Let me tell you how your son survived. In the early hours, the day after you left, there was fighting everywhere in the city. There were gunshots everywhere, and bombs were going off. The rebel forces intruded into people's homes and took whatever they could, including women and lives. Despite the fighting that was intensifying by the hour, we, or should I say *your children*, insisted on staying in the apartment on the corner of the 8th Avenue and West 37th Street, waiting and hoping for your return. It seems a different lifetime, now." Brady stops to reflect. In that moment, Saskia suddenly realizes that she has been so busy rejoicing with her children that she has almost ignored Brady. And she has yet to thank Brady for saving her children's lives.

"Anyway," Brady continues. "Your son's survival comes down to his choice of breakfast. As he bowed down to look for a cereal in the back of a lower cupboard, the ceiling collapsed. He was sheltered by the kitchen top. Being tugged deep into the cupboard, almost certainly saved his life. In that moment, I think, we all agreed that we could no longer stay in the apartment and wait for you. We had to get leave!"

Ava and Max take over, as they talk over each other eager to explain how they left the city. "We didn't want to leave without you. We were crying. We didn't know if and when we would see you again. Every day we have been talking about when you would come," Ava says.

"It is totally unbelievable that you are sitting here with us, now, having supper," Brady says.

They sleep in bunk beds in what was once stables. It still smells of animals and their manure. Some families have their own tents that they were given by one of the aid organizations on their way out of the city. The red crosses have been painted over to better blend in with the natural surroundings. Afterall, they don't want to call upon them unwanted attention. Some families have started building houses. They are planning to stay. People help each other. They have a vegetable garden and are preparing to grow crops next autumn.

After three days, the Ranger looks up Saskia. He has been wandering around the settlement, chatting, making friends, and breaking hearts. He nonchalantly strolls over to Saskia, while saying, "Kate and Aria Vega are trying to get in touch with you. They called me over my car radio. I didn't know that was possible. Anyway, they are ripshit! They demand we continue the journey to Skyman. We have to go. Now!"

Saskia gets annoyed just looking at him. She says, "Says who!"

The Ranger works himself up. "Says Kate and Aria Vega! They've got the entire rebel force backing them up. Rebels are cropping up everywhere, absolutely everywhere! Even here..."

Deep down, Saskia knows, the Ranger is right. They must go, and she is determined that Ava and Max must come with her. She is not again leaving her children in the midst of a raging civil war. They set off the subsequent morning. Their truck is brimming with essentials. Brady unexpectedly opts to join them at the eleventh hour. "You're all I've got now," she mutters, her gaze averted. Saskia's heart lifts; Brady is on board. Her children are overjoyed.

During an extensive conversation with Kate over the phone, Saskia finds herself wondering how Kate manages to allocate so much time to seemingly trivial matters while concurrently overseeing a war. Amidst their discussion, Kate goes into meticulous detail about Saskia's imminent encounter with Skyman. It is still unclear to Saskia, if Kate knows that she has had a longish off-on relationship with Skyman. Saskia even speculates if that is why Kate is sending her, instead of someone more devoted to the cause. "Skyman has grown even more influential, Saskia," Kate expounds. Saskia wonders what mask Kate is wearing today. "He's destined to become the next president of the United States!" Kate's unwavering admiration for Skyman has always been transparent. Yet, Saskia knows him as just an ordinary man.

When, two days later, they enter the country estate of Skyman, they hold their breath in awe. "Keep driving!"

Saskia insists, as the Ranger slows the truck to almost standstill. The house stands tall. A colossal cottage constructed from massive fieldstones procured locally from the Hudson River riverbed. Window frames, doors, and the roof structure are all crafted from white pine, coated with a yellowish hue adorning a warm ambiance. The roof, composed of slate, absorbs the morning sun's gentle warmth.

As the truck snails the long way up the hill to the estate, Saskia's mind wanders, reflecting on the point at which financial and tech prodigies succumb to the belief in their own genius. When does practicality give way to insatiable greed? Skyman's ego was immense even before the big attack. She has only known him as pretentious beyond reason. He artfully conceals his deep self-regard, masking it with feigned humility. Saskia holds a simmering resentment toward him, his greed, and ambition. She harbors no grand ideas that whatever Skyman and his accomplices will replace the old establishment with will be any better or more equitable and just.

As she sits in contemplation, Saskia muses that the most profound betrayal occurs when wealthy people turn against their fellow wealthy people, or when the disadvantaged people turn against their own. Inevitably, someone somewhere will respond in kind. The cycle of warfare shall persist.

THE END